AMIRA DANALI

Brushing Off Business

Things will get better ♡

First published by Amira Danali Books 2024

Copyright © 2024 by Amira Danali

All rights reserved. No part of this publication may be reproduced, stored or transmitted in any form or by any means, electronic, mechanical, photocopying, recording, scanning, or otherwise without written permission from the publisher. It is illegal to copy this book, post it to a website, or distribute it by any other means without permission.

This novel is entirely a work of fiction. The names, characters and incidents portrayed in it are the work of the author's imagination. Any resemblance to actual persons, living or dead, events or localities is entirely coincidental.

Amira Danali asserts the moral right to be identified as the author of this work.

First edition

ISBN: 9798335210713

This book was professionally typeset on Reedsy.
Find out more at reedsy.com

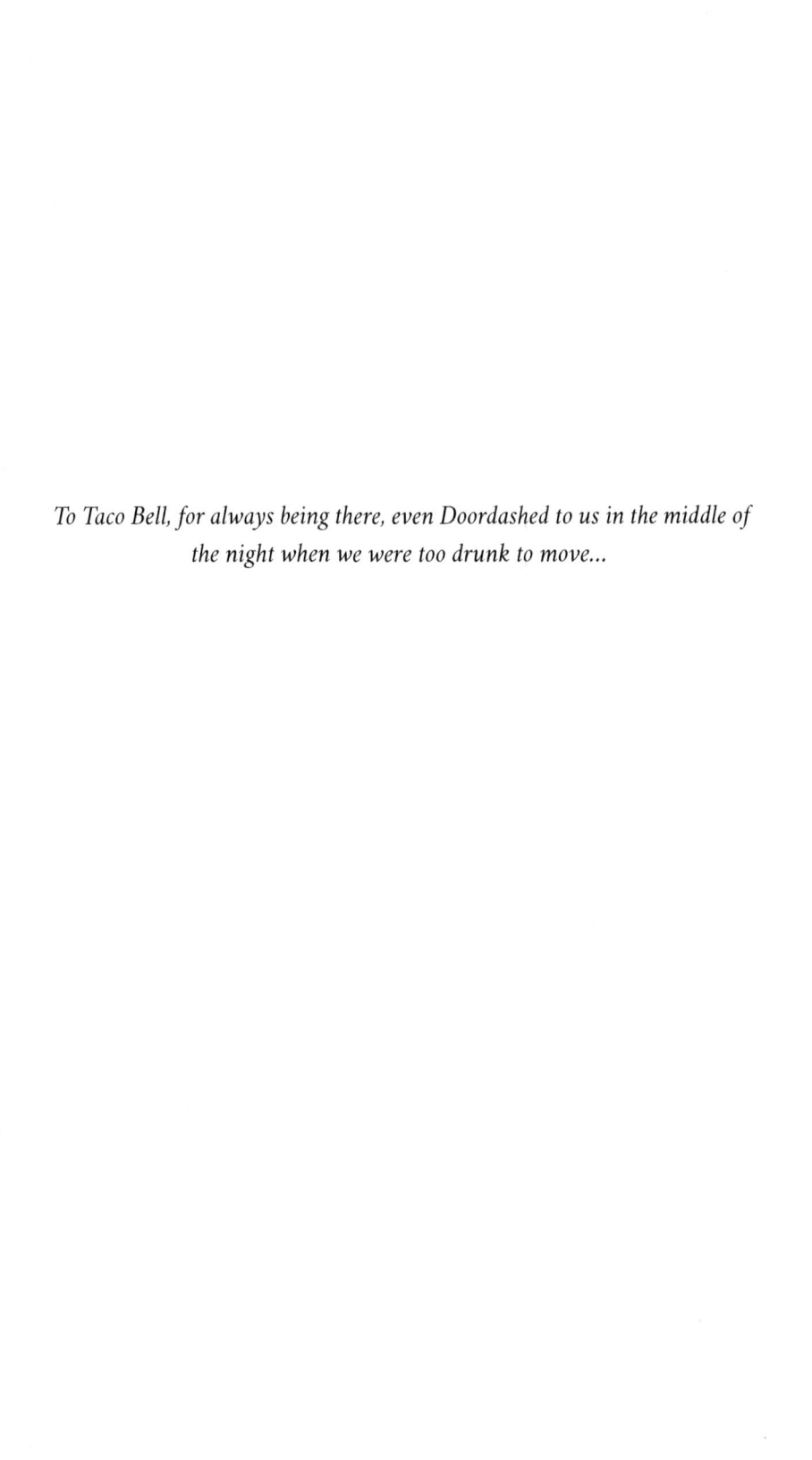

To Taco Bell, for always being there, even Doordashed to us in the middle of the night when we were too drunk to move...

Contents

Acknowledgement	iii
Chapter 1	1
Chapter 2	12
Chapter 3	20
Chapter 4	31
Chapter 5	41
Chapter 6	53
Chapter 7	63
Chapter 8	74
Chapter 9	78
Chapter 10	85
Chapter 11	91
Chapter 12	96
Chapter 13	103
Chapter 14	109
Chapter 15	114
Chapter 16	128
Chapter 17	138
Chapter 18	145
Chapter 19	153
Chapter 20	157
Chapter 21	166
Chapter 22	170
Chapter 23	177

Chapter 24	182
Chapter 25	188
Chapter 26	193
Chapter 27	199
Chapter 28	203
Chapter 29	210
Chapter 30	216
Max	222
Chapter 32	231
Chapter 33	238
Chapter 34	243
Chapter 35	249
Chapter 36	255
Chapter 37	261
Chapter 38	267
Chapter 39	274
Chapter 40	279
Epilogue	284
About the Author	293
Also by Amira Danali	294

Acknowledgement

To start this off, I'd first like to thank you guys, for taking a chance on my book. I know that the book market has been flooded these days with tons of incredible novels written by incredible authors and for that, I'd like to thank you for picking mine, even if just for a few days.

I'd also like to thank my college roommate, Kate, for inspiring the wine-loving, always there for you, no-nonsense character in my book, Kait. Crazy name change, I know. No one ever would have gotten it was you...

Thank you to Ruchi, my amazing beta reader, Margaux, my fabulous cover artist, and Tuna, my America-hating best friend for helping me pick between the Capri filter and the Chroma filter.

To my family, for being there for me. To my college friends-turned-family (sorry, I know, I keep bringing up college, but I did just graduate two months ago), whose antics inspired some of the stories in this book. To the United Airlines Standby list for putting me at the top as I wait in this airport gate, writing this.

And finally, to the amazing city of Chicago. A city that I fell in love with over college (third time's the charm). Thank you for holding all of my friends for me while I move and start a new life in Boston. I'll be coming back soon.

Chapter 1

"Shit," I muttered under my breath, the realization hitting me like a ton of bricks. I should have taken a closer look at the invitation. I really, *really* should have taken a closer look at the invitation. If I had, maybe I would have realized sooner that I wasn't going to a *bridal* shower. Maybe it wouldn't have taken me standing frozen in the center of the brightly decorated living room, surrounded by cooing guests and pastel-hued decorations, to realize how much I had fucked up. How much I will probably never hear the end of this.

How had I gotten myself into this mess?

It was a simple mix-up – an innocent misunderstanding that had spiraled into what soon will be one of the most mortifying experiences of my life. I had been so busy the past few weeks with GenTech's newest project pitch that when I received the text from Kait this morning reminding me that the shower was today, I didn't think twice about it. I had nodded to myself, changed from my fuzzy socks into my more comfortable running heels, and ran seven blocks to the nearest Target. In my haste to get here on time, I had grabbed what I thought at the time was a suitable and funny gift from the store.

For context, Kait was engaged. She had been engaged for the past three years. It was only natural to peek at the invitation I received in the mail then promptly lost two weeks ago, see the vague pattern of 'B___ Shower' and let my brain fill in the blanks. But as I soon discovered, this was not the setting I had thought; it was a freaking baby shower, complete with diaper cakes and onesie garlands.

For God's sake, her great-grandmother Irene was here. All 5'1 and 100 pounds of the 98-year-old woman was crouched in a love seat, practically sinking into it. Who even goes to a baby shower when you're 98? If it was me, I would have played the age card and hung out at the Bingo table all day.

My cheeks burned with embarrassment as I clutched the offending gift in my hands, desperately searching for an exit strategy. All the other ladies had already sat down, waiting for Kait to open her very many cute and pastel and perfectly appropriate gifts, while I was trying to figure out if anyone would question me going to the bathroom, sneaking out a window, and never returning.

"Alina, come on! I can't wait to see what you got me." Kait beamed at me, her cheeks rosy and blushing with what I thought was a post-taco sheen, but now I realize was, in fact, a pregnancy glow all along. No wonder she didn't chug a marg like she used to in college.

"I actually have to-"

"Nope! It's Saturday. You're taking today off work. I've decided it, so will you please sit, so I can open your present?"

So this was what it was to feel like a deer in headlights. For some reason, I always assumed it would be a quicker more fleeting feeling but nope, this is in fact lasting what feels like years.

Fuck. My. Life

She gave me a sweet smile and patted the seat next to her. As Kait's eyes pleaded with me, I felt a sinking sensation in the pit of my stomach. Everyone was staring, confused. Even fucking Lacey was staring at me with a curious, evil smirk on her face. God, I hated Lacey.

Chapter 1

Ever since middle school when she would make those snide remarks about my light-up Sketchers. I loved my light-up Sketchers, and she made me hate them, all with a sweet little angelic look on her face. Why is she even here? How in the world did my sweet, kind, funny best friend from college manage to meet the demonic pig-tail-wearing blonde from my middle school nightmares?

With a resigned sigh, I shuffled over to the circle of chairs, my cheeks flaming with embarrassment. I handed Kait the blue gift bag, my fingers trembling slightly as I watched her eagerly unwrap it. Some glitter fell onto the carpet and I cringed.

The room fell silent, all eyes on her as she pulled out the contents of the bag. There was a moment of confusion, followed by a collective gasp as Kait's gaze fell upon the item nestled within the sparkly tissue paper I paid extra for.

Her eyes widened in shock, then crinkled with laughter as she held up the glittery pale dildo for all to see. For a moment, there was silence. I held my breath, praying to a God out there that this wouldn't be the end of Great Grandma Irene. Lacey in all her bitchiness gave me a smirk and I almost punched her. The silence was deafening.

Then, to my surprise, a laugh broke out.

Great Grandma Irene's laughter rang out above the din of the crowd – a hearty, genuine laugh that filled the room with warmth and affection. I didn't even know a woman that frail could make a noise that large. After a beat, the rest of the room erupted into uproarious laughter, the tension dissipating in an instant as Kait doubled over with mirth.

"Oh my God, Alina, you didn't!" she exclaimed between giggles, her cheeks flushed with amusement. She reached into the bag and pulled out a colorful neon pamphlet, reading aloud.

"Limited edition sparkle-peen – sparkle-peen? Alina, you did not."

I put my head in my hands, not able to look at anyone in the face

3

Brushing Off Business

right now. Kait furthered my humiliation by clearing her throat and continuing on, her voice echoing through the room, detailing the absurd instructions printed on the pamphlet.

"With maximum quenching. Put in the freezer for four hours before use, then let your wildest fantasies come true…" She trailed off then looked at me expectantly, obviously seeking an explanation.

"You know… from college. We just finished marathoning Twilight and you said you would give anything to ride RPatt's vampire dick." I mumbled between my hands, still unable to lift my head from my hands. I might just stay here forever.

"You thought this was a bridal shower, didn't you?" She asked me knowingly, amusement dancing in her eyes. I nodded awkwardly, wanting to disappear into thin air.

"I can't believe you remembered that but couldn't remember what kind of shower this was on the invitation." Kait teased.

As the room erupted into laughter and good-natured teasing — except for Lacey of course that prude bitch — I couldn't help but join in, recognizing the absurdity of the situation. Kait and I had been friends for nine years, ever since we met during our sophomore year in college. She understood my tendency to get wrapped up in work and never held it against me when my personal life became a bit scattered. It was one of the reasons we worked as well as we did.

She gave me a comforting hug and a playful wink before turning her attention back to the crowd.

"Okay! Who's next?"

After my gift mishap, the rest of the shower went on swimmingly. Luckily, the rest of the gifts *were* baby-appropriate, one of which was a milk-pumping kit that genuinely looked like a medieval torture device. It gave me goosebumps just thinking about the whole breastfeeding

Chapter 1

process. Hopefully, Kait's kid didn't end up breastfeeding until 4 years old the way I see some kids do on social media, or 11 years old like that kid in Game of Thrones.

As I hurried out of the baby shower, my mind immediately shifted back into work mode. The looming presentation on Monday weighed heavily on my thoughts. There was still so much to do and no matter how much work I got done, it just felt like time was always running out. I have been working on this proposal for the past two months to expand GenTech into international markets. Every minute of every day was dedicated to this presentation.

Because it wasn't just any presentation – it was my opportunity to finally demonstrate my skills, business acumen, and potential to take on greater responsibilities within the company in front of the board of directors, one of which being my boss Jack who tasked me with this responsibility. I couldn't afford to let anything distract me.

As I stepped into the elevator, my focus remained squarely on the tasks ahead. The doors slid shut in front of me, and just as the elevator began its descent, a series of sneezes echoed through the confined space. Irritation surged through me as I turned to a corner to see a tall man standing behind me, his nose red and eyes watery.

'Great', I thought. Of all the elevators in this building, I had to get stuck in one with a sick person. I discreetly scooted to an opposite corner, trying to breathe as little as possible. If I was going to be stuck in this shoe box of an elevator for the next few seconds with Patient Zero, I had to prevent getting sick as much as possible.

I couldn't afford it right now.

My fingers itched toward my purse, where I knew my Purell was, but I held myself back. It would've soothed the intense discomfort I was feeling, but it also would've been rude, and my dad taught me better than that.

The man seemed to notice my light shuffle and glanced at me

sheepishly, offering a weak smile.

"Sorry about that. I think I caught a cold."

I gawked at him, unsure what to say until a deafening creak pulled my eyes away from him and up to the ceiling where the light was now flickering just as the elevator jolted to a sudden stop.

Dear God no.

Kait had told me of how these elevators were built in the late 80s and how oftentimes they'll come to a stop for no reason other than their age, only to continue a few minutes later. It didn't help that the intense humidity that was Chicago in August was starting to creep in through the seams of the walls, beading sweat on my skin. I really should have taken the stairs. It would have been 9 floors of hell, but it would have been better than this.

Another sneeze erupted from the man behind me, accompanied by a stifled groan, as if he were trying to suppress it. Panic fluttered in my chest as I glanced at him, realizing we were now trapped between floors.

"Are you kidding me?" I cried, my frustration bubbling to the surface once again. "This is the last thing I need right now."

Just when I managed to take four hours off of prepping for the presentation, fate decided to throw me a curve ball.

The man shifted uncomfortably, his apologetic expression doing little to assuage my frustration. He started speaking to me in a congested voice, wiping his nose with a tissue.

"I'm really sorry about this. I was gonna take the stairs, I promise… but my body's exhausted."

I stared at him.

"I'm Max, by the way." He said, offering me a lazy smile, his tired eyes peering over at me under his tortoiseshell frames. They framed his face nicely, highlighting his bright eyes, a vibrant shade of green that reminded me of freshly cut grass in the spring. His hand started

Chapter 1

to lift towards me as if planning for a handshake, but then he seemed to have second thoughts and gave me a friendly wave instead.

A pang of guilt washed over me. Here was Max, a complete stranger, offering a friendly gesture despite his obvious exhaustion, and all I could muster was irritation. I swallowed my pride and forced a small smile.

"I'm Alina. Bennet." I replied, waving in return. "Nice to meet you, Max."

Max started grinning, his smile lighting his whole face up. As his grin widened, his eyes seemed to sparkle with delight, momentarily distracting me from the tense situation we found ourselves in. Despite the flickering light and the cramped space, there was something unexpectedly comforting about the warmth in Max's expression.

"Nice to meet you too, Alina," he said, his congested voice softening with genuine warmth. "Though I wish it were under better circumstance-ACHOO!"

Interrupted by his own sneeze, his body jerked involuntarily, the sound vibrating the walls of the elevator. His brown hair flopping around with the motion almost brought a genuine smile to my face.

Taking a deep breath, I forced myself to remain calm. There was no point in getting worked up over something I couldn't control. However, I couldn't help the ball of lead forming in my stomach as the gravity of the situation began to sink in.

We were trapped in a malfunctioning elevator, with no way of knowing when we'd be freed. Kait said it normally only lasted about five minutes, but I had read too many thrillers growing up that I couldn't imagine being in here for less than five hours.

My dad once got stuck in a hotel elevator while getting ice and we didn't see him for hours. Eventually, he came back to the hotel room, but his jacket and hair were all dusty, and it turned out the firemen had him climbing the elevator shaft. We didn't even know he was stuck in the elevator. He didn't have service.

Oh, God. My eyes widened and I shoved my hand in my purse, pulling out my phone. Zero bars. There suddenly wasn't enough air in the elevator.

Max, sensing my incoming panic attack, reached out a reassuring hand and gave my shoulder a gentle squeeze, his worn leather bracelets brushing against my collar.

"Hey, don't worry," he said, his voice steady despite the flickering lights and the occasional creak of the elevator. "We'll be out of here before you know it. These things happen all the time."

His words offered a small measure of comfort, but I couldn't shake the lingering sense of unease.

"I hope you're right," I replied shakily, forcing a weak smile onto my face. "I really can't afford to be stuck here for too long. I have a huge presentation on Monday."

Max's eyes widened in understanding.

"Ah, the dreaded Monday presentation," he said with a sympathetic nod, the motion causing his unkempt brown hair to flop with it.

Just then he let out another sudden, explosive sneeze, catching me off guard with its intensity, his hand jerking off my shoulder so he could sneeze into his elbow. Another frustrated groan left his mouth, and he shuffled back to his corner of the elevator.

He slid down against the wall and landed on the floor, sitting with his knees up in front of him. "Well, if we're going to be stuck here for a while, might as well make ourselves comfortable," he said with a slight smile.

I stayed standing, leaning against the opposite wall, keeping my distance. "I think I'll stick with standing, thanks. Gotta stay prepared in case we need to make a quick escape."

Max chuckled, his laugh turning into a cough. "Smart move. I probably should have thought of that before plopping down. I don't

Chapter 1

even know if I can get back up after this."

"Always be prepared."

"Where's that from again?"

"I think it's the boy scouts."

"Were you a boy scout?" He asked, sniffling into his tissue.

I stared at him, my eyebrow raised.

Max looked around blearily while waiting for my answer before his eyes landed on my face and widened. "Crap! Sorry! No, you definitely were not a Boy Scout. I think I just had a stroke or something. You do not look like a Boy Scout. If anything, you look like an angel, which you probably are one because I do feel like I'm dying right now and I'm just really glad you're here, even if this is the last place you want to—"

"Okay, okay," I interrupted, holding up a hand. "Slow down there, Shakespeare. I get it, you're not at your best. Just try to breathe, alright?"

Max laughed weakly, nodding. "Got it. Sorry, my filter tends to break down when I'm sick. My friends are always making fun of me for it. I'm normally much smoother than this, I swear."

"Noted," I said, a smile tugging at my lips. "And no, I wasn't a Boy Scout. But I did manage to light a bonfire once, so I could see where you got my rugged outdoorsy wilderness vibe from."

I don't even know why I said that. Something about this stranger had my filter breaking down too. Maybe it was that he was sick and vulnerable.

"Not quite the vibe I was getting from you, I'm sorry to say," Max's eyes sparkled with amusement.

I scoffed and decided, fuck it, and slid down my side of the elevator until I was sat on the ground opposite him. "What do you do when you're not infecting people in elevators?"

He rasped a laugh, rubbing at his eye with his hand. "I make a good spaghetti carbonara." He offered.

"You know that's not what I meant."

"But it's the more interesting answer."

"I was hoping for something a little more juicy."

He chuffed and looked me dead in the eye, his eyes darkening with a seriousness that seemed foreign to him. "I don't use guanciale. I don't even use pancetta. I just use plain bacon. If you tell anyone, though, I will have to contact the authorities and pursue legal action against you."

I burst out laughing, unable to help myself. "Your secret is safe with me. I promise not to report you to the pasta police."

Max grinned, the serious look evaporating as quickly as it had appeared. "Thanks. That's a load off my mind."

We smiled at each other, and I was puzzled by how comfortable I felt right now, in this broken elevator, with this sneezy man, a million things I have to do today all forgotten for the moment.

"So, what's this big presentation you're working on?"

I sighed, running a hand through my hair. "It's for a proposal to expand GenTech into international markets. I've been working on it for two months, and it's kind of my chance to prove myself to the board of directors."

"Wow, that sounds intense," Max said, adjusting his glasses. "No wonder you're on edge. But I'm sure you've got it all under control."

I raised an eyebrow. "You don't even know me. How can you be so sure?"

He shrugged, a playful glint in his eyes. "Just a hunch. You've got that 'I can conquer the world' vibe."

I laughed despite myself, feeling more at ease in this conversation than I have the past week. Something about him just drew the truth out of me, honest and unfiltered. "I wish I felt that way. Lately, it's more like 'I hope I don't accidentally start a wildfire and kill everyone.'"

Chapter 1

"If you do start a wildfire, use your rugged outdoors wilderness connections to call the Boy Scouts. They'd know what to do."

I rolled my eyes, but couldn't suppress my smile.

Max chuckled, his laugh turning into a cough, which quickly turned into a sneeze. "Sorry about that," he mumbled, wiping his irritated nose with a tissue.

Oh, how I wish it was socially acceptable to whip out a bottle of Purell in moments like these.

Finally, with that last ceremonial sneeze, the elevator jolted back to life, the lights stabilizing and the doors sliding open. Relief washed over me as I shot up, gave a quick wave to the man on the floor and a smile that he returned, and rushed out, eager to put the unexpected encounter behind me and focus on the gargantuan list of things I had to do that day. But as I stepped into the bustling lobby, I couldn't shake the lingering thoughts of the sniffling man with the floppy brown hair.

Chapter 2

I'm dying.

I've died.

This was the end of me.

I always thought 29 was too young to die, but it's happened. The sneezy man from the elevator infected me with the plague.

As sunlight filtered through the curtains, shining unwanted onto my side of the bed, I groaned and buried my head deeper into my pillow. My limbs felt like lead, and every muscle in my body ached with a dull, persistent throb. With a heavy sigh, I reluctantly opened my eyes, greeted by the unwelcome realization that I was, in fact, still alive.

"I'm dying," I moaned to no one in particular, then promptly cringed at the hoarse whisper that came. The room spun slightly as I attempted to sit up, my head pounding in protest at the movement. A quick glance at the clock confirmed my worst fears: it was Monday morning, and I was one Benadryl away from slipping into a fever-ridden coma.

With a sinking feeling in the pit of my stomach, I hobbled over to my bathroom drawer, reaching inside for the thermometer I never thought I'd need, dreading the confirmation of what I already knew.

Chapter 2

As the digital display blinked to life, the numbers stared back at me accusingly: 103 degrees. Great. Just great.

I thought I was fine. As soon as I got off the elevator and out of sight, I squirted an ungodly amount of hand sanitizer onto my hands and thought I had caught it in time. Even as I worked all day long yesterday trying to finalize this presentation, I thought I had managed to get away with it. I was a little tired, but I figured that was just me being rundown from all the work I had been doing.

Realization washed over me like a wave crashing against the shore. I couldn't get out of bed, let alone make it to work or attend my presentation in this state. With a heavy heart and a groan of frustration, I sank back against the pillows, resigning myself to the fact that today was not going to go as planned. Reluctantly, I dialed Jack's number, awaiting the soothing timbre of his older voice. At 67, Jack was one of my favorite people in the office. His extraordinary experiences, extensive travel, and general satisfaction of a life well lived lent him a voice that could rival Morgan Freeman with how soothing and fatherly it was.

"Alina? What's wrong?" he asked as soon as he picked up, his tone filled with concern.

"Why do you think something's wrong?" I tried to joke, but my shaky voice and coughing gave me away immediately.

"Because you sound like you've just been run over by the 'L,'" he chuckled, "and you never call me."

"Just a bit under the weather," I admitted, feeling the weight of defeat in my words. "Actually, a lot under the weather. I woke up with a fever, and I can barely move."

There was a pause on the other end of the line, and I could almost picture Jack furrowing his brow in concern.

"I'm sorry to hear that, Alina."

"Thanks."

"Let's reschedule the proposal pitch. You take the next few days off. Remember, we have the auction this Friday."

"But the board of direc-"

"You let me handle them." Jack's stern voice interrupted my blubbering. "Don't worry about the presentation, Alina. Your health comes first. We can always reschedule. Just the fact you're calling me tells me all I need to know. Just focus on getting better, alright?"

I nodded, even though he couldn't see me, feeling a pang of anxiety rolling around in my stomach.

"Okay... Thanks, Jack."

As I hung up the phone, a sense of defeat washed over me. Rescheduling the presentation was the last thing I wanted to do, but my body left me with no other choice.

With a heavy heart, I crawled back into bed, resigned to the fact that my plans for the day – and possibly the next few days – would have to be put on hold. In the past few months, Jack had become more than just a boss to me; he was a mentor in every sense of the word.

I appreciated how he took the time to listen, to understand, and to offer advice that went beyond the boardroom. He had a way of making me feel valued, like my success mattered to him as much as it did to me.

In a world where bosses often felt distant, Jack was refreshingly human, and for that, I was truly grateful. With how much he fought for me to be the project lead of GenTech's international expansion, the last thing I wanted to do was to let him down.

A soft buzz from the bedside table interrupted my thoughts just then. My head turned to observe the light commotion, but the motion was halted by the throbbing behind my eyes. An exasperated groan left my mouth, my arm reaching next to me to locate my phone.

Kait: Good luck baby, love you! You're gonna kill it today :)

Chapter 2

My legs kicked off the blanket, the offending material having overheated my body to the point I felt like I was in a pizza oven. *Should I tell her the truth and risk worrying her and the fetus, or should I lie and risk her finding out and getting angry?* I rolled a response over in my brain, then ultimately replied.

          Alina: Rescheduled it. Dying.
Kait: Symptoms?

Alina: Head pounding, sneezing, eyes sore, neck sore, everything sore, nose Niagara falls-ing. 103. keep you and your fetus away from me.

Kait: Stay alive for an hour
          Alina: Kait no
          Alina: Kait?
Alina: Kait you better not infect yourself by coming over, I'll never forgive you

Thud. Thud. Thud.

A loud knocking jolted me out of my fever-ridden haze. I speedily rushed over to the door at my grand pace of 2 miles per hour, but not before giving my bed a longing glance. Through the peephole, all I could see was a blur of white holding a plastic bag. With a resigned sigh, I opened the door to find a man, or what I could only assume was a man, being that he was covered from head to toe in some sort of makeshift personal protective equipment.

A pair of sunglasses rested on his nose bridge, drawing slight attention away from the N95 medical mask that occupied the bottom half of his face. A yellow raincoat wrapped around his large body, stretched tight with pink daisies patterning it, a little too small for him. Latex gloves covered his hands, the edges overlapping with his long sleeves under the thick raincoat cover.

In his hands, he carefully held a Tupperware containing some sort of liquid — chicken soup I'm guessing, based on the floating chicken and vegetables bobbing around the top of it. A smile started forming at the corner of my lip at the man in my doorway, a sheepish expression on his face evident despite the layers covering it.

"Hey Adam."

"Hi."

"Kait sent you?"

"Yep."

I turned around and plopped onto my couch, letting him enter and close the door behind me. He took his shoes off, placed them on the shoe rack next to the door, then walked himself to my kitchen, the rest of his protective equipment staying on.

I heard the telltale sounds of kitchen equipment clanging against each other and only prayed he didn't scratch one of my non-stick pans. I just bought those new after my old ones got recalled for leaching microplastics into food. I almost kept them too if my cousin Harper hadn't barged her way in here with her emergency key and thrown them in the dumpster when I wasn't home.

"What's with the armor?" I attempted to holler, the action inciting a series of coughs to hack from my lungs.

"Can't risk any germs getting to Kait or the bean." He hollered back, unfazed by the coughing. I heard a sloshing sound followed by the hum of the microwave.

"Were the sunglasses and raincoat really necessary?" I asked.

"Don't want your plague spit hitting my eyes, and I read that raincoats are hydrophobic or something. I'll probably run all my clothes through the dryer after this."

"Can you not just say waterproof? And isn't the dryer thing for bedbugs?"

"I don't know" he shrugged, the sounds of the rubber raincoat stretching over his body accompanying the movement.

"I'm just sick. I don't have bedbugs." I heard the shrill beeping of the microwave, followed by heavy footsteps in my direction. Adam placed a steaming bowl of soup on the coffee table with a spoon and a glass of water, then sat down on the armchair next to me.

A snort escaped me at the sight of him, the ridiculous outfit providing a stark contrast from how this man normally looks. He was a lacrosse star in high school and a playboy in college. The man was 6'3 and had a full head of hair. It was hard walking with him without him getting accosted by someone asking for his number.

From his backpack, he pulled out a sleeve of crackers and a tissue box and placed them on the couch arm above my head. A warmth washed over me at the caring actions of this man, my best friend's fiancé of three years. I mustered all of my strength to put myself into a vertical position on the couch and started ripping into the crackers, glancing at his sunglasses-covered eyes.

"You didn't have to come. I really don't want you or Kait to get whatever I have." I mumbled quietly, mouth partially full of saltines.

Adam looked at me with a sympathetic smile, his concern evident in his eyes.

"Kait was worried. She also wanted me to tell you she made the soup."

"So she poured a jar of Progresso into a Tupperware and added a bunch of black pepper."

"Exactly."

As I took the soup from the table, I couldn't help but feel a surge of gratitude for having friends like Kait and Adam. We've seen each other through our worst. Sometimes I think back to senior year in college when they took me on my first date — and then quickly helped me escape my first date 30 minutes later — and I feel a tinge of sadness that our carefree college days are behind us. Soon our little trio would become their little trio, and I'd be alone again.

"Heard you had to miss a big something at work today." He gave me an apologetic smile. They knew how deeply I wound myself in work, sometimes not going anywhere but my office and apartment for days at a time, too focused on a new project or initiative. A lump formed in my throat and I nodded, my eyes watching an orange carrot chunk bob around in the soup.

"Wanna talk about it?"

"It was a presentation," I confessed, stirring the soup absentmindedly. "A big one. I've been preparing for it for months."

Adam's sympathetic gaze only amplified my sense of disappointment, the weight of the missed opportunity heavy on my shoulders. Yet, as I met his eyes, I found solace in the silent understanding between us.

"It's just frustrating, you know?" I continued, my voice barely above a whisper. "To have everything planned out, only for it to be derailed by something as mundane as a fever. I swear to God if I ever end up in an elevator with a sick person again, I will wrench those doors open and squiggle out onto whatever floor or half floor it ends up on."

Adam nodded in understanding, his expression filled with empathy and slight amusement even under the layers of the sunglasses and face mask. For a moment, we sat in silence, the only sound was the soft hum of the air conditioning unit in the background and my occasional sniffles. Then, with a gentle squeeze of my shoulder, Adam offered me a reassuring smile.

"Well, you'll knock it out of the park when you're feeling better," he said with unwavering confidence. "And in the meantime, you've got me, Kait, and the bean to take care of you."

A light laugh flowed through me, and I couldn't help but smile at

Chapter 2

the thought of a little Kait running around, wreaking havoc all around them.

"Are you guys finding out the sex on Friday?" I asked curiously.

He emitted a loud guffaw, the sound slightly muted by the mask, and shook his head.

"I told Kait it would be fun if it were a surprise as a joke and she almost shoved my head into a tree. You know Kait. She likes to be prepared."

I did know Kait and if I knew her like I thought I did, she already had a prioritized list of things to do if it were either a boy or a girl. Ever since college, she's known that she wanted to be a mother. We always joked around about "lead baby" because our college apartment was built in the 70s and we had to sign a clause about the potential of lead exposure when signing our lease, but I never thought about when she actually would have a child one day.

I've never thought about if I even wanted to have a child one day. My train of thought was interrupted by an obnoxious sneeze that jerked my whole body, some soup sloshing out the sides of the bowl onto the pillow under it.

Adam flung himself back against the armchair dramatically like he had just been shot and gazed at me bewildered.

"Jesus Christ woman!" He bellowed before gathering himself up and putting his backpack on. "Lots of love, but I need to go. This probably goes against 3 different OSHA standards."

As I watched Adam stumble out the door, his squeaky rubber-clad figure gradually fading from view, I couldn't help but snort in amusement. The large former football player and wrestler cowering over a sneeze played in my mind once again. Kait and her bean are gonna be so loved. With a sigh, I put the bowl down and turned back to my room, the warmth of his visit lingering long after he had gone.

Chapter 3

Whatever that guy had, it was lethal. After three days of dying in bed, coming back to work in the middle of the work week was an overall less than pleasant experience. The thousands of emails greeting me in my inbox were a lovely gift, and the scathing comments from one of the board members on my 'lack of professionalism' was just the cherry on top. Like he had never been sick before.

Now, it was Friday afternoon, and the weight of the morning's events still hung heavy in the air as I sat at my desk, sorting through a stack of paperwork. Despite a few hiccups, the presentation had gone better than I had expected, but the adrenaline rush had faded, leaving me feeling slightly drained.

After a week of constantly feeling like I was on the verge of death, the mental exhaustion had started to kick in and I was ready to go home and pass out for three days. Unfortunately, GenTech was hosting a charity auction tonight at the Memoria Art Gallery.

Just as I was about to leave the office to start getting ready for tonight, my phone rang, startling me out of my thoughts. Glancing at the caller ID, I saw my dad's name flashing on the screen. It wasn't unusual for

Chapter 3

him to call, but something in the back of my mind told me this wasn't going to be an ordinary conversation.

"Hey, Papa," I answered, trying to sound upbeat despite the fatigue in my voice.

"Alina, *sayang*, how did the presentation go?" His deep voice sounded cheerful yet tired, and for a moment, my heart clenched with concern. At 64, my dad was getting older, and I could hear it in every strained syllable.

"It went well, Papa," I replied, trying to inject as much enthusiasm as I could muster. "I nailed it, actually. Luckily, the board was able to reschedule it for this morning and after apologizing to them about the whole situation, it went perfectly. The board loved the proposal, and I think we're one step closer to expanding into international markets."

I left out the part where the board chewed me out for canceling on them at the last minute and wasting their time, but he did not need to know about that.

There was a brief pause on the other end of the line before my dad spoke again, his tone softening with pride.

"That's my girl," he said, his voice thick with emotion. *"Anakku dari bintang."*

My child of the stars.

It always made my eyes watery whenever he called me that. I felt a lump form in my throat as I listened to the wistfulness in his voice.

When I was younger, my dad loved recounting the story of my birth. He had set up his telescope to observe Comet Hale-Bopp, which he'd been anticipating for two years. Just as he was about to look through it, my mother called in a panic, saying I was arriving three weeks early. He dashed down the hill, leaving his telescope behind, and four hours later, I was born. After ensuring my mother and I were settled, he held me up to the hospital window, trying to point out the comet to me. He named me Alina for the light that seared through the sky that night.

"Born during the Hale-Bopp comet sighting," he'd tell people with sparkling eyes. "It was as if the heavens were celebrating your arrival."

My dad, an Indonesian Chinese astrophysicist of his time, was always one to weave magic into mundane moments. He'd regale me and my sister with tales of stars and galaxies, making sure we knew where we came from. It was always super cheesy of him, but we still sat in our beds every night, excitedly waiting for another cosmic story.

As he spoke, I couldn't help but smile, remembering those nightly stories, the memories bittersweet from what happened shortly after.

I cleared my throat, trying to dislodge the lump in my chest.

"I uh- I have to go, Papa. Big charity auction tonight, and you know me. I need all the time to get ready that I can get." I laughed lightly, hoping to end the conversation before it made me cry.

There was a moment of silence on the other end of the line before my dad spoke again, his voice holding a cheerful quality.

"Okay, *sayang*. Come visit soon, okay?"

"Okay. Love you, Papa."

"Love you, honey."

As I set my phone down, I couldn't shake the feeling of melancholy that washed over me. Everyone knows how hard it is to be alone. No one ever tells you how much harder it is to watch your parent be alone. I try to visit him when I can, but something always seems to get in the way. Sometimes it's work. Sometimes it's friends. Sometimes I just can't handle going back to that house and the memories it holds.

Taking a moment to collect myself, I drew in a deep breath, steeling my resolve as I packed my bag and left the office.

As always, I was alarmingly early. I thought I would finally be able to show up to an event fashionably late. I thought this was the day. I

Chapter 3

even took a bath instead of a shower earlier and let my hair air dry. But even with luxuriously taking my time doing my makeup and hair and trying on four different gowns in my apartment, I somehow still managed to show up to the Memoria Art Gallery ten minutes early.

After Facetiming Kait for an hour and anxiously debating between the four dresses, we finally settled on a stunning deep green gown, a choice that Kait said accentuated my olive skin tone perfectly. The dress hugged my curves in all the right places, its flowing skirt cascading elegantly to the floor as I moved and I felt confident and poised in it as it moved around me.

The For Our Kids charity auction was an annual event that united the top tech companies in Chicago for a night of debauchery, art, and generosity. All proceeds from the event went towards the donation of tech products like computers and tablets for kids of lower-income families to help them in their academics.

The idea behind the auction was formulated after a study went viral on how students with technological resources such as iPads performed better in school, therefore creating a systematic divide in children of differing social classes. So even if a large proportion of the attendants came for the open bar and the opulent environment, it ultimately did a lot of good for a cause that I was passionate about.

As I stepped into the grand foyer of the Memoria Art Gallery, the air was alive with anticipation and excitement. The walls were adorned with exquisite artworks, each piece a testament to the creativity and talent of the artists. Guests mingled, their laughter and animated conversations filling the space with a certain energy you couldn't really get elsewhere. The sound of a live band echoed through the hall, adding to the festive atmosphere and creating a pleasant euphony in the room.

I took a moment to soak in the ambiance and peered at the abundance of people, all smartly dressed and glowing with the free-flowing alcohol, a large smile on my face. But before I could even take a moment to look around for the open bar, a sly figure appeared in front of me, blocking my view with an excited grin.

"Alina! Such a great job on the proposal." Jack's bright white teeth gleamed at me.

I snorted. "I thought so too until they reamed me out for canceling in the first place. Remind me never to get on an elevator with a sick guy again."

Just the thought of the abrasive discipline I received made me want to crawl into bed and lay there listening to Fight Song by Rachel Platten on repeat.

He laughed lightly, the sound airy and raspy from age.

"They'll get over it. Just look around you, they probably already have."

I peered around the room then and just like he said, there were board members laughing and chatting, drinks in their hands, smiles on their faces.

I guess with the bright colors and energetic ambiance of tonight, it was difficult not to forget all the troubles of the week. I felt the tension in my shoulders relax and it became a little easier to breathe.

Jack took my distraction as an opportunity to wave a waiter over and removed two flukes of champagne from his tray, discreetly placing one in my grasp.

"There's a reason you were promoted to Senior Operations Manager when you were."

He took a long sip, his eyes pensive. "Youngest in the company. You deserved it. Don't worry too much about the old rat bastards. Relax, Alina."

Jack Friedman was, himself, one of the 'old rat bastards'. For the past 25 years, he has served as GenTech's Director of Operations, a position that I would love to take up one day. A position I've been

Chapter 3

working tirelessly hard for my whole career to prove that I can take up one day. I gave him a genuine smile then, appreciating his unwavering support.

"Was this how you were able to woo Mr. Friedman? With flowery words and champagne?"

I tipped my champagne flute in his direction.

"Of course not. Mr. Friedman was exposed to my ruggedly good looks and mysterious nature. It was only a matter of time for him." He joked back.

If there was one word I would never use to describe Jack Friedman, it would be 'mysterious'. He was probably the chattiest adult I knew, oftentimes telling you stories and details you didn't need to know.

I laughed then, a genuine laugh that rarely made its way out in work environments. Jack and his husband had been together for over 40 years at this point, and when gay marriage was legalized in 2015, they jumped at the chance to finally get married like all their friends had. It was something I admired about him, how he had faced adversity in the workplace and made it as far up the chain of command as he did.

"I'm assuming you're about to network your ass off?" He asked knowingly.

"You know it." I replied with a smirk.

"That's my protégé." He playfully clinked his flute against mine, giving me a wink and leaving me to go socialize – I'm sure about golf or his retirement or Mr. Friedman, or even the new Mexican restaurant he was obsessed with that he claimed had an 'orgasmic queso that ignites something within him'.

The bubbles danced in the crystal flute, a fleeting moment of effervescence amid the swirling emotions within me. Jack's intuition never ceased to amaze me; he could always read me like a book, even in the midst of a crowded room.

As I took a sip of the crisp champagne, the lively chatter of the auction guests filled the surrounding air, blending with the soft strumming of the band nearby. A large group of people were settled around one of the spotlighted pieces hanging on the wall, but with the crowd, I couldn't see what it was.

Not that it would matter for me if I could, I barely understood modern art. I knew that art was subjective, but I swear that once I saw a crowd praising a piece that was just a black background with one white dot placed slightly off centered. I didn't get it. I probably never would. With that, I shook my hands, held my head up higher, plastered a polite smile on my face, and then got a head start on the long night of networking ahead.

I hated networking. Well, I loved some parts of networking; I loved the connections you could make that could change the trajectory of your whole career, the chance to meet new people and maybe learn something new, but the forced small talk and constant schmoozing? Not so much. However, tonight was different. Normally at these auctions, I could schmooze my way through the room with ease, but tonight, something felt off.

The pressure of the morning's presentation still lingered, leaving me mentally drained and less eager to engage in the usual social banter. As I navigated through the crowd, trying to muster up my usual charm, my attention was unexpectedly drawn back to that one piece, now empty of surveyors.

Its vibrant colors and intricate details caught my eye, momentarily captivating my thoughts and providing a brief reprieve from the usual socializing. I walked closer towards it, trying to figure out what it was exactly that beheld my attention so intensely.

A man? No. A woman standing on the edge of a cliff, gazing at the horizon. It was just the shadow of a woman really, her back facing the audience, but it felt like she was sad. And lonely. There was a sense of quiet strength in the figure's demeanor, the almost nonexistent clouds straying far away from her as if they couldn't bear to be near her pain. I have attended a great deal of these auctions, but I have never been so thrown off my element by a piece. I stood there, transfixed by it. As I continued to study the painting, a voice broke through the silence, pulling me back to reality.

"It's quite a captivating piece, isn't it?" A young woman next to me asked, a polite smile on her face.

I blinked, momentarily disoriented by the interruption, before offering a small smile in return.

"Yes, it certainly is," I replied, tearing my gaze away from the painting to acknowledge her.

It looked like she might have been a gallery assistant, her all-black, sleek outfit, slicked-back hair, and perfectly done makeup giving her away.

"It's the centerpiece of the auction. The way the artist blended the colors and conveyed emotion in such a profound manner is truly remarkable," she continued, her voice carrying a hint of reverence. I nodded, appreciating her enthusiasm for the piece, but having no knowledge of anything in the art world, I wasn't sure what else to say to her.

She continued on. "The artist behind it has become notorious for his emotional pieces. Most of the showcased pieces tonight are actually his. It's weird, though, he kind of came out of nowhere a few years ago. An M. Reynolds, I believe."

I didn't know much about the timeline of artists and I wasn't sure how odd it was that he gained popularity quickly, but I could admit that I was impressed. For an event of this magnitude, it was rare for more than one or two pieces to have been made by the same artist, much less most of them. Luckily, everyone was called to sit for the auction and dinner before I had to open my mouth and ultimately lose face in front of her.

With a polite thank-you to the gallery assistant, I took my assigned seat at one of the many circular tables, each spot having an elegant table setting with a sea bass dinner and numbered paddle. The dinners at these were always said to be delicious. I've never been able to enjoy one — too wracked with nerves and plans for the next conversation.

As I settled into my seat, the ambient chatter of the crowd enveloped me, punctuated by the occasional clink of cutlery against fine china. Glancing around the room, I couldn't help but marvel at the opulent decor and the sea of elegantly dressed guests, each one exuding an air of sophistication and refinement. Before long, the lights dimmed, and a hush fell over the room as Jack took to the stage.

I didn't know he was giving a speech. Normally one of the other directors does it, sometimes the CEO. His commanding presence demanded attention as he began to speak, his words echoing with authority and gravitas.

"Hello everyone. I'm Jack Friedman, the Director of Operations at GenTech and I would love to welcome you all to our annual For Our Kids charity auction. Now, before we dive into the bidding wars and break out the checkbooks, I must say, I'm truly impressed by the turnout tonight. I guess the promise of free wine and fancy art was enough to lure you all out from behind your computer screens." Jack's charismatic delivery elicited a ripple of laughter from the audience.

"Now, before I'm ushered off the stage like a senile old man so that you can get started with the main event, I wanted to make an announcement." He got serious then. It sent a ripple of anxiety through me, making me shift in my seat.

"I am pleased to announce that after 40 years here at GenTech, I will be retiring. Come the end of January, I will no longer be working at GenTech or any company." There was a rise in chatter amongst the crowd. I felt my heart drop to my stomach.

"Very sad, I know," He chuckled. "They really wanted me to retire

Chapter 3

end of December, you know, fiscal year and all that, but I'm a stubborn bastard and I'll go when I choose to go! Even if it's just 30 days later."

The crowd laughed then. Jack Friedman was an icon in the tech world. He started at the very bottom and worked his way up rapidly, always remaining a jokester and always remaining real. He never let success change him. Most of the people in this room probably knew him from his persistence in wanting to be friends with everyone. He never forgot a single detail people told him, no matter how small and insignificant a person thought it was.

I had no idea how.

It took intense concentration for me to remember anything. I never would have been able to be in one of those superhero movies where they received a prophecy once and seemingly memorized it on the spot.

"So thank you all for your support these past 40 years," He looked at me then, his gray eyes piercing even 100 ft away, "Starting next week, GenTech will be conducting an internal search into my replacement. I have nothing but optimism for whomever they'll pick to fill my shoes. So without further ado, let's start the auction. But first, I originally wanted to spotlight the artist of the night, Mr. Reynolds who has benevolently contributed over 4 of his pieces to the auction, one of which being the centerpiece of the gallery entitled 'Echoes in the Silence'."

"Unfortunately, he is running behind," he chuckled, "so let's honorarily raise our glass to the tardy artist of the night. Thank you all, Mr. Gusteau, you can take it away."

All 200 of the attendants raised their glass to the man, before the stocky auctioneer took his place and began the bidding.

◇◇◇

Not one hour later, I was elbow deep in my panna cotta when I felt a gentle tap on my shoulder. Already knowing who it was, I turned with a smile and found Jack towering above me, a mischievous glint in his eyes. As I opened my mouth to confront him about his bombshell of a retirement announcement, he cut me off.

"Alina, my dear, I know you have a lot to say and we can talk about it Monday at the office, but first, I'd like you to meet someone very special," he said, gesturing behind him with a flourish.

"It's the artist of the night. Mr. Max Reynolds."

Then he stepped aside, revealing the tall figure lurking in his shadow. I blinked in surprise, my spoon poised midair. It was the man from the elevator.

Chapter 4

How could this be possible?

The artist of the night. The creator of the mesmerizing painting that had put me in a trance earlier. The illustrious Mr. Reynolds.

M. Reynolds.

Max Reynolds.

Max.

Max from the elevator a week ago. Max, who was a complete stranger but comforted me anyway when our elevator got stuck. Max, who infected me with his flu/cold/plague and sent me out of commission for a whole week, making me reschedule and look bad in front of the board.

He offered a tentative smile, his eyes betraying a hint of nervousness. I let my eyes leave his, a peculiarly vibrant shade of green, and inspected his person. His floppy brown hair was tousled and unkempt, a wild mane of waves with a few tendrils resting on his tortoiseshell frames. His clothes were a canvas of their own, adorned with specks of paint and smudges of various colors, evidence of a day spent immersed in his art.

A lightweight linen button-down shirt in a soft white hung loosely over a white tee, the sleeves rolled up casually to reveal his forearms. Slim-fit chinos in a neutral khaki tone replaced his well-worn jeans, while suede loafers in a complementary shade completed his ensemble. With his leather necklace and his casual, paint splattered clothing, Max stood out in the room like a sore thumb.

His hands, stained with some sort of medium — I wanna say charcoal? — fidgeted nervously at his sides, causing his leather bracelets to tangle up together on his wrists. Despite his disheveled appearance, there was an undeniable charisma about him, a magnetic pull that would have pulled me in… had this man not hot boxed me in an elevator with his flu.

"Yes," I said flatly, "We've met."

His eyes widened in recognition, an abashed expression crossing his face. Jack simply looked befuddled, and sensing a tension in the air, he tried his hand at humor.

"Well. That's one less thing I have to do now. Getting closer to this retirement thing already!" Jack bellowed, a slight shake to his laughter giving away the awkward situation.

Luckily for him, Max took the reins and smoothed over the awkwardness with a gracious smile.

"It's a pleasure to officially meet you, Alina," he said, extending his large hand in a gesture of goodwill.

Despite my lingering annoyance, I couldn't ignore the genuine warmth in his tone. Reluctantly, I shook his hand, the tension between us momentarily easing.

Calluses.

Which sent a rush of perplexity through me. I hadn't realized artists would have those.

Yet his touch was delicate, the nimbleness of his touch conveying his probable talent for precision. Why did almost all artists get blessed with the gift of agile fingers? It was a lucky day if I was able to open a

Chapter 4

damn pickle jar.

I gave him a polite smile and a nod in return, my emotions simmering under the surface. I wonder if he knew just how badly that elevator encounter had affected me. He didn't seem the type to have entered that elevator with malicious intent, and part of me did feel bad for him that he had to leave his apartment in his condition.

But why? What did he need exactly? Did he need to get some groceries because his fridge was empty? Was he looking for medicine? Did he not have anyone that could take care of him? Was he just ignoring that he was sick and knowingly putting everyone at danger for something stupid like a date or a burger?

I took one more look at his face, his perfectly healthy face flush colored by the reddening of his cheeks, and felt my temper start up again beneath me. His hand in mine lingered there gently and he continued to stare at me. Jack, timely as ever, cleared his throat, breaking Max from whatever daydream he seemed to be in. Max's hand withdrew quickly and returned to his side, making a fist before flexing, leaving an odd sensation of warmth lingering in its wake.

"Sorry about that," Jack said with a knowing smile, oblivious to the situation between Max and me. "I just wanted to introduce him to my protégée first before he got bombarded by the masses. But now we've gotta share!"

With a wink, Jack took Max with him to the stage at the front of the room and took the mic. Max's juniper colored eyes stayed on mine until the last second.

"Alright, folks, gather 'round!" Jack's voice boomed through the room, drawing everyone's attention. "I know we're at the end of the auction, but I have the great pleasure of introducing tonight's featured — and tardy as hell — artist, Mr. Max Reynolds!"

As Jack gestured towards Max, a ripple of applause swept through the crowd. Max stepped forward, a humble smile playing on his lips as he acknowledged the applause with a gracious nod.

"Thank you, Jack," Max said, his voice carrying a hint of nervous excitement. "And thank you all for being here tonight. It's truly an honor to have my work featured at such a prestigious event, and I'm grateful for the opportunity to share it with all of you." The crowd anxiously awaited his next words, but they never came. He just continued smiling at everyone, nervous but confident.

He gave the crowd a nod and stepped off the stage, immediately getting bombarded by executives and the like.

I drank more champagne.

✧✧✧

An hour passed and yet the night was nowhere near done. Most people would see the poster and assume that a party full of tech people and former engineering majors would end early and uneventfully, but they'd be surprised by how much STEM people like to get down. Even in college, we had a stigma for being boring and preferring the company of our computers to actual people, but in my experience, the ones partying the hardest and closing the bars were always the engineers.

Probably because we needed it the most.

I had been dancing with some work friends for the past ten minutes when I left to the refreshments table to get some more of the caprese crostinis. Put anything on a mini crunchy toast and I was a happy camper. As expected, it was at that moment that Jack sidled up beside me, a proud grin etched across his face.

"You know, Alina," he whispered, "you seem not your usual go-getting, executive schmoozing, always-trying-to-get-ahead self tonight. Might I ask what's wrong?"

"Just sad I'm down to my last two crostinis," I lamented, wearily, a

Chapter 4

mourning expression on my face as I gazed at the two objects in my napkin.

He gave me a no-nonsense look.

I sighed. "Something just feels different tonight, I guess. Maybe I'm still contagious."

Jack frowned, his wrinkles deepening.

"Mhm. What's the situation between you and Max Reynolds?"

I dropped a crostini.

I almost whimpered as I looked at it splattered on the floor before turning my attention back to Jack and responding, "Nothing. He's just the man who trapped me in an elevator and gave me the plague."

Jack looked at me for a beat before bellowing in laughter. I took the distraction to pick the fallen crostini up with a napkin and throw it away in the nearby bin, wishing I could go back to a minute ago when it was safe and delicately tucked into my napkin with its partner.

Jack doubled over, his aged laughter ringing in my ears, "He's the one?"

"Yep."

Jack started wheezing. "What a small world!"

"Apparently so." I snorted before breaching the topic I really wanted to ask about. "Wait a second… you just dropped a major bomb earlier, then shoved this man in my face. You're really retiring?"

He got serious and nodded.

"It's time."

I let out a soft sigh, the weight of his impending retirement settling in my chest. Jack had been more than just a boss to me; he had been a mentor, a friend, and a constant source of support throughout my career at GenTech. The thought of him stepping down was both daunting and bittersweet.

"I'll miss having you around," I admitted quietly, my voice tinged with a hint of sadness.

I normally tried to avoid getting sentimental in work settings, as it gave people in the office a wrongful reason to skip over me when assigning tasks and promotions. All my career, I had to act differently to get ahead, but I always felt I could be genuine with Jack. He has never once punished me for being a woman.

Jack smiled warmly, his eyes reflecting the sentiment.

"I'll always be around. They can't get rid of me as easily as they think. And, with me stepping down, I'm hoping someone will be able to step up."

He gave me a pointed look.

"You think they'd consider me? Especially after they made it clear they now believe I don't respect their time and schedules." I asked wryly.

"You might have to prove yourself more than other candidates would. But they'd be stupid not to." We smiled at each other then, a soft expression on our faces.

For a minute, it was silent.

Then Jack did what he did best, lightening the mood with a subject change.

"You know those four pieces of Mr. Reynolds' we auctioned off earlier? They fetched quite a pretty penny. Looks like we've got a rising star on our hands."

I glanced over at Max, who was still surrounded by a throng of admirers, each vying for his attention and eager to congratulate him on his success. Despite the chaos around him, he remained composed and gracious, his eyes sparkling with a mixture of excitement and gratitude. It was almost annoying how effortlessly charming and likeable he was.

"You know," Jack continued, drawing my attention back to him, "You should consider adding some of Max's pieces to your collection, Alina," Jack suggested with a knowing smile. "They'd look great in

Chapter 4

your office."

I chuckled lightly, appreciating Jack's attempt to shift the conversation away from retirement and onto lighter topics. We both knew I would never purchase these pieces. For one, they were extremely out of my budget, and for two, I didn't decorate my office.

"Maybe I'll consider it," I joked, my gaze drifting back towards Max, who seemed to be handling the attention with casual charm. Jack was always egging me about how minimalist and plain my office was. I always retorted back with a study on how women who have colorful offices get taken significantly less seriously than their male counterparts. Besides, with how much his four pieces sold for tonight, they definitely weren't in my price range anyway.

As Jack excused himself to mingle with other guests, I found myself wandering towards a quieter corner of the gallery, seeking a moment of respite from the bustling crowd. Leaning against a nearby wall, I took a deep breath, allowing myself a moment to collect my thoughts. It was probably time to go home soon. I wanted a bath. And my bed. And a peanut butter brownie Kait had sent a tray of yesterday.

It wasn't long before I sensed someone approaching, their footsteps echoing softly against the polished floor. Glancing up, I found Max standing before me, a warm smile on his pink lips.

"Alina," Max greeted, his voice soft yet confident. "I hope you don't mind me interrupting your moment alone. Didn't realize how bloodthirsty these art buyers would be. Haven't gotten a single minute to myself." He joked.

I glanced up at him, my expression guarded.

"Depends on why you're interrupting."

Max's smile faltered slightly, but he persisted.

"I just wanted to say thank you for handling the situation earlier with grace. I know our last encounter wasn't ideal."

I arched an eyebrow, crossing my arms over my chest.

"You mean when you sneezed on me multiple times in an enclosed space?"

He winced at the reminder, his cheeks flushing with embarrassment, then ran a hand through his hair.

"I'm really sorry about that. I normally don't sneeze on pretty women in elevators. Hope you didn't get sick or anything because of me."

Ignoring that comment, I replied, "I did."

I almost left it at that, but something in me made me continue, "I had to reschedule a monumental event in my career last minute because I was so sick."

Max looked horrified, a tinge of anguish crossing his face.

"Alina, I am so sorry," he said earnestly, "I would never knowingly infect anyone in any other circumstance. It's just that I ran out of food in my apartment when I was all fever-ridden and I desperately needed to buy some soup because I finally wasn't throwing everything up and-"

He stopped himself and shook his head, starting again. "I held off as long as I could… if that helps at all."

My heart broke a little in my chest.

He didn't have anyone to take care of him. He didn't have an Adam or Kait bringing him homemade soup and crackers the way I did. I softened my gaze slightly, relenting just a fraction.

"I'm sorry. That was… in poor taste of me. It wasn't really your fault. And apology accepted, I guess. Just try not to get too close this time."

Max nodded, a small smile playing on his lips.

"Noted. I'll keep my distance."

He shuffled two steps to the side, his eyes looking at me in amusement. It almost made me laugh, but I choked it down.

There was a moment of awkward silence between us, the tension palpable in the air as we both stared at a nearby sculpture.

Chapter 4

Then, with a forced casualness, Max changed the subject.

"I haven't been to a gallery in a while, it was kind of weird seeing things that I painted hung up like that." He trailed off before turning to me again, "So, what did you think of the artwork here tonight?"

I shrugged nonchalantly, glancing around the gallery. "It's... impressive, I guess."

Max raised an eyebrow, clearly sensing my reluctance to engage in small talk.

"Not a fan of art?"

"It's not that," I replied curtly. "I just, I don't fully understand it, that's all."

His eyes widened slightly and he took a step back towards me.

Before Max could respond, I interjected with an excuse, eager to escape the awkwardness of this conversation.

"I should go. It's getting late, and Uber prices are probably about to skyrocket any minute now."

He closed his mouth immediately, putting his hands in his pockets and nodding. The motion drew my eyes to his throat, where the tendons flexed subtly with each movement.

He had a prominent Adam's apple, undercut by a leather necklace that normally I would think looked obnoxious on anyone else, but somehow worked for him. A faint shadow of stubble lined the curve of his jaw, and his neck was strong and well-defined.

"Yeah, I probably should go back to thanking my buyers," he said with a small smile. "But hopefully, we can start fresh next time."

I hesitated for a moment before nodding, offering a tentative smile in return.

As I walked away, I couldn't shake the feeling of unease that lingered in the pit of my stomach. Despite his seemingly genuine apology, there was something about Max that still rubbed me the wrong way. And until I figured out what that was, I wasn't about to let my guard down around him.

Chapter 5

Come Monday morning, everyone was back in the office, their hangovers cured by the long weekend and the post-auction burgers at Au Cheval. I've been wanting to go there for a while. Cheeseburgers are my number three favorite food after all, yet somehow I had lived in the Chicago land area my whole life and never been there.

Every time I go, the line always just puts me off. Not to mention, with my apartment being in Streeterville, I would have been going the complete opposite direction.

Coming into the office after a reluctant week off was like coming home. The soft hum of the office buzzed around me as I sat at my desk. Papers were neatly stacked in front of me, my computer screen displaying a flurry of emails and spreadsheets demanding attention. The afternoon sunlight filtered through the blinds, casting warm, golden rays across the room and illuminating the space with a gentle glow.

As I diligently focused on my work, the rhythmic clacking of my keyboard was interrupted by a knock on my open door. Glancing up, I saw Jack, my boss, standing in the doorway. He closed the door shut behind him before striding purposefully towards my desk. His usual

air of authority was tempered by an unmistakable twinkle in his eyes.
With a slight tilt of my head, I regarded Jack with curiosity, intrigued by his sudden burst of enthusiasm.

"What's up, Jack?" I inquired, setting aside my work to give him my full attention.

"Alina," Jack began, his voice carrying a note of excitement, "I have some news to share with you."

I arched an eyebrow, intrigued by Jack's sudden enthusiasm.

"Ah, the suspense is killing me," I quipped, the tone of my voice deadpan.

Jack leaned in slightly, a grin spreading across his face.

"Well... first I want to know; what do you think when you look around the office?"

I furrowed my brows in confusion, leaning back against my chair and taking a gander of the office. As expected, Carla and Shay were at the water cooler, probably gossiping about the events of the weekend, Dan was ducking into the restrooms to take his third bathroom break of the morning, and the scent of popcorn was wafting through the air from Kelsey's desk.

"That Kelsey needs to stop microwaving popcorn in the office?" I asked wryly. I loved popcorn as much as the next girl and I understand Kelsey's an intern still in college, but every girl learns at some point that as good as it smells, it's not really a good look for clients to have a whole corporate building smelling like it.

I personally always wait to pop my popcorn at home.

His face fell slightly before he continued on.

"I was thinking more... aesthetically."

I took another look around, my confusion deepening.

"It's nice? Minimalist?"

He interjected, stopping me from offending him more.

"Well. You're wrong. It's boring and we need more color!"

Chapter 5

I frowned momentarily. I've always liked how sleek and professional the office looked. I even made my own office bare and minimalist. My own internship in college proved that when you decorated your desk with knick-knacks and colorful trinkets, you get taken less seriously.

"I'm not following."

Jack whiffled, the air leaving his mouth in an unsteady stream, causing his lips to flap amusingly. Almost like a horse.

"Our office is boring. Our logo is boring. Our website is boring. Everything here is boring. It makes me bored, it makes our clients bored, and it doesn't facilitate a creative environment. We're a tech company for Christ's sake, we should be innovating and letting the creative juices flow and in order to do that, we need a hell of a lot more visual simulation in this space."

"Aren't you leaving soon?"

He gave me a pointed look. "Yes. And I want to make my mark on the office before I go. Leave the world a better place than you found it, and all that."

I nodded, understanding that Jack was going through with whatever plan he had concocted no matter what anyone said.

"Okay. And how do you plan to," I paused, searching for the right words, "facilitate the flow of everyone's juices?"

Nope.

Those were not the right words.

I cringed loudly and looked at Jack, he was also shaking his head, a grimace on his face, causing his crow's feet to indent deeper into his face.

"Let's pretend you didn't say that."

"Mhm."

"Okay!" He picked a ball of lint from his jacket, then turned to me again with a suspicious excitement in his face.

"I have taken it upon myself, with the approval of the board, of course, to commission an artist to handle the rebranding of our brand, our logo, our website, as well as the artwork for the building."

Oh, Jack. Leave it to him to completely shake things up before he leaves.

"That's... a big job. Have you found one?" I asked.

"Yes, actually," he announced proudly. "And guess what? He's supposed to be arriving today."

My interest piqued at the mention of a new artist. I leaned back in my chair, crossing my arms as I regarded Jack with curiosity.

"That's great news," I remarked, my tone laced with anticipation. "Any idea when he's supposed to get here?"

Jack's grin widened.

"Actually, he should have been here about five minutes ago," he admitted, a hint of amusement in his voice. "But you know artists, always fashionably late."

I chuckled at Jack's remark, nodding in agreement.

"True, they do tend to arrive at things whenever 'the vibes call to them'," I conceded, but a flare of irritation simmered in me.

I have never really been able to admire people who were constantly late. It was just a complete disrespect of the other person's time and unless they had a good reason, I could never not get irritated by it.

Especially, if it was to do it fashionably to assert a level of 'coolness'.

"Well, I'm sure he's almost here. I can't wait for you to meet him." He said with a knowing grin that puzzled me even more.

"Where did you find a guy like this again? Part artist, part graphic designer, part digital illustrator?" I asked.

"Actually, he was at the au-"

Jack was interrupted by a knock at the door. He turned to it with a start, then looked back at me with a mischievous grin on his face.

I was starting to get a little scared.

Jack was a great boss — a great guy in general, but sometimes he

Chapter 5

scared me a little. Like most men his age, he had a mischievous streak in him and more often than not, it always bit me in the butt.

"Come in!" I spoke loudly, making sure to hold an air of fake confidence in my voice.

In high school, my cousin Harper told me a statistic that she read that stated that it takes a mere seven seconds to make a first impression. It doesn't even matter what you say — people will thin-slice a person based on how they look and how they sound.

Naturally, as a self-anointed control freak, this freaked me out, which was why I always injected a healthy dose of assertiveness and poise into my voice when meeting someone new. And why I never entered a work environment in anything but my best.

The door swung open, revealing a familiar figure standing in the doorway.

Max.

Again.

The artist Jack had been talking about was Max.

He entered the room with a casual yet confident demeanor, his eyes scanning the space before settling on Jack and me. He wasn't wearing glasses today and his piercing green eyes sparkled with amusement, more prominent on his face without the normal filter over them.

"Mr. Friedman, thanks for inviting me here." His deep voice sounded into the room, eyes making contact with mine. He held a disposable coffee cup in his hand. So that's why he was late. He had made us wait for him on our very busy day for ten minutes because he was grabbing himself a coffee. My mood soured a smidgen.

He hadn't stopped looking at me since he got here, probably plotting another way to take me out of commission for a week. "Alina, it's lovely to see you again."

I gave him a minute smile.

"Likewise."

Jack was positively gleaming with mirth. He clapped his hands in front of him and said, "Well, now that we're all here, let's get down to business."

He gestured for Max to take a seat, and then motioned for me to join them at the round table in my office. I complied, feeling a mixture of curiosity and apprehension about what Jack had in store.

"Alina, Max," Jack began, his tone businesslike yet cheerful, "Max here will be taking on the task of beautifying our logo, website, and office space and Alina" He paused, a mischievous twinkle in his eye. "I will be placing you in charge of this project."

My stomach lurched and I immediately protested. My eyes shot to Jack's with objection.

"Jack, I can't take this project, I'm busy with our international expansion plan."

He didn't waver one bit.

"Alina, you can do both."

"I'm not sure I can. I'm not even in marketing–" I protested.

Jack gave me a pointed look and his voice took on a lighter but more calculated tone.

"I know you can. And," he paused, "when the directors see the new logo on all of our merchandise and products, they'll think of the person responsible for it. When they click onto the new and improved website, and look around the office at the beautiful space, it might even give that person a leg up in the deliberations when hiring for my position in a few months."

My words died in my throat. He was right. He also was hinting something to me that he probably wasn't supposed to. I saw Max look between the two of us, a quiet understanding dawning on his face. He hadn't said a word since his greeting, the only sign he was still here being his fingers fidgeting on the table beside his coffee cup.

If Jack was right and I missed an opportunity to put myself ahead

Chapter 5

because of my wariness of a single man, I would never be able to forgive myself. This wasn't me. I didn't fight my way through this company and work endless nights and weekends just to get in my own way.

Jack looked at me for an answer, and I just nodded in agreement.

"Excellent. Now, I want the two of you to collaborate on this project. Alina, I'm putting you in charge of overseeing the entire rebranding process. And Max, I expect you to work closely with Alina to bring your vision to life."

I blinked in surprise, not expecting to be assigned such a significant responsibility. Max, on the other hand, seemed unfazed, his smile widening as his hands paused in their fidgeting.

"Of course, Jack," I replied, trying to keep my tone professional despite my inner turmoil. "I'll do my best to ensure everything runs smoothly."

"Excellent!" Jack exclaimed, clapping his hands together once more. "I have full confidence in both of you. Now, let's discuss the details of the project and how we can make our brand truly shine."

Shit.

✧✧✧

After half an hour of outlining the project details and our deliverables, Jack took his leave, leaving me and Max in my office alone.

I couldn't help the sense of unease that settled over me.

It wasn't just the missed opportunity that weighed on my mind; it was also the prospect of working closely with this man, the very person who inadvertently caused my setback. As I gathered my thoughts and prepared to give Max the rundown of the project, I couldn't shake the feeling of tension that hung in the air between us.

Taking a deep breath, I turned to face Max, determined to maintain a professional demeanor despite the undercurrent of discomfort.

"Alright," I began, my voice steady as I handed him a printed document outlining the project guidelines. "It looks like Jack wants us to install six large paintings on our floor by December as well as one brand-new logo, and an updated website. This gives us three months to plan, design, paint, and install."

Seeing the inquisitive look on his face, I clarified, "We share the building with two other companies."

He nodded at me, then accepted the document with a small smile, his eyes crinkling with amusement as he scanned through the pages.

"Quite the comprehensive list," he remarked, his tone laced with amusement. "I take it you run a tight ship around here."

I resisted the urge to bristle at his comment, reminding myself to stay focused on the task at hand.

"I expect nothing less than excellence," I replied, my tone firm but polite. "This project is important, and I need to ensure that everything runs smoothly."

Max nodded in understanding, his amusement never leaving his face as he met my gaze with a hint of respect.

"Understood," he said, his voice slightly more serious now. "I'll make sure to meet your expectations, Alina."

Why was he so easygoing? It would have been much easier to ignore him and keep him at arms length had he been more like the cocky, arrogant, holier-than-thou artists I had seen on TV. But his face hadn't lost its radiant smile since he got here. Even the way he leaned back in his chair should have vexed me with its unprofessionalism, but it didn't. It just seemed to be a natural position for him.

As we delved into the specifics of the project, Max's easy going demeanor began to irk me. It was as if he didn't fully grasp the gravity of the situation or the importance of the project at hand. He just kept looking at me, making my skin prickle every time I tried to refocus us

Chapter 5

on the project.

"Okay then. I guess we can sign the contract now," I reached over to grab a pen for him, watching his hands fidget, bringing my attention to his long, almost perfectly clean fingers, save for a splotch of paint on his forearm he must have missed.

He absentmindedly reached for his coffee, the steam from the lukewarm liquid curling upwards in lazy tendrils. With a sudden movement, his hand brushed against the cup, sending it toppling over and spilling its contents onto the documents on the table.

I watched in disbelief as the dark liquid spread across the surface, seeping into the papers and leaving a stain in its wake. My initial shock quickly gave way to frustration, and we both leapt up.

I frantically scrambled to salvage the soaked papers, hurrying to my desk to grab my backup roll of paper towels. It paid to be a control freak. Max's expression shifted from amusement to genuine contrition as he hurried to assist me in cleaning up the mess.

"I'm so sorry, Alina," he apologized, his voice tinged with regret. "I didn't mean to—"

"It's fine, just help me clean this up, please." I said gently, trying to keep my exasperation concealed.

He nodded and sprang into action, grabbing a few paper towels and helping to mop up the spilled drink. His hands deftly moved beside mine, and I couldn't help but notice a little scar on the knuckle of his index finger. My gaze lowered to his paint splattered fingers before I got distracted by a familiar aroma.

"Is this…" I took a deep whiff, identifying the nostalgic scent. No. It couldn't be.

"Is this hot chocolate?"

I stopped my cleaning and looked at him.

His eyes widened before he gave me a sheepish shrug.

"I don't do well with caffeine."

He looked almost embarrassed, and the sight of it made me want to laugh a little.

"So you got a hot chocolate." I asked, a look of bewilderment on my face.

"With a lid, it looks just like coffee! People take me more seriously," he paused, seemingly trying to justify the typically childish choice, "and it's tasty."

I couldn't help but chuckle at his explanation, the tension from the earlier mishap dissipating with the shared moment of amusement.

"Fair enough," I conceded, offering him a small smile. "At least it smells better than the stale coffee and popcorn that usually lingers around here."

My typically icy exterior was all but forgotten, dismantled by the thought of this grown man going up to a coffee counter and ordering a hot chocolate. I bet the barista was just as thrown aback as I was. Max returned the smile, his eyes crinkling at the corners as he continued to help clean up the mess.

A beat passed as we finished mopping up the mess.

"Thanks," I murmured, grateful for his assistance.

"No problem," Max replied, his voice warm and reassuring.

Once the spilled papers were replaced with new ones and the disposable cup thrown away, we both straightened up, surveying the now tidy table with a sense of satisfaction. The only evidence of the mess having occurred in the first place was the scent of milky hot chocolate wafting in my office, not that I minded – it was a nostalgic scent.

"Looks like we make a pretty good team," Max remarked, a hint of amusement in his tone.

I couldn't help but smile at his observation.

"Hold up there, Picasso, we haven't even started the real work yet. Now sign the contract."

Chapter 5

✧✧✧

After taking him on a tour of the office so he could see what he was working with, we decided to call it a day on the project so he could conceptualize some ideas. I was just hoping we could do it, it seemed like a huge task to undertake for a novice artist. As we headed towards the elevators, I found myself feeling strangely positive about the project. Despite our rocky start, there was something undeniably disarming about his presence.

"Hey, Alina," Max called out, his voice breaking through my thoughts.

I turned to face him, raising an eyebrow inquisitively.

"Can I get you a coffee? You know, to make up for the elevator incident?" he asked, his expression hopeful.

I felt a surge of surprise at his unexpected invitation, my initial instinct to decline warring with a newfound curiosity. After all, it wasn't every day that a stranger who got you sick invited you for a coffee. However, I had so much to make up for from last week that I couldn't afford to leave the office, and I didn't want to blur any lines in this arrangement.

"Thanks, Max, but I'll have to pass," I replied, trying to keep my tone polite yet firm.

He just kept smiling that damned smile at me.

"No worries, Alina. Maybe another time."

I nodded, grateful for his understanding.

"Yeah, maybe."

As the elevator doors slid open, Max stepped inside. The whole scene was a little too familiar for me. A light chuckle made its way out my throat and I waved at him from the other side. His eyes lit up and he waved back.

"I'll have some mockups ready by tomorrow for the paintings. Come by my studio at noon, I'll send you the address."

The elevator doors closed before I could say anything.

Chapter 6

The next day, I found myself standing in front of a nondescript building, double-checking the address Max had sent me. This was an apartment building. This was Kait's apartment building. Did he not say it was his studio? A wariness crept in and just in case, I sent my current address and Max's name to Kait. You never knew what could happen. I did not want to take my chances in a world where Criminal Minds was based on actual real-life cases.

Taking a deep breath, I pressed the buzzer and waited. After a moment, the door buzzed open, and I stepped inside, making my way up to the third floor.

When I reached Max's door, I hesitated for a moment before knocking. Despite our progress yesterday, I couldn't shake the feeling of uncertainty. What if today's meeting didn't go smoothly? What if this was all a big mistake?

Before I could dwell on it any longer, the door swung open, revealing Max standing on the other side. He greeted me with a warm smile, gesturing for me to come inside. As always, he looked just slightly disheveled. His brown Henley was slightly rolled up at the sleeves and wrinkled, and the cuffs on his jeans looked slightly distressed.

He was also barefoot. I forced my eyes up and looked into his eyes, once again, framed by his tortoiseshell glasses. There was something about a man in glasses that me and Kait always gushed over in college. It was a very specific, very niche demographic, and the glasses had to be just the right kind.

Once, Kait forced Adam to try switching out his contacts for a pair of hipster glasses, but he couldn't handle it and he thought he looked stupid, so he threw the glasses away one day and told her he had been robbed. She was heartbroken. But, if Kait ever met Max, I feared the complex that Adam would go through. Max could have been the spokesperson for this genre of men.

"Hey! Welcome to my humble abode," he said, stepping aside to let me enter.

I stepped into the studio, taking in my surroundings. The space was filled with artwork in various stages of completion, and that feeling I felt at the auction came over me again. Too busy looking up at the decor, I didn't even notice my heel snagging on a rug, propelling my body forward. Before I destroyed my face on the glass coffee table, a pair of strong arms caught me from behind, steadying me with surprising ease.

"Whoa there, careful," Max murmured in my ear, his voice tinged with amusement as he helped me regain my balance. I felt goosebumps dot my neck at the intimacy of our position. Maybe Kait was right and it had been too long since I had been with a man.

Embarrassment flooded through me as I straightened up, cheeks flushing with color.

"Thanks," I muttered, feeling annoyed by my clumsiness.

Max chuckled, his eyes crinkling at the corners as he regarded me.

"No problem. It wouldn't be a visit from you without a little excitement, right?"

Chapter 6

I rolled my eyes playfully, relieved that he wasn't making a big deal out of my stumble.

"Yeah, I seem to have a talent for that."

As I composed myself, I finally took a proper look around the studio. The walls were adorned with paintings of all shapes and sizes, each one more captivating than the last. There was a rawness to the artwork that spoke to me on a visceral level, and I couldn't help but be drawn in by the intensity of Max's talent… and the home furniture surrounding the space.

"If I had known you were inviting me to your apartment, I would have picked a different location." I remarked dryly.

Max chuckled at my comment, his eyes twinkling with amusement.

"Yeah, I guess I should have clarified that my studio is also my living space. It's a bit unconventional, but it works for me. And, this way, I can *make* you a coffee to make up for our origin story."

I raised my eyebrows at him.

"So this was all a trick, then?"

"Naturally." He then gestured at his coffee maker and gave me an expectant expression.

"Now, how do you like your coffee?"

"I may not forgive you at the end of this coffee."

He laughed.

"I'll have to take my chances."

"Why do you even have a coffee maker? You don't drink coffee."

"It has a really good hot chocolate setting."

My jaw dropped to the ground.

"You can't be serious."

"Oh yes, I am. What flavor?"

"Black." It wasn't my preferred way of drinking coffee, but I found that black coffee was most respected, so I had grown to tolerate the taste of it.

He guffawed and gave me an exasperated look.

"Do you even like your taste buds?"

I sputtered, feigning offense.

"Do *you* like your taste buds?"

"Real mature. Great middle school comeback. How do you *actually* like your coffee?"

I sighed. "2 creams, a sugar, and a dash of cinnamon please."

Max grinned, then gestured towards a cozy-looking couch nestled in one corner of the studio.

"Why don't you go ahead and take a seat and we can go over our ideas for the series when the coffee's done? I haven't started on the logo yet so we can talk about that too."

I nodded and headed in the direction of the couch. Max flashed me a mischievous grin before heading over to the coffee maker to start brewing our drinks. As he worked, I settled onto the couch, taking a moment to admire the artwork adorning the walls before taking out my tablet of ideas from last night's research.

When Max returned with our beverages, I accepted mine with a grateful nod, taking a tentative sip. It was... surprisingly delicious. It had been a while since I had gotten a coffee like this and I missed it.

I rolled the liquid over my tongue and basked in the warmth it spread down my stomach. It had the perfect amount of milkiness from the cream, and the cinnamon smell was drifting through the air. I had forgotten how cold my hands naturally ran, so I cradled the warm mug with both hands.

"Not bad," I admitted, earning a pleased smile from Max.

His eyes bore into me warmly, as he spoke, and I had to break eye-contact first, settling my gaze on the brightly colored mug in my hands.

"Am I forgiven?" he teased, settling into the couch beside me with his own mug of what I was sure was hot chocolate.

"Okay."

Chapter 6

✧✧✧

As we began to discuss our ideas for the project, I quickly realized that we had very different visions for the final outcome. Max's creativity was evident in his desire to infuse the space with vibrancy and color, while I was more focused on maintaining a professional, corporate aesthetic.

"It's important that we strike a balance between creativity and functionality," I explained, trying to articulate my perspective. "We want the space to feel inviting and inspiring, but it also needs to be practical for the employees who will be using it on a daily basis."

Max nodded thoughtfully, but I could see the disappointment flicker in his eyes.

"I understand where you're coming from, Alina, but I think we have an opportunity to push the boundaries here. Look, I drew out some ideas last night."

He pulled out a couple of concept sketches from his sketchbook and immediately I wanted to reel back. They were beautiful, but they weren't right for the company.

"Those are nice, but I think they may be too intense for the space. What if we did something more like these I found last night?" I picked up my tablet from the coffee table and showed him the images.

He scrunched up his nose and pushed his glasses up.

"Alina, don't you think those are a little… unimaginative?" He winced, almost as if he forced himself to voice that opinion. "It's just GenTech is a tech company, and I feel that the series should be more creative and vibrant, not straight-edged and plain."

I frowned.

"I appreciate your enthusiasm, Max, but we need to consider the expectations of the company as well. They're looking for a space that reflects their brand identity and values."

For a moment, there was a tense silence between us as we grappled with the conflicting priorities. Eventually, Max let out a sigh, running a hand through his hair in frustration.

"I suppose we'll need to find a way to compromise then," he said reluctantly.

I nodded, feeling a sense of relief that we had at least acknowledged the challenge ahead.

"Agreed. Let's brainstorm some ideas that incorporate elements of both our visions and see if we can find some common ground."

As we continued to exchange ideas, it became increasingly clear that finding common ground would be no easy feat. Max was adamant about injecting bold colors and avant-garde designs into the project, while I remained steadfast in my belief that the space should exude professionalism and sophistication.

"I just worry that if we go too far in the direction of creativity, we'll alienate the more traditional members of the company," I explained, gesturing towards the concept sketches on the table. "We need to strike a balance that appeals to a wide range of tastes and preferences."

Max leaned back against the couch, his expression thoughtful.

"I see what you're saying, Alina, but I also think we shouldn't be afraid to take risks. Innovation often comes from pushing beyond the boundaries of what's expected."

I couldn't help but admire his passion. Regardless, I held my case and firmly replied.

"I agree that we shouldn't shy away from innovation. GenTech was founded on innovation. But we also need to be mindful of the practical considerations. The space needs to be conducive to productivity and collaboration."

He nodded in understanding, but I could sense his frustration simmering beneath the surface.

"I just don't want this project to end up feeling… sterile," he admitted,

Chapter 6

his voice tinged with disappointment.

I nodded, looking down at my shoes.

"This is a big project. Every time anyone in the office looks at these pieces, the logo, the website, they're going to know that I was the one who signed off on them. I don't want to mess this up." I said quietly.

Max's expression softened as he regarded me with empathy.

"Alina, you're not alone in this. We're a team, and we'll figure it out together," he reassured me, his voice gentle yet resolute. "And hey, if we do mess up, we'll learn from it and come back stronger. That's just how it goes in this line of work."

Max's words offered a measure of comfort, but the weight of my responsibilities still hung heavy on my shoulders. If anything, the stakes felt even higher now, knowing that my actions could have far-reaching consequences not just for the project, but for my career as well.

That may have been how it goes in the art world, but my position wasn't as easy going. If I messed this up, I wouldn't be considered for Jack's job at all. They'd hire someone else and I'd miss what could be my one chance. I'd also disappoint Jack, and that might have been worse than everything else.

"I appreciate your optimism," I replied, mustering a small smile. "But in my position, there's little room for error. One misstep could cost me everything."

His brow furrowed with concern, and for a moment, I could see the gears turning in his mind as he searched for the right words to say.

"Alina, I know you're under a lot of pressure, but remember, you didn't get to where you are by playing it safe," he said earnestly, then put a large hand on my arm. "You've got the talent, the dedication, and the drive to see this through. Trust yourself."

He let go of my arm, gave a shrug of his shoulders, and sucked his teeth. His unwavering belief in me was both humbling and empowering. It sent a warmth down my body that I embraced. It had been a while since I had been comforted like this and it was slightly bizarre that he was the one providing it. Taking a deep breath, I straightened my posture and met his gaze with renewed resolve.

"Let's get back to work. We've got a project to finish."

With a shared nod of determination, we returned to our brainstorming session. With a newfound sense of collaboration, we continued to bounce ideas off each other, each of us building upon the other's contributions. It was a refreshing change from the earlier tension, and I couldn't help but feel grateful for Max's willingness to meet me halfway.

As we delved back into our discussion, I found myself more open to considering Max's creative ideas. While our visions still differed in some respects, I began to see the value in incorporating elements of his bold aesthetic into the project.

"Maybe we could integrate some of these vibrant colors into the accent pieces," I suggested, pointing to one of Max's sketches. "It could add a pop of energy without overwhelming the space."

Max's eyes lit up with enthusiasm as he considered the suggestion. "That's a great idea."

He frantically opened a new page in his sketchbook and put the idea to paper. He barely seemed to breathe when he was drawing, as if he was a kid holding their breath opening their presents. His tongue was poking out the side of his mouth as he drew, and his hand moved frantically across the page, a flash of color catching my eye.

Was that... a friendship bracelet? It had pink and white beads and was clearly homemade. My eyes widened as I realized that I had never seen a grown man wearing a friendship bracelet. First the hot chocolate, now the friendship bracelet. Who was Max Reynolds? Where did this man come from? He clearly had friends, so why was no one taking care of him when he was sick last week?

Chapter 6

My train of thought was interrupted by Max ripping the page off his sketchbook and handing it to me with a grin.

"What do you think?"

I took the sketch from him, studying it with a critical eye.

"I love it," I admitted, unable to hide the smile that tugged at the corners of my lips. "It's exactly what we need to elevate the space."

Max's grin widened, a sense of pride evident in his expression.

"Great! I'll start working on fleshing out the details, and we can reconvene tomorrow to finalize our ideas for the other five pieces. Then we'll get to work on the logo."

With a sense of excitement bubbling within me, I nodded in agreement.

"Sounds like a plan."

As we exchanged a few more ideas and finalized our plans for the next steps, I couldn't help but admire Max's dedication to the project. Despite our initial differences, he had shown a remarkable willingness to compromise and find common ground.

"Thanks for being so open-minded, Alina," Max said, breaking the comfortable silence that had settled between us. "I know it's not easy to let go of your vision, but I really have a feeling this is going to be something special."

"Thanks for compromising with me. Sorry if I cramped your 'artistic flow' or anything with my rebuttals."

He barked a laugh, his eyes crinkling at the corners.

"Artistic flow?"

Color bloomed in my cheeks and my eyes widened in embarrassment. I turned away and cringed.

"Is that not a thing?"

Max's laughter filled the room, warm and infectious.

"Well, it might be a thing, but I've never heard it put quite like that before," he said, still chuckling. "You think I'm a hippie, don't you?"

"Um."

"My god," he guffawed. "Unbelievable."

My defense mechanism kicked into gear and I exclaimed, "No! I don't, seriously."

"Nope. You hesitated," he stood up, making me follow his lead. "I'm kicking you out before you wound my feelings further."

I groaned as he snickered and led me to the door, jumping slightly when I felt his hand lightly touching the small of my back. Just before I opened the door to leave, his hand lightly wrapped around my arm and stopped me in my tracks. He let go before gazing at me with a twinkle in his eye.

"Tomorrow at noon? Meet here? I'll have your coffee ready." He looked hopeful and I couldn't help but smile at him.

"Okay."

He smiled back.

"Okay."

Chapter 7

"So you're in charge of an art project?" Kait's shocked voice pierced my ear through the phone.

"Yep, that's right," I confirmed, my voice tight with tension as I weaved through the bustling office. Kait's enthusiasm was infectious, momentarily distracting me from the chaos unfolding around me.

"But you don't know anything about art." Kait replied with confusion in her voice.

"Okay, bitch, I do know things about art," I countered, offended.

"Genuinely, what do you even know about art?"

I paused, pursing my lips, unsure what to say. Unfortunately, it was enough for Kait's voice to turn smug and teasing.

"Mhm."

"Okay, maybe I'm not an art expert, but I know enough to appreciate it," I retorted, a hint of defensiveness creeping into my voice. My parents always remarked on my severe defensiveness. I wasn't sure why it came out so strongly in moments like this.

Maybe it was because I felt like I had something to prove, especially now. Perhaps I did need to hit up Kait's therapist Chelsea like she had been pestering me to do for 8 years.

"Anyway, tell me everything! Who's involved? What's the project about?" Kait's excitement bubbled through the phone line, prompting me to quickly fill her in on the details.

"His name is Max Reynolds. He's an artist, and he's been commissioned to work on rebranding GenTech's image," I explained, my voice steadier now as I delved into the details.

"Max Reynolds? That name sounds familiar," Kait mused, her curiosity piqued. "What kind of work does he do?"

"He's known for his futuristic, vibrant pieces. He also dabbles in a lot of mediums: charcoal, sculpture, paint, graphic design…" I trailed off, my mind drifting to the colorful sketches I had seen in Max's studio. "His style is… unconventional, to say the least. And he kinda just came out of nowhere apparently, but his stuff was all over the FOK auction last week and-"

"*What?*" Kait cried, a hint of outrage in her voice, "Damn it, the one year I don't go as your date and something interesting happens!"

"Wow. It's almost like you weren't even there that year the CEO of Hudson Tech's wife accidentally set a curtain on fire with a cigarette," I retorted dryly.

Apparently, the woman had been trying to quit smoking for three months by going cold turkey. Another woman was outside smoking and had a few extra cigarettes. Lady Hudson bummed one and tried to hide her smoking behind a curtain. The curtain never recovered.

"I've seen fire before," Kait responded indignantly. "I've never seen you rattled in a work setting before. What was his name again? Max Roberts?" I could hear the telltale sound of typing through the phone.

"Reynolds." I corrected her.

"Max Reh-nolds," I heard her enunciating before a sharp gasp came through the phone.

"He's hot!"

Chapter 7

"What! Kait, no-"

"Allie baby, he's a cutie! He's got that whole nerdy artist sex hair glasses thing working for him. Why didn't you tell me this?" Her tone was accusatory.

I sighed, feeling a blush creep up my cheeks.

"Because that's not what's important here. We're working together, and it's purely professional."

Kait's laugh echoed through the phone.

"Sure, keep telling yourself that. What's the real reason?"

I hesitated, knowing exactly how she'd react to the next part.

"You remember that guy I told you about? The one from the elevator?"

"The one who basically hotboxed you with his germs? Wait... don't tell me... it's him?" Kait's voice was incredulous.

"Yeah, that's him," I admitted, unable to keep the embarrassment out of my voice.

"No way!" Kait exclaimed. "This is like something out of a rom-com! You're telling me the hot artist from the elevator is the same guy you're working with now?"

"Yes, and it's not a rom-com, Kait," I groaned. "It's my life, and it's already complicated enough without you turning it into some kind of crappy romance movie."

"Oh, come on, Alina. This is fate! You can't just ignore the fact that the universe is clearly trying to set you up with this guy," Kait argued, her tone a mix of teasing and genuine excitement.

"I don't have time for fate," I shot back, trying to maintain my focus. My attention was drawn to my office door, a panicked Jenna on the other side of it signaling me to come over.

"I have a project to manage and now a crisis at work to deal with. Speaking of which, I really need to go."

"Fine, fine," Kait conceded, her voice softening. "But promise me you'll at least consider the possibility that this could be something more than just a work relationship. You deserve a little happiness, Allie."

"Thanks, Kait," I said, touched by her concern despite the exasperation I felt. "We'll talk later, okay?"

"Okay, good luck with your crisis," Kait replied. "And don't forget to keep me updated on your sexy artist."

"Bye Kait."

"WAIT, he lives in my building, doesn't he?!"

"Bye Kait!"

◆◆◆

By the time noon rolled around, I found myself standing in front of Max's door again, ready to knock. I had been poised with my fist in the air ready to knock for two minutes now, but something in me held back for some reason. I was completely frozen. Kait's words were rolling around in my head. Why did she have to say that? I hadn't dated in five years, and I had no plans to start now. I probably would never allow myself to. I knew that. She knew that. Everyone knew that.

So why was I hesitating?

Just as I shook my head, determined to knock, the door swung open, and a pair of grass-green eyes met mine through the door frame.

"Why were you just standing there?" Max asked, a hint of amusement in his voice.

"I was not just standing there. I just got here!" I retorted, feeling the heat rise to my cheeks.

Max raised an eyebrow, a smirk playing on his lips.

"I heard the elevator ding three minutes ago." He pointed at the elevator, a mere five feet away from his apartment, a used paintbrush

Chapter 7

in his hand. It drew my attention to the splotch of paint on his temple. Caught, I fumbled for a response.

"I... uh, I needed a moment to collect my thoughts."

"Sure you did," he said, still smiling. "Come on in. Your coffee's getting cold." He stepped aside to let me in, his eyes twinkling with that ever-present mischief.

I entered the studio, immediately enveloped by the familiar scent of coffee and the sight of Max's vibrant, half-finished artworks scattered around. Trying to push Kait's words out of my mind, I focused on the task at hand.

"How was your day?" He hollered behind his back.

"It was fine, thank you."

A moment passed.

"Aren't you going to ask me about my day?" His voice had a teasing quality to it, and I suppressed a laugh at his candor.

"How was your day?" I conceded.

"It was good until an overhead bird pooped on me."

This time, I did laugh.

"Oh, that's horrible," I couldn't help the giggles going through me, "did you at least get back at it?"

He craned his head behind him and looked at me with a mock puzzled expression.

"Alina, are you asking if I murdered it in my need for vengeance? It was a bird. God, you're stone-cold. I pray other Operations Managers are more merciful than you are." He shuddered and walked over as I snorted at his response.

He was so random, it was kind of endearing. But this was work, and I had to stay professional.

He handed me a steaming mug of coffee and settled down on the couch.

"So, what's on the agenda today?" he asked.

This time, the mug in his hand had a little pink tea bag floating in it. I don't think I had ever seen a man drink a raspberry tea. I took a sip of the coffee, savoring the warmth. Two creams. A sugar. And a dash of cinnamon. I smiled into my mug before plastering on my professional, stoic expression.

"We need to finalize the concepts for the other pieces, then the logo. I trust you to rebrand the website solo," I said, sitting beside him and pulling out my tablet. "I think we made great progress yesterday, but we still have a lot to cover."

Max nodded, but his eyes searched mine, as if sensing my unease.

"Are you okay? You seem... distracted."

I forced a smile, trying to shake off my anxiety.

"I'm fine. Just a lot on my mind."

He leaned back, studying me for a moment before nodding.

"Alright, let's get to work then. We have a lot to do."

Max stood up and walked over to his desk, retrieving a small canvas.

"Here's a mockup of what we finalized yesterday," he said, placing it on the easel in front of me. "Of course, once we approve all six paintings, I'll make a much larger scale version." He gave me a grin, the dimples in his cheeks deepening in his face.

The piece was stunning, capturing the essence of the company's innovative spirit through bold, intertwining lines and vibrant colors.

"It looks even better today," I said, genuinely impressed. "The board is going to love it."

"Glad to hear that," Max replied, a satisfied smile spreading across his face. "Now, let's brainstorm for the next piece. I was thinking we could do something that represents the company's commitment to sustainability."

I nodded, intrigued by the idea.

"Maybe we could use recycled materials as part of the piece? Incorporate elements that reflect eco-friendliness."

Chapter 7

Max's eyes lit up.

"That's a fantastic idea. We could use old circuit boards, pieces of glass, maybe even some organic materials."

"Exactly," I said, feeling a spark of excitement. "It would be a great way to highlight the company's tech roots while also showcasing their commitment to sustainability."

Max nodded, already jotting down notes.

"We could create a mosaic, with the circuit boards forming the backdrop and the glass and organic materials adding texture and depth."

"I like that," I agreed, leaning forward. "And we could use different shades of green to represent various aspects of nature. Maybe even incorporate some LED lights to make it more dynamic."

"LED lights," Max echoed, his grin widening. "That's brilliant."

I smiled, feeling a sense of accomplishment.

"It's coming together nicely."

Max looked up from his notes, his expression sincere behind his large frames.

"You've got a great eye for this, you know."

I shrugged off the compliment, keeping my tone professional.

"It's just part of the job."

He studied me for a moment before speaking again.

"Do you ever allow yourself to take credit for your creativity? You have a real talent, Alina."

I felt my guard rising.

"I appreciate that, but let's stay focused on the project. What other ideas do you have?"

Max seemed to sense my reluctance to engage in personal conversation and smoothly transitioned back to the task at hand.

"I was thinking we could also work on a piece that embodies the company's global reach. Something with maps, maybe?"

"That's a good idea," I said, grateful for the change in subject. "We could use different materials from various parts of the world to create a textured, multi-layered map."

Max nodded enthusiastically.

"And we could even incorporate some interactive elements, like touch-sensitive areas that light up when you press them."

I felt a genuine smile creep across my face.

"That sounds amazing. Let's sketch out some ideas and see what we come up with."

We spent the next hour brainstorming and sketching, bouncing ideas off each other with an easy rhythm. Despite the lingering tension from our earlier conversation, we managed to stay focused on the work. We even managed to get down four of the six concepts for the paintings despite our three-month deadline. That was, until Max smiled at me and started talking.

"So… are you from Chicago?" He asked, his gaze turning back to his sketchpad as he drew out our ideas.

There it was again though, that pink and white friendship bracelet adorning one wrist, the other carrying a few leather bracelets. How did his bracelets not get damaged with the amount of pencil lead they probably picked up? I felt my skin start to prickle and I shook my head jerkily.

"Chicago suburbs. Geneva," I corrected him.

Chicagoans had this complex where they couldn't stand it if suburbians said they were from Chicago. I never quite understood it, but they could get quite heated about it. From what I knew, other states didn't care as much. My college friend Amy always told people she was from Houston when she was really from Katy, and no one gave a fuss about it.

I wanted to break off this conversation before it went over the working relationship — friendship line. But out of politeness and

Chapter 7

mild curiosity, I asked him the question back.

He shook his head and smiled gently to himself.

"Texas. Austin."

I gave him a cool stare and replied, "You don't sound like you're Texan. Or look it, really."

He barked a laugh, the motion causing his hair to flop around and fall in his eyes. Kait was right, he did have sex hair.

"Sorry I left my spurs and lasso at home," He jokingly apologized, "And the big city Texas kids don't really have an accent, it's just a basic American one. Besides, I've lived here for 11 years now, if anything I sound more Midwestern."

I laughed lightly before stopping myself and nodded through my slight discomfort. This was meant to be a professional working relationship. We weren't meant to do this opening up thing.

"Why'd you move here?" I pried further. Amy had told me that Austin was an oasis of sorts, full of hills, lakes, music festivals, and young hipsters. Why would he want to move to windy city Chicago, when I'm sure Austin had a great art scene?

"College." A tranquil look washed over him. Out of the corner of my eye, I saw him start to fiddle with the friendship bracelet adorning his left wrist.

"Let me guess," I joked. "Art history?"

He snickered and moved his face closer to mine, holding eye contact with me. He had a look on his face that I hadn't seen before.

"Aerospace Engineering."

I blinked, caught off guard.

"You're an aerospace engineer?"

"Yep," he said, popping the 'p' with a grin.

11 years ago meant he would have to be around 29. Just like me.

"You don't *look* like an aerospace engineer." I questioned.

He pulled back and examined me, a playful look on his face.

"Do you just have like a set roster of visual expectations for every type of person?"

A laugh came over me and all lines were forgotten because what I did next definitely crossed some boundaries.

I lightly smacked his arm, rolling my eyes.

"Shut up."

A brilliant grin landed on his face and he just gazed at me, not saying anything, his eyes bright. I felt a heat bloom in my cheeks, and I just hoped my olive skin-tone was enough to mask it. I cleared my throat and pushed forward.

"Why'd you start doing art instead?" My voice was soft, hesitant as I stomped on the working-friendship line.

A dark look came over his eyes and his smile faltered for a split second before his usual carefree, easygoing expression returned.

"Another time."

Disappointment bloomed in me. I knew getting personal was a bad idea. It always was. It was never a good idea to mix up work and relationships, even if it was just a friendship. At the end of this project, he would go back to his world and I would go back to mine.

Hopefully, with a new position I had been working my ass off the better half of my career for.

Trying to steer the conversation back to safer ground, I glanced at the sketches in front of us.

"So, about this sustainability piece…"

Max took the hint and returned his focus to the artwork.

"Right. So we'll need to gather some materials. I know a few places where we can get old circuit boards and glass. Do you know of any sources for organic materials?"

"I can ask around," I replied, relieved to be back on familiar territory. "I'm sure the company has some contacts we can use."

"Perfect," he said, his enthusiasm rekindled. "Let's start putting

Chapter 7

together a list of what we need and then we can start sourcing everything."

We spent the next hour immersed in our work, the earlier tension fading into the background. Despite the occasional personal question, we managed to stay on task, our ideas flowing easily as we collaborated.

Yet, as focused as I was on the project, I couldn't quite shake the feeling of being just a bit off balance. Max's unexpected background and his easy charm were disarming, and I found myself treading carefully, determined to keep the boundaries clear. This was work, after all, and I needed to remember that.

Chapter 8

The quaint streets of the western suburb of Geneva welcomed me as I stepped off the Metra, a sense of nostalgia mingling with apprehension in the air. It had been a while since I made this journey, and the two-hour train ride was the perfect place to get more work done on my computer. I made my way through familiar streets, passing by familiar landmarks, until I found myself standing in front of Grahams 318, a cozy coffee shop nestled on Third Street.

Pushing open the door, I was immediately enveloped in the comforting aroma of freshly brewed coffee and the gentle hum of conversation. The warm ambiance of the place paired with the absolutely stunning display of house made pastries brought a nostalgic smile to my face. This was my dad and I's favorite place. This place had a weekly rotation of fun themed donuts and growing up, we would spend every Sunday morning here, trying out every flavor.

It became our ritual.

I ordered a black coffee and all five of the nine themed donuts (we both shared a mutual hatred of cake donuts) and found a quiet corner near the window. As I waited for my drink, I glanced out at the street,

Chapter 8

taking in the familiar sights of my hometown.

It had been years since I had last visited Geneva, and the memories that flooded back were bittersweet. The laughter of childhood summers, the scent of freshly cut grass, the warmth of family dinners—all tinged with the ache of the reminders of her.

It wasn't long before my dad arrived, his warm smile and salt and pepper hair lighting up the room as he spotted me sitting by the window. I stood up to hug him and almost cried at the smell of lemons in his hair. He took a seat opposite me, his presence a comfort I had missed.

"Alina, *sayang*, what a pleasant surprise," he said, reaching across the table to squeeze my hand. "It's been too long since I've seen you."

I returned his smile, grateful for the familiar warmth of his touch.

"Hey, Papa. I thought I'd come and visit for a bit. I've missed you."

He nodded, his expression softening with affection.

"Visit more." He said plainly, a stern tone in his voice.

He looked at the spread of donuts on the table and then looked back up at me, grinning brilliantly, the lines in his face deepening as his dark brown eyes twinkled.

I simply nodded back with guilt.

He picked one up, a Flintstones raspberry filled donut, split it in half, then distributed the two halves between us. We clinked our donuts, then took simultaneous bites, savoring the sweetness of the donut as we chewed.

As the donuts disappeared one by one, I found myself opening up to my dad about what had been happening at work. I explained the whole situation with Jack—the tension, the pressure, the constant push and pull of conflicting interests. As always, my dad listened attentively, his expression a mix of concern and understanding.

"Wow, Alina, Director of Operations" he remarked, his voice filled with admiration. "I'm so proud of you, sayang. It sounds like all your hard work is finally paying off."

I nodded, feeling a swell of pride at his words.

"Thanks, Papa. I haven't gotten it yet, though. It's a lot of pressure. If I don't do well in these projects, I could miss out on the chance of a lifetime."

"That sounds like a tough situation, sayang," he said, his voice laced with empathy. "But remember, you can't let one position dictate your happiness or your success. You've been a powerhouse since you were born, but you're still human, Alina. Even Luella is out there doing what she needs right now."

I tensed at the mention of my sister before taking a deep breath and letting it go. I nodded, grateful for his words of wisdom.

"Thanks, Papa. It's just been really stressful lately. I'm... not sure how much longer I can keep this up."

He reached out to pat my hand, his touch reassuring.

"You'll figure it out, Alina. You always do. Just remember to take care of yourself in the process."

I loved him, but he didn't understand. This was what I had been working towards my whole career. I didn't date, I barely had any friends other than Kait and Adam, and all I thought about was work. I don't have anything else.

"I'll try, Papa," I promised halfheartedly, a sense of guilt settling over me. "And thank you for always being there for me, even when I'm a mess."

He chuckled softly, the sound warm and familiar.

"That's what dads are for, sayang. Now, enough about work. One of these is custard filled, I can feel it."

For a moment, time seemed to stand still, and all that mattered was the simple pleasure of indulging in a childhood treat with him. Then, I noticed a subtle tremor in my dad's hand as he held his half of the donut and it was like a bucket of cold water was thrown over me.

Chapter 8

"Papa, are you okay?" I asked, my voice tinged with worry as I reached out to touch his hand.

He looked up, his smile faltering for a moment before he quickly masked it with a reassuring expression.

"I'm fine, Alina. Just a little tired, that's all."

But I could see the strain in his eyes, the faint lines of fatigue etched into his face. The sight sent a pang of guilt through me, knowing that I hadn't been there for him as much as I should have.

"You don't have to pretend with me, Papa," I said softly, my heart aching at the sight of him struggling. "I know you've been having a tough time lately."

He sighed, his shoulders sagging with weariness.

"It's just old age catching up with me, sayang. Nothing to worry about."

But I couldn't shake the feeling of unease, the nagging fear that something more serious was at play. My dad had always been strong and resilient, his indomitable spirit a source of inspiration for me.

He was Dr. Zaki Santoso, one of the most prized astrophysicists of his time. He was the same man who would hold me on his shoulders at games so I could see the action better.

Seeing him like this, vulnerable and fragile, filled me with a sense of helplessness I had never experienced before.

He saw my worried expression and smiled his deep smile again, the motion causing his eyes to crinkle in the corners. He split another donut in half and wordlessly handed a piece to me. I took it and once again we clinked our donuts before eating them in the comforting silence.

Chapter 9

"Are you sure you wanna do this? Isn't this like torture for you being pregnant?" I asked, concern etched in my voice as I uncorked a bottle of Sauvignon Blanc.

Kait scowled playfully, adjusting her position on the blanket.

"It's tradition. With how busy you are, this was the only way we could keep connected. I want my Allie-time."

I smiled gratefully, pouring us each a glass of wine.

"Cheers to that."

The late afternoon sun cast a warm golden glow over Polk Bros Park as Kait and I settled onto a patch of grass, our picnic blanket spread out beneath us. It had been three months since our last 'biweekly' wine date, and both of us had been itching for some much-needed girl time.

We clinked our glasses together before I took a sip, the crisp taste of the wine soothing my frazzled nerves. Kait just lifted her glass, took a deep whiff and groaned gutturally, putting it down on the blanket between us.

"Maybe this was a mistake," She cried before glaring at her belly, a noticeable bump finally forming at five months. "Why would you do this to me? *I am your mother!*"

I snorted and took another sip of the wine before retorting.

"Kait, I really don't think the bean is at fault here. You should blame Adam for impregnating you with his spawn."

She groaned again and took another inhale of the wine.

"Ugh, don't remind me," Kait grumbled, shifting uncomfortably.

I chuckled, placing a hand on her shoulder in solidarity.

"We all salute you for your sacrifices. May the baby pee on him as much as possible when they're born. They're gonna be a force to be reckoned with, with y'all two as parents."

Kait laughed and looked at me for a moment before nodding to herself with a serene smile.

"*She* will be."

A beat passed. Then another.

I stared at Kait, putting my wine down, my eyes wide with excitement.

"Did you just say 'she'?"

Kait's grin widened as she nodded, confirming my suspicions.

"Yep, we found out at the last ultrasound. It's a girl."

I couldn't contain my joy any longer. With a high-pitched squeal, I launched myself at her, tackling her gently to the ground in a hug.

"Oh my god, that's amazing! I'm so happy for you!"

Kait laughed, her voice filled with delight as she hugged me back.

"Thanks, Allie. It's been killing me not being able to share the news with you."

I pulled back, still grinning from ear to ear.

"I can't believe it! You're going to be the best mom ever."

Kait's expression softened, a fondness in her eyes.

"You really think so?"

I nodded emphatically.

"Absolutely. You've always been great with kids, and this little girl is going to be so lucky to have you as her mom."

Kait's eyes turned watery as she reached out to clasp my hand.

"I'm gonna be a mom." She said quietly, almost in disbelief.

My eyes started to sting with the telltale signs of a cry coming on.

"You're gonna be a mom." I echoed.

We held hands for a second before she broke away to wipe a tear away.

"Bitch," she said jokingly, her voice still strangled from the crying, "taking advantage of my pregnancy hormones and making me cry in a public park."

"I cried too!" I returned, defensively.

"You've always been a sympathy crier. How many times in college did you cry on the couch because I was crying on the couch?"

"How dare you?"

She shrugged playfully and kept looking around at all the park goers.

"I was always the stone-cold, mysterious, cool girl and you were the sympathy crier. It's why we worked."

We both knew that wasn't true. She always *thought* she was the cool, mysterious one, but the woman sobbed at every emotional hiccup. I was a sympathy crier, though. And we did work.

She took another whiff of her wine and groaned even louder than before, throwing a fist in the air. I laughed and sipped my wine again, pouring some more into both our glasses.

For a moment, we simply sat in companionable silence, enjoying the tranquility of the park and the sound of the nearby lake. I saw her get teary-eyed looking at a woman tie her daughter's shoes, and not once did I think about work. Then a buzzing caught my attention.

I glanced down to see a text from Max.

> Max: *Real question, what if we did a dog in a coffee cup for the fifth painting.*

Chapter 9

I looked at the picture he had attached and snorted at the image of a bulldog in a coffee cup wearing a beret for some reason. I felt a warmth spread through me at his message, a genuine smile tugging at the corners of my lips.

"Who's got you smiling?" Kait's voice penetrated the quiet. I turned to her and saw her wiggling her eyebrows at me.

"No one, it's just work." I responded coolly.

"Who is it?" She reiterated, her voice taking a serious tone.

"It's just Max," I announced, showing Kait the text.

Her eyes lit up with mischief as she grabbed my phone from my hand.

"Let me see," she demanded, scrolling through the message before handing it back to me. "He's cute. You should text him back."

I rolled my eyes, but couldn't hide the blush creeping up my cheeks.

"It's not like that, Kait. We're just coworkers, nothing more."

She raised an eyebrow skeptically.

"Sure, just coworkers who work together in one of their apartments and text each other for nonwork reasons."

"You know full well his apartment is also his studio, and this *was* for a work reason!"

"Sure." She said sarcastically.

I waved her away.

"I'm at a big point of my career right now and he would just be a distraction. He probably doesn't even like me, I think he just still feels bad about the elevator incident."

"Allie, he definitely likes you. Men don't just text their coworkers for no reason." She tried reasoning with me before, her eyes gleamed with mischief. Before I knew it, she had typed out and sent a text without me. I cried out and stole my phone back, needing to see the extent of her damage.

> *Alina: Hmm. Not too 'ruff' an idea... What should we name our coffee cup dog?*

I looked at Kait my expression repulsed.
"Kait this is bad."
"Nah. Everyone needs a little excitement now and then."
"No, Kait," I corrected her, looking like I just ate something sour. "This is just bad in quality. Do you and Adam not flirt anymore? Why is it this awful?"
An offended look came on her face and she yelped, slapping my arm. She opened her mouth, I'm sure to defend her honor, but a light buzzing interrupted her. Our eyes both widened and we looked at the response.

> *Max: Our coffee cup dog? I like the sound of that :)*

"Dude, he so likes you." She deadpanned.
"Kait," I sighed softly, "you know why I can't." She looked at me sadly, realizing the real reason, then nodded and dropped the subject.
We both consumed our wines in our own fashions and gazed at the people and the lake. We started this ritual when we graduated from college and while we had been really good at sticking to the biweekly schedule, the past few months had been hectic for the both of us. We both started talking about the most recent development in the Bachelor series and as Kait and I chuckled over our banter, a familiar voice interrupted us from behind, "Hey, y'all!"
We turned to see Adam jogging towards us, a grin plastered on his face.
"What are the odds of running into you two here? I was just on my biweekly run and I felt like this park today, it's so funny seeing you two here on your girl date!"

Chapter 9

He really needed to get acting lessons. He was panting heavily, his breath resembling someone who had never run a day in his life.

I exchanged a knowing look with Kait, both of us aware that Adam had likely orchestrated this encounter.

"Hey, baby," Kait greeted him with a smirk, handing him her wine glass as he approached. "Fancy meeting you here."

Adam shrugged, taking the glass and settling onto the blanket beside us.

"What can I say? I have impeccable timing."

I chuckled, rolling my eyes.

"Impeccable? I'm sure that's what it was."

He feigned offense, holding a hand to his chest.

"Ouch, Alina, I'm wounded. Can't a guy join his two favorite ladies for a drink in the park?"

Kait laughed, nudging him playfully with her elbow.

"And what about the rest of your 'run'? We wouldn't want you to have to cut it so soon for us! Go back, baby, maybe you can finally break a mile."

Adam blew a raspberry and laid his head against her chest, a hand on her just barely showing belly.

"It's okay, baby, I'll cut this one short for you. But you owe me."

Kait just laughed.

I leaned over to flick him on the forehead and stared him down, "*My* Kait date."

He shrugged his shoulders, "My Kait."

I glared at him, "*Our* Kait."

A scared expression took over his face and he nodded somberly, "Our Kait."

I laughed, watching Kait nudging him playfully with her elbow.

"You can always join your two favorite ladies in the park, Adam. Just admit you missed us."

Adam grinned unabashedly and sat up. "Fine, you got me."

He gulped down Kait's entire glass of wine with no concern.

"Jesus Christ Adam, this was a nice bottle!" I reprimanded him.

"Sorry," he caught his breath, "Kait's been buying all these wines just to sniff them and I've had to drink all of them, or she would've started crying about the 'wine gods not forgiving her for wasting wine'. It just tastes like water to me now."

Kait smiled at me sheepishly, then replied with a shrug of her shoulders.

"Yeah, he's my wine-sniffing scapegoat."

We burst into laughter, the sound echoing through the park as the afternoon rays of sunlight bathed us in golden warmth. Despite the playful teasing, the three of us had a bond that was stronger than any other friendship I had ever experienced.

Kait and I nodded to each other and made room for her man to join us. As he settled in beside us, the three of us began catching up, laughter filling the air as we enjoyed each other's company in the tranquil setting of the park.

Chapter 10

Come early October, Max had sent me a calendar invite to meet at his studio to work on the project. I didn't even know how he had gotten access to my calendar, or how he knew it was the best way to reach me. I guess after countless times texting me to work together only for my schedule to be fully booked every time, he found a way.

We had finalized the concepts for all five sketches about two weeks ago and I hadn't seen him since. Thankfully, he never mentioned the dog-in-a-teacup text chain again. Most men I knew would have thrown a fit after my not responding, but nothing seemed to faze Max. He just moved on, sent me a calendar invite with a note to just enter his studio, and all was right again.

As I stepped into Max's studio, the familiar scent of acrylic paint filled the air, instantly transporting me back to the countless hours we had spent here together. I looked around for the tall man with the messy brown hair and stopped when I saw him hunched over his latest canvas, his focus so intense that he didn't notice my arrival. A cup of coffee with what I could smell was a dash of cinnamon perched next to him on the windowsill.

"Hey," I greeted him with a smile, but as I took a step forward, my foot caught on a small stool holding open paint cans, sending them toppling to the ground in a cascade of colors.

Max turned around in surprise, his eyes widening as he took in the colorful mess at my feet. For a moment, there was silence. I winced and opened my mouth to apologize, but was interrupted by Max's raucous laughter bursting into the room.

It was a deep belly laugh and it had him hunched over his knees trying to catch his breath. I was caught off guard by how nice his laugh was. It had a smooth quality to it and was rich in the way it echoed throughout the room. My resolve broke and I burst into laughter as well, joining in, the tension evaporating as we looked at each other.

"Well, that's one way to make an entrance," Max chuckled, hurrying over and reaching out to gently hold my elbow. "You okay?"

I nodded, still laughing as I brushed the paint from my clothes.

"I'm fine. Just a little clumsy, I guess."

"Stop falling all over everything, woman. You're a walking hazard, I swear."

"It's not my fault, you're the one that has all this," my face screwed up as I looked around at all the paint cans and charcoals and canvases propped up against random objects in the room, "clutter everywhere."

"It's called organized chaos and for that, you're never invited over here again." He teased.

His hand was still holding my elbow, and I felt his thumb stroking my arm gently. Goosebumps prickled all over my arm, radiating from the skin under his large hand.

"Oh no. How will I ever get through the day now I don't have to worry about stabbing my foot with a putty knife when I walk?" I rolled my eyes, suppressing a laugh.

"Shots fired. And I'm just kidding, you're always welcome here. In fact, come over all the time." My cheeks pinkened as his tone turned serious and I didn't know what else to do other than roll my eyes again. What did *that* mean? It felt almost like he was... flirting with me? Was Kait right?

No. I shut that idea down as soon as it came and glanced back at him.

Max grinned, his eyes twinkling with mischief.

"Looks like we've got some cleaning up to do."

But before I could even think about grabbing a mop, Max scooped up a handful of paint and flicked it at me, splattering my clothes with vibrant streaks of color.

For a second, I stood there frozen with my mouth agape. Then Max gave me a challenging look and cocked his head in that infuriating way of his, and the wrath of a war general came over me.

I reached for a nearby paintbrush and dipped it into the puddle of paint on the ground. His eyes widened, as if he didn't expect me to accept the challenge. But I loved surprising people, and hopefully the next expression he made would be worth it.

"Okay buddy, you asked for it!" I swiped the brush across his arm, leaving a bright blue streak. Max gasped dramatically, clutching his arm as if I had gravely wounded him. "Oh, you're in for it now!"

He threw his glasses onto the couch and dipped his fingers into a pot of red paint and smeared it across my cheek. I stood there, shocked for a moment, before deciding to retaliate. Submerging my hands in a puddle of yellow paint, I dipped my fingers in and flicked it at him, splattering his shirt with the neon streaks. Max's eyes widened with mock horror.

"You missed a spot," Max teased, pointing to a clean patch on my shoulder. He dipped his hands into the green paint and left a handprint on my shoulder.

"There, much better."

I laughed, grabbing a can of purple paint and pouring a bit into my hand before launching it at him. It splashed across his chest, leaving a wide, purple streak. He shook his head, smiling, and stepped closer, dipping his hands into more paint.

Before I could react, he was upon me, and we were both splashing, smearing, and flicking paint at each other with reckless abandon. The studio floor turned into a chaotic rainbow, our clothes and skin covered in a wild palette of colors. We danced around each other, our playful battle escalating into a full-blown paint war.

What started as a playful exchange soon escalated into a full-blown paint fight, with both of us laughing uncontrollably as we splattered each other with paint. I couldn't remember the last time I had felt so carefree.

"Truce!" I called out, laughing as I ducked behind an easel, trying to catch my breath.

Max stood across the room, panting and grinning from ear to ear.

"Only if you admit defeat!"

"Never!" I grabbed a nearby paintbrush and launched a final attack, streaking red paint across his cheek. He retaliated by splattering a handful of blue paint at me, which I ducked, resulting in a splatter on the wall behind me and my tripping and landing on the ground, bringing him down with me.

"Okay, okay, truce!" Max finally agreed, both of us laughing uncontrollably.

Spent from the energy of the paint fight, we both laid on the floor, too tired to do anything else, too covered in paint to risk moving around his apartment. We turned to face each other still laughing when my breath caught in my throat.

Slowly, Max reached out and used his thumb to wipe a smudge of paint from my eyebrow, his touch gentle and surprisingly intimate. He leisurely used his fingers to brush my paint-covered hair out of my face, his hand landing on the side of my head, lightly brushing my ear.

Chapter 10

My heart skipped a beat as our eyes met, and for a moment, it felt like my heart was about to jump out of my chest. All I could think about was how jealous I was of how long his eyelashes were. They almost brushed against his cheekbones whenever he blinked.

"You know, I thought this kind of thing only happened in movies," I laughed quietly, grinning at him.

"Maybe we're just living a really good one," he replied, his smile softening.

His words hung in the air between us.

Before I could even think about getting up, he closed the distance and pressed his lips to mine. The kiss was soft and tentative at first, a gentle exploration of new territory. His lips were warm and inviting, and I felt a jolt of electricity shoot through me as our mouths moved in sync.

Max's hand cupped my cheek, his thumb gently caressing my skin. I stiffened, shocked by what was happening before my body betrayed me and leaned into his touch, deepening the kiss, losing myself in the moment. His other hand slid around my waist, pulling me closer until there was no space left between us. The world outside faded away, and all that mattered was us, laying in a sea of paint in his living room. All I could feel was his soft lips against mine. I hadn't been kissed in years. I hadn't been kissed like this ever.

When we finally pulled apart, we were both panting, our foreheads resting against each other. I could see the depth of emotion in Max's eyes, mirroring my own feelings. His gaze never wavered, filled with a mixture of hope and vulnerability.

"Go out with me." He asked softly, his voice barely a whisper. My heart stopped. His gaze never left my eyes. I wonder what he saw when he looked into them.

"What?" I croaked. He was still cradling my face and I wasn't sure how I'd feel when he let go.

He smiled, a bit more nervously this time. When he spoke again, his voice was slightly louder but gentler than ever, a wavering note lacing his words.

"Go out with me. Please."

For a moment, I was at a loss for words. I felt a mix of excitement and panic bubbling up inside me. Max was undeniably attractive. As Kait said, he had the 'cool artist sex hair glasses thing' going for him. And our connection was definitely there.

Not once had I ever felt so at ease with a person and we had only known each other for around two months. Would it be so bad for me to say yes? Would the world end if I picked him?

Could I afford to let my guard down and let someone in? Every fiber of my being screamed to protect what I had built. Yet, laying there, paint-splattered and staring into Max's hopeful eyes, I couldn't deny the longing I felt.

His pleading green gaze bore into me, and my heart broke slightly in my chest. I'd never had a man beg me for something before. I don't think I ever wanted a man to beg me for something again. I opened my mouth to say yes.

But then, my instincts kicked in. I had worked too hard to get to where I was, and mixing business with pleasure was a risk I wasn't willing to take. Loving someone the way my dad loved my mom wasn't a risk I was willing to take.

I let go of the breath I was holding and what came out was so weak I was afraid he couldn't hear it.

"*No.*"

Chapter 11

"*No.*"

He nodded, as if expecting it, the slightest hint of disappointment peeking through his sunshine exterior, and I felt my stomach drop.

"Max," I began, my tone softening as I collected my thoughts. "I really appreciate the offer, and I like you, I do. But I think it's best if we keep things professional. I've got a lot on my plate right now with work, and I'm really focused on my career and-"

"It's okay." He breathed out. I could feel his thumb gently stroking my cheekbone, and I swallowed to keep my emotions in check. "You don't have to explain yourself. I understand, and I apologize if I made things awkward, it doesn't have to be."

A traitorous tear made its way down onto my nose bridge and I cursed the gods for making me such an easy crier, but Max didn't say anything about it. He just brushed it away with his thumb before getting up and holding a hand out to me. I accepted his hand, and he pulled me up with a gentle, comforting strength. My heart ached as I looked at him, covered in a rainbow of colors, his eyes still holding that soft, kind look.

Max glanced around the paint-splattered studio and then looked back at me.

"You should go get cleaned up. The bathroom's down the hall in the bedroom. Extra towels in the cabinet. I'll take care of this mess."

I hesitated, the weight of the conversation still pressing down on me. I would shower at Kait's but she and Adam were out of town visiting her parents and I left my spare key at home.

"Are you sure? I made the mess; I should help clean it up."

He shook his head, a gentle smile on his face.

"Really, it's fine. Go ahead. You don't want that paint drying on your skin and hair."

Reluctantly, I nodded and made my way to the bathroom. The small room was cozy, with a mix of functional and artistic touches that screamed Max's personality. I turned on the shower, letting the hot water cascade down and wash away the remnants of the paint fight. As the water soothed my skin, my mind kept replaying that moment. The vulnerability in his eyes, the way his thumb had gently brushed away the paint from my eyebrow—it all felt so intimate, so real.

I sighed, trying to push the thoughts away. I knew I had made the right decision for myself, but it didn't make it any easier. The hot water helped relax my muscles, but my mind was still racing with a mix of regret and longing.

After what felt like both an eternity and just a few minutes, I stepped out of the shower, wrapped myself in a towel, and took a moment to collect my thoughts. I couldn't hide in the bathroom forever.

When I emerged, I found a pair of sweatpants and a T-shirt folded neatly on a chair that had been placed directly in front of the bathroom door. A chuff made its way out of my mouth at the thoughtful gesture and as I inspected the clothes, both clearly too large for me, I couldn't help but pull them to my nose and inhale.

Fresh paint and cinnamon.

Chapter 11

I put them on, noticing the pant legs making a puddle on the floor, and rolled them up before tucking my soiled clothes into a plastic bag. I eyed his hairbrush on the dresser but left it alone, leaving my messy black hair to curl around my face. It had been a while since I had given it freedom from the straightener and now I remembered why.

When I entered the living room, I found Max still diligently cleaning up the studio. The vibrant splashes of color were mostly gone from the floor, and the space was starting to look more like the organized but chaotic, creative haven it had been before. He still looked covered in paint himself, but he must have washed his face because the paint was isolated to his body.

"Feel better?" Max asked, glancing up from where he was scrubbing the floor.

"A lot," I admitted, feeling a pang of guilt. "Thanks for taking care of this."

He waved off my thanks with a smile.

"No problem. It's good to clean acrylic immediately." He put away the rest of the paint cans as I stared at him.

"Looks like you've got everything under control," I said, trying to break the lingering tension with a light tone.

He straightened up and gave me a smile, though it didn't quite reach his eyes.

"Yeah, all good now. Thanks for not making too much of a mess," he joked.

I laughed, though it was a bit forced.

"I'll try to be less of a walking disaster next time."

Max chuckled, the tension between us easing slightly. "You know, if you weren't a bit of a disaster, life would be a lot less colorful."

I rolled my eyes playfully. "I think we've had enough color for one day."

He smiled, but there was a lingering sadness in his eyes that made my heart ache. He must have noticed my expression because he quickly changed the subject.

"Come on. I calendar-ed you over so you could see the first finished painting of the series. Wanna see it?"

I perked up, genuinely curious.

"Yeah, I'd love to."

Max led me over to an easel in the corner of the studio, where a large canvas was covered with a cloth. With a flourish, he pulled the cloth away, revealing the painting underneath. My breath caught in my throat.

It was stunning. The piece captured the essence of our project perfectly—a vibrant, dynamic representation of cultural fusion and creativity.

"Max, this is incredible," I whispered, stepping closer to take in the details. "You've really outdone yourself."

He smiled, his eyes lighting up with pride.

"Thanks. I wanted to capture the spirit of what we're trying to achieve."

"You did more than that," I said, reaching out to trace a particularly striking line of color. "This is exactly what I hoped for. Maybe even better."

Max watched me, his expression softening.

"I'm glad you think so. I was a bit nervous about showing it to you."

I turned to look at him, surprised.

"Nervous? You? Come on, you're one of the most self-assured people I know."

He shrugged, a sheepish grin spreading across his face.

"Not around you."

My smile paused. He turned back to the painting as if he hadn't just said that. We stood there in silence for a moment, both of us absorbing the beauty of the painting.

Chapter 11

Finally, Max broke the silence.

"Do you want to go over the next steps for the project? I haven't touched the website yet, that feels more like a final task thing." he asked, his tone professional.

I nodded, grateful for the return to familiar ground.

"Sure, let's do that."

Chapter 12

"Alina, you're burning the midnight oil again," Jack said, leaning against the door frame of my office. His tie was loosened, and he had the look of someone who had also seen too many late nights recently.

I looked up from my laptop, rubbing my eyes.

"Just trying to make sure everything is perfect for the international expansion pitch. There's no room for mistakes."

Jack walked in, taking a seat across from me.

"You know, you don't have to carry all this weight on your own. We're a team. Give some of it to Kelsey, that's what interns are for." He gave me a sneaky wink which made me laugh tiredly.

"Kelsey, who set the microwave on fire yesterday with her 400th popcorn of the year? I think I'll pass."

He looked at me sternly, his mentor mode shifting into gear.

"You can't control everything, Alina."

"I know," I said, offering a tired smile. "But this project is my ticket to your position. I need to prove that I can handle the pressure."

Jack nodded, understanding.

"How's the board reacting to your efforts so far?"

Chapter 12

"Mixed," I admitted, sighing. "They're impressed with the data, but they're still hesitant after the whole rescheduling debacle. I can't afford any more slip-ups."

Jack leaned back, crossing his arms.

"You've got this. No one else is as prepared or as passionate about this project as you are. The board will see that."

"I hope you're right," I replied halfheartedly, "They've moved up the final presentation date to January 10th, do you know what that's about?"

He nodded with a grimace, "Yes. Now that I'm leaving, they want to announce my successor by January 25th. But! At least this means you know that you're seriously in the running." His expression transformed and he beamed at me with his old-man smile.

A chuckle slipped past my lips, and I looked up from my laptop to grin at him.

"I guess so," I said, glancing at my phone. "By the way, how's the competition looking?"

"Fierce," he said with a wry smile. "There's about three other candidates they're looking at, but if anyone can outshine them, it's you. Just remember to take care of yourself in the process."

I laughed softly. "I'll try. Thanks, Jack."

He stood up, giving me a reassuring pat on the shoulder.

"Anytime. Get some rest tonight, okay? We need you sharp."

He left, and a quietness settled around me. I turned back to my screen, but my thoughts did what they had been annoyingly doing on repeat this week and traitorously wandered to a certain artist.

It had been a week since my and Max's last conversation, and our correspondence had remained strictly professional and only through text message. I missed the easy banter and the creative spark that seemed to flow between us, but it was better this way.

I could dedicate all of my focus to getting the promotion this way.

And neither of us could get hurt this way.

He never brought up what happened in his studio, which I was thankful for, and his texts were still very 'Max' texts. In fact, he didn't seem fazed at all by what happened – he was just his happy, sociable, easy going self again.

So why did that make a pit form at the bottom of my stomach? His latest text informed me of a supplier he had found for the environmental piece. It was deeply informative with addresses, pricing, and even comparisons to other suppliers, but a part of me wished there was more.

✧✧✧

Later that evening, I packed up my things and headed home, my mind still buzzing with plans and strategies. As I walked through the door, I was greeted by silence. My apartment felt emptier than usual, a stark contrast to the bustling office environment. I dropped my bag on the couch and headed to the kitchen to make some tea.

I turned on the kettle, staring blankly at the rising steam. It always brought an old image to my mind of my mother hunched over a tea kettle, a towel over her head to trap the steam. She always said it was like a free facial and it was the secret to staying young. A pang of resentment simmered within me, and I shook my head to clear the memory.

My mind raced with thoughts of international markets, board meetings, and Max's texts. It was a relief that he was unfazed by our last encounter, yet it stung a little that he was able to move on so easily. I shook my head, trying to clear my thoughts. I had more pressing matters to focus on.

As I waited for the water to come to a boil, a buzz came through my phone. My heart skipped a beat before I grabbed my phone to read

Chapter 12

the text.

> Harper: Airbnb-ing a cabin in the woods for the next few months. Idk how long lol just letting you know so you don't report me missing :D

A twinge of disappointment washed over me before my brain processed the text. What the fuck? I immediately FaceTimed her. A beat passed before she picked up, and her cheery smile filled the screen.

"Harper, what?"

"Hey girl!" She greeted me, her eyes flashing with nervousness for a split second before she masked her expression again with her constantly happy expression. My cousin was one of the smile-iest people I had ever met. Nothing ever seemed to bring her down from her naturally cheery disposition. I used to think she was on something every day, but she slept over once and I didn't see her take anything. With her blonde hair, tan skin, and perfect smile, she was the human epitome of a ray of sunshine.

"What do you mean you're Airbnb-ing a cabin in the woods? AND for a *few months?*"

"Exactly that?" Her tone took a confused quality and she tilted her head like a puppy. She really was a puppy. Everyone who met her loved her, though. She was easy to love like that. She also was the only person I kept in touch with from my mom's side of the family, which was entirely her effort.

I tried to shut her out, but she was persistent. She kept coming to family dinner, she rode her bike with me to school, she even egged the car of my first boyfriend after he had dumped me without telling me– I had to find out from a mutual friend. And now she was a huge part of my life.

"What about work? And John?"

A sorrowful expression took over her face, which had me taken aback. I don't think I had ever seen her sad before. This was new, and I didn't know how to take it.

"John cheated on me." My usually exuberant cousin said plainly, her eyes looking off towards the side.

A rage filled me at the thought of her boyfriend of 4 years cheating on her. How does a person do that to someone they love? How does anyone do that to *Harper*? She was as close to perfect a person could be.

"What?"

She sniffed and wiped her nose with her sleeve before continuing, "I tried to surprise him at our apartment. He had been on a business trip for two weeks and I missed him, you know?"

She sniffed again, harder this time. I could see her eyes welling up with tears, and my heart broke for her.

"I left work early and got all dressed and waxed – I *waxed,* Alina. I waxed – and then I laid on our couch ready for him to come home, and when he did, he wasn't alone."

"That fucker."

She nodded before a dam broke, and her face crumpled as she sobbed.

"H-he had been in town fo-for three days! At her place!" She cried. "An-and all our friends knew!"

Her words were choked with tears, each sob ripping through me as if it were my own. I felt an overwhelming need to comfort her, to bridge the gap between us and somehow take away her pain.

"Oh, Harper," I whispered, my voice trembling with empathy and anger. "I'm so sorry."

She nodded, her face buried in her hands.

"I thought he loved me. I spent four years with him. I was ready to marry him, Alina. I even started looking at wedding venues."

Chapter 12

I clenched my jaw, trying to contain my fury.

"He doesn't deserve you. You are worth so much more than him, Harper."

Harper sniffled and wiped her eyes.

"That's why I need to get away for a while. Clear my head, find myself again. This cabin seemed like the perfect place to do that. I already told my boss and she gave me a sabbatical and I gave all my cases to Will and I trust him and I already feel like the fresh air is helping."

I nodded, understanding her need to escape.

"I get it. Just promise me you'll stay in touch. Let me know if you need anything, okay? Send daily updates so I know you haven't been eaten by a bear."

"Of course," she said, managing a small smile. "Thanks, Lee-Lee. I knew you'd understand."

We chatted for a few more minutes, with me reassuring her as best as I could from a distance. After we hung up, I sat there for a moment, the silence of my apartment pressing down on me. Harper's heartbreak was a stark reminder of how fragile relationships could be. It was another reason to keep my focus on my career and avoid the complications of a relationship.

The kettle whistled, snapping me back to the present. I poured myself a cup of tea and settled on the couch, letting the warmth seep through the mug and into my hands. As I sipped, my phone buzzed with another work email—just one of many that demanded my attention. I glanced at it but decided to ignore it for now. I needed a moment to just breathe.

I curled up on the couch, sipping my tea and letting the silence wash over me. The quiet was a stark contrast to the constant noise of the office, and it felt almost unnerving. I closed my eyes, trying to relax, but my thoughts kept drifting back to the same artist with the tortoiseshell frames and floppy brown hair.

Chapter 13

The sound of metal ricocheted off the target at the next lane, and I winced in complete fear of my life. Neon lights illuminated the rustic wood interior of the local axe bar, casting a warm glow over the scattered patrons and the long rows of axe-throwing lanes. I sat at a high table with Kait and Adam, savoring the rare night out. I had planned to stay home and do more research about India's tech market but I couldn't do much when they showed up at my apartment and forced me to join them.

"This place is awesome!" Kait exclaimed, her eyes wide with excitement. She glanced at Adam, who was sipping his craft beer. "I can't believe we haven't come here before."

Adam chuckled. "Just as long as you don't go too crazy with the axe throwing, alright? We don't need any pregnancy-related injuries."

Kait rolled her eyes playfully. "Please, I'm gonna be so good at this they're gonna want to hire me."

Kait always thought she was going to be amazing at everything she did.

She was always just okay.

"Sure, honey, and then you'll probably be dispatched to the moon to be the first contact point for the aliens and then yo-."

Sarcasm oozed from his voice before she glared at him, causing his eyes to widen fearfully. He shut up and lifted his beer to his mouth, sipping at it quietly instead.

I smiled, watching them banter. It was good to see Kait so happy, especially with everything she had on her plate. She had been stressing about this baby a lot recently now that she knows it's going to be a girl.

I just know their apartment was covered head to toe with various lists. I took a sip of my drink, feeling the stress of the day slowly melt away.

Kait suddenly gasped, her eyes fixed on something across the room. "Oh my God, Alina, look who's here!"

I followed her gaze and felt my stomach flip. There, at another table, was Max, laughing with three other men. Even in the dim light, his floppy brown hair and tortoiseshell frames were unmistakable. I hadn't seen him in over a week. Our communication has been limited to working texts these days.

The three men with him were equally striking: a grumpy-looking guy with jet black hair and striking blue eyes who looked really familiar, a smiley Hispanic man with warm brown eyes and brown hair, and a blonde who looked like he had stepped straight out of a magazine taking his turn to throw his axe.

"Oh my god, I knew it was a good idea to stalk him online. I'd recognize him a mile away now and- *oh* he looks even better in person!" Kait whispered conspiratorially. "Come on, you have to go say hi!"

I shook my head, feeling a mix of anxiety and curiosity.

"No way. We're here to relax, not to make things complicated. I'm leaving work behind tonight."

Kait gave me a look that said she wasn't taking no for an answer.

Chapter 13

"Oh, come on, Alina. He's not work. Besides, you deserve to have a little fun, too. And look at them, they're all hot!"

A throat clearing next to her had her looking remorseful and caressing his hair.

"You're hotter, babe."

A gleeful smile took over his face, making him look at his drink with bashfulness, he didn't even see as she moved her head behind him and shook her head, her nose scrunched.

I snorted, making his eyes dart towards me, and I coughed, looking away and taking a sip of my drink.

"Go." Kait demanded.

"No, Kait," I said weakly, "we should just enjoy our night. He's work and work stays behind tonight."

"Max!" Kait hollered. Oh, god no. Multiple heads turned in our direction. She then turned to me with a mischievous grin. I was going to kill her. I glared at her, sending her the message. She just smiled victoriously, while Adam cringed behind his drink.

Max looked up, his eyes widening in surprise. She nudged me forward, pretending it was me who had called out. Spotting me across the room, he smiled and waved, gesturing for me to join them.

Oh he looked nice. He was dressed more formally tonight in a pair of dark jeans and his usual paint splattered shirt was replaced with a dark button down. I felt a mix of indignation and reluctance as I made my way over to their table, unable to ignore Kait's insistent nudges.

"Alina! What a pleasant surprise." His eyes twinkled.

"Hey," I replied, trying to keep my voice steady. "Fancy seeing you here."

"It's nice to see you." This normally was a standard, ingenuine greeting people gave each other, but Max said it like he meant it and it made my stomach feel warm. "I got so used to seeing you every day, the past week has been weird."

"Yeah, I um haven't seen any calendar invites in a while." I joked, clearing my throat awkwardly when I heard how it came out.

His expression fell the slightest bit before he smiled at me with his pearly teeth again.

"I didn't know if you wanted to see me," He blushed and ran a hand through his hair. "I had to stop myself from sending one four times."

I stared at him, feeling a warmth in my cheeks. He wanted to see me? He kept it professional because that's what he thought *I* wanted? It was… but I didn't realize his words would affect me like this.

All week I thought he had been keeping a distance because he was angry with me from our last meeting, but by his tone it sounded like he had already accepted it and was giving me space for me.

We stared at each other for a moment before a throat cleared, interrupting our eye contact. I broke away first to see his three friends staring curiously at us. The blonde one was just tilting his head and inspecting us, holding his axe by his side a few feet away.

My eyes drew to his axe-holding wrist and I was startled by another beaded bracelet matching Max's. Looking around the table, they all wore one. Bewilderment filled me at the sight of four grown men wearing beaded friendship bracelets.

Max looked at me a few more seconds before turning to his friends and grinning.

He gestured to his friends.

"Let me introduce you. This is Ezra," he said, indicating the quiet looking guy, "Rowan," the Hispanic guy with warm eyes, "and Cas," the striking blonde.

Ezra Bates. No wonder he looked so familiar. The black haired man with the blue eyes was Ezra Bates, the tech genius behind the newest VR systems. The man revolutionized AI and was always on all the tech magazine covers. He was a legend. So how was Max friends with him?

Chapter 13

They all greeted me warmly with pleasant smiles and a hint of confusion that lingered in their gazes, and I felt a wave of relief wash over me.

Max gestured to the empty seats around their table. "Why don't you join us?"

I hesitated, gesturing behind me at my old table with Kait and Adam without looking.

"I actually am here with some peop-"

But before I could finish, Kait and Adam appeared beside me, beaming.

"Hey there!" Kait chirped, sliding into the conversation seamlessly. Adam nodded at Max and his friends, that weird restrained male greeting me and Kait always made fun of.

I sighed before accepting my fate, gesturing at the duo. "This is Kait and Adam."

His friends all introduced themselves in return warmly. I wonder if they knew about the kiss – if Max had told them. I didn't tell Kait, but that was mostly because I knew that she would have killed me for what happened.

"Our table was getting lonely, so we thought we'd join you guys if that's okay!" Kait announced gleefully.

"Nice to meet you all." Adam mumbled, clearly reluctant to be here.

Max grinned, motioning for them to sit down. "The more, the merrier!"

Kait happily obliged, settling into the seat beside me.

"So, who's the best player so I know who to beat?"

Immediately, all the guys pointed at Cas and he smirked over at her. He ran a hand through his blonde hair and looked her dead on, "Prepare to taste defeat, I'm not above wiping the floor with a girl."

Laughter filled the air as we merged into one group, sharing stories and exchanging jokes. The competitive spirit quickly took over, and soon we were all laughing and cheering each other on.

Despite his grumpy demeanor, Ezra turned out to be a surprisingly good axe thrower, hitting the target with precise accuracy. Rowan and Caspian weren't too shabby either, and Max, well, he was just as charming and easygoing as always. It felt good to let loose and forget about work for a while.

At one point, Kait yawned, her energy waning.

"I think it's time for us to head out. Baby here needs some rest," she said, patting her belly.

I glanced at my phone, noting the time. It was still relatively early, but I knew Kait needed her rest.

Adam nodded. "Yeah, we should get going."

I moved to join them, but Kait and Adam both shook their heads.

"You stay and have fun," Kait insisted. "We'll be fine."

"It's okay," I offered, standing up from the table.

Kait waved me off.

"No need, Alina. You stay and enjoy yourself. We'll catch a ride home."

"No, I'll come with," I intervened, desperately. I wasn't tired but I felt like enough lines had been crossed tonight. "Besides, you guys are my ride."

"I can drive her home later." Max offered, raising a hand. He was too nice. He also was getting in the way of my escape plan.

"It's really okay," I started before Kait interrupted me.

"Perfect!" She walked backwards to the exit, a victorious smile as she dragged Adam beside her. "Text us when you get home. Byeeeeeee!"

And then they were gone. I was really going to kill her.

"Looks like you're stuck with us," Max said with a grin.

Crap.

Chapter 14

The conversation resumed, but I couldn't shake the feeling of unease that settled in the pit of my stomach. I didn't want to overstay my welcome or impose on Max and his friends.

"I can just take the bus," I said after a while, reaching for my purse.

"No." Ezra's tone was firm. "It's late and you're a young woman, and if my sister has taught me anything, it's that we shouldn't let you go alone. Max will drive you home later."

Max nodded. All my words left me. After a second, I sighed and nodded, sitting back down.

I felt a bit awkward at first, but Max and his friends quickly made me feel included. We continued throwing axes, and the competitive, yet friendly atmosphere helped me relax.

At one point, Max handed me an axe and leaned in a little closer.

"So, how have you been?" he asked, his voice soft and genuine.

"Busy," I replied with a small smile. "But good. My other project is coming along well. Ours is going so smoothly with you holding the reins that I haven't had to worry much about it."

"That's great to hear," he said, his eyes meeting mine. Then his eyes turned more serious. "I've missed our conversations."

My breath caught in my throat before I nodded and looked at my axe. Suddenly, it was the most interesting thing in the world.

"Me too," I admitted quietly, feeling a warmth spread through me. "It's been... different."

Before the conversation could go any deeper, Ezra called out, "Alina, you're up!"

I stepped up to the line, taking a deep breath. With a steady aim, I threw the axe, and it landed with a satisfying thud in the target. Kait could suck it.

"Nice throw!" Rowan cheered, and the others joined in.

"So, how do you all know each other?" I asked, curiosity getting the better of me.

Max chuckled, sharing a knowing look with his friends.

"We actually all went to Riverview University together. Lived in the same house for a few years."

Rowan nodded, a grin spreading across his face.

"Those were some wild times, let me tell you."

I couldn't help but smile at their camaraderie.

"And now? What do you all do?"

Rowan gestured to himself. "I own a Spanish fusion restaurant in River North. It's been keeping me busy, but I love it."

"What restaurant? Maybe I've been."

Rowan smirked. "Alegria."

My jaw dropped. Alegria was one of the most popular restaurants in Chicago. The wait times were magnanimous. Most of the people from my office had been wanting to go there for months, but couldn't because of how long it took to get a reservation.

Caspian chimed in, his eyes sparkling with mischief. "I'm an architect. Been working on some pretty cool projects lately."

"I'm in tech." Ezra grumbled to us behind him, cocking his arm back

Chapter 14

to throw the axe.

"And the friendship bracelets?" I asked, hesitantly. For all I knew, it was a secret, but I was too curious not to ask.

For the first time, Ezra smiled softly as he inspected his bracelet.

"My sister Emmy made them for us our senior year in college. She said it was to 'represent the brotherhood.'" The guys all laughed.

Ezra continued on. "We all complained but she threatened to gut us if we ever took them off."

I laughed at the image and nodded, understanding the bond behind the bracelets. "Sounds like a real threat."

Max grinned, his eyes sparkling with amusement. "Trust me, she's not one to mess with."

"Speaking of," Cas chimed in, "why is your sister such a tyrant?"

"Maybe if you hadn't stolen her property, she wouldn't feel the need to mess with you." Ezra looked at him pointedly, then turned to me. "She's *also* an architect."

Cas scoffed then and told the group.

"We had been competing for the Bradshaw property for a month now and she's all pissy that I won it."

"Yikes, dude, that's a douche move. Didn't she really want that property?" Max cut in with a wince.

Caspian's grin widened.

"Don't worry, she got her revenge. She snuck into my car while I was sleeping and somehow managed to change the horn of my car to emit a woman's moan every time I honk it."

I couldn't help but burst out laughing, imagining the scene.

"That's diabolical. You'll have to get her back somehow."

Max chuckled, adjusting his tortoiseshell frames and peering at me.

"Believe me, he's already plotting his revenge."

The rest of the evening passed in a blur. By the time we finally decided to call it a night, I felt lighter, more relaxed than I had in weeks. When we finally said goodbye outside, Max led me to his car and abided by his promise of driving me home.

Despite my initial protests, I found myself seated in his car, the soft hum of the engine filling the silence between us. The streets were quiet, illuminated only by the soft glow of streetlights, casting long shadows across the pavement.

I stole a glance at Max as he drove, his hands steady on the wheel, his profile illuminated by the soft glow of the dashboard lights. There was something comforting about his presence, something familiar and warm that made me feel safe, despite the late hour.

"Thanks for driving me home," I said softly, breaking the silence that had settled between us.

Max glanced at me, a small smile playing at the corners of his lips.

"Of course. I wouldn't want you walking home alone at this hour."

I nodded, grateful I didn't have to take the bus in the dark. As we drove, I couldn't help the yawns that came over me. I couldn't remember the last time I went out and didn't spend the whole time stressing about a project or a deadline.

As the city passed by in a blur outside the window, I couldn't help but feel a sense of dread creeping in, a fear of the unknown that lurked just beneath the surface. To my surprise, the car was quiet the entire way. It also didn't irk me the way most awkward silences did.

This was comfortable, and I basked in it.

When we arrived at my apartment building, I felt a wave of relief wash over me.

Max nodded, his expression softening.

"Thanks for joining us tonight, Alina. I had a great time."

I forced a smile, the weight of his words settling heavily on my shoulders.

"Me too. Your friends were lovely."

He nodded, his eyes meeting mine before flickering down to my lips

Chapter 14

for just a second. I couldn't help it as my eyes drew down to his, my throat swallowing as the car suddenly felt quieter and warmer. They looked so soft, and puffy, and pink… and I had to clear my throat to snap myself out of it.

Thankfully, he didn't say anything, or maybe he didn't notice as his soft gaze lingered on mine for a moment longer before he reached over and opened the door for me. Stepping out onto the sidewalk, my cheeks flushed and throat parched, I couldn't help but feel a sense of relief wash over me. The cool night air wrapped around me like a familiar embrace, grounding me in the reality of my own solitude.

"Goodnight, Alina," Max said softly, his voice carrying on the gentle breeze.

"Goodnight," I rasped.

He waited until I walked into the building to drive away.

Chapter 15

Tuesday morning, I sat at my desk, engrossed in the latest market analysis report when my phone buzzed with a notification. With a sigh, I set aside my work and picked up my phone, expecting yet another email demanding my attention. Instead, I was greeted with a text from Harper.

Already familiar with this routine, I smiled as I opened the message and was met with a picture of Harper, standing in front of a towering tree, her arms wrapped around its trunk in a tight hug.

Based on the angle, she probably had set her phone against a different tree and self-timed it, just like in her countless other updates of just her and a new tree she found around her area. As I studied the photo, my phone buzzed again, drawing me out of my reverie.

I glanced at the top of the screen to see a new notification. My jaw fell. A calendar invite. From Max. My first one in two weeks. A subtle smile made its way back onto my face, unknowingly.

As I read the details, I felt a mix of surprise and anticipation. It was for today, in a few hours. He wanted me to come by the studio to see the second finished painting in the series. This was the sustainability

Chapter 15

piece that we wanted to incorporate recycled materials into. How had he already finished it? He just found a supplier for the materials a few days ago.

It had only been three days since we last saw each other at the axe bar and he drove me home. His friends were amazing and while I did still plan to kill Kait for forcing me to talk to them and then leaving me stranded with them, I was glad I stayed.

But it didn't change anything. I still didn't have time for a relationship and even if we got into one, I wouldn't be able to give him all of me. I don't think I would ever be able to give someone all of me.

A part of me considered declining the calendar invite to keep the space cool between us but I really did want to see the second piece. When we were bouncing ideas off each other for it, it quickly became my favorite and I was excited for what it would become. He had been sending me different ideas for logos over email the past few weeks which I had gotten used to seeing in my inbox, but seeing him in person, in his studio apartment again... This was different.

I also had to get over this need to put distance between us. He seemed to have no hard feelings about my rejection so I had no reason to avoid him.

With a nervous exhale, I pressed accept.

✧✧✧

As I made my way to Max's apartment later that day, I couldn't help but notice how familiar the journey was becoming. It seemed like I was visiting more often than I expected, and each time, the knots of apprehension in my stomach loosened just a little bit more.

When Max opened the door, a small smile tugged at the corners of my lips. There was paint on his forehead. A thin line of green that must have made its way there when he wiped his forehead or something.

"Hey." He grinned.

"Hey." I smiled.

As he led me to the corner of his apartment where his art was displayed, I couldn't contain my curiosity. He stood me in front of a covered canvas and wordlessly handed me a freshly made, still-hot cup of coffee. I looked at him in astonishment, then took a sip.

Two creams. A sugar. And a dash of cinnamon.

With bated breath, he unveiled the painting, and I felt my breath catch in my throat. The sustainability piece was even more breathtaking than I had imagined. The way he had incorporated the recycled circuit boards and glass onto the canvas was nothing short of genius, and I found myself completely captivated by the intricate details.

Max leaned against the wall, his eyes fixed on the painting.

"So, what do you think?" he asked, a hint of uncertainty in his voice. I took a sip of my coffee, savoring the warmth as I studied the piece. Like all his other paintings, I couldn't take my eyes off of it.

"It's amazing, Max," I said, my voice filled with genuine admiration. "You've really captured the essence of GenTech's sustainability efforts. It doesn't even scream at you or anything, it's just… a beautiful painting that happens to be about the environment."

A smile tugged at the corners of Max's lips, his eyes lighting up with appreciation.

"Thanks. I couldn't have done it without your input."

I shook my head, feeling a rush of humility.

"No, you're the one with the talent. I just offered a few ideas here and there."

Max's smile widened as he shook his head, but he didn't counter me. He seemed to know I wouldn't accept it, and for a moment, we simply stood in silence, lost in the beauty of the painting before us.

Soon enough, conversation flowed easily between us, as if the

Chapter 15

tension that had been lingering between us had finally dissipated. I knew I should have just taken my leave before it got personal again, but I didn't want to. Something in me deeply wanted to stay and talk to him.

Max continued leaning against the wall while I sat on the couch, a contemplative expression on his face.

"You know, I never thought I'd enjoy axe throwing as much as I did the other night," he admitted with a chuckle. "I have to say, it was surprisingly cathartic."

I laughed, recalling the thrill of hurling an axe through the air.

"Yeah, it was definitely a… unique experience. I didn't even want to go, Kait and Adam forced me. But once I got over the fear of being beheaded, it was fun."

Max nodded, a smile playing at the corners of his lips.

"Well, I'm glad Kait convinced you to give it a try. She was certainly something. Your friends were great. I'm glad I met them."

"Your friends were pretty amazing too." I replied.

His smile deepened in his face and he adjusted his glasses as he responded.

"It was nice," he paused, "having you there."

I smiled, feeling a warmth spread through me at his words.

"Yeah, it was nice to get out of my head for a while."

"Are you always in your head?" He tilted his head and peered at me strangely.

"Most days I can't find my way out." I laughed wryly, playing it off as a joke.

His expression remained unchanged, and just as he leaned forward to respond, my phone buzzed with an incoming text. I glanced down at the screen to see a message from my neighbor, his words sending a surge of panic through me. My whole body froze and I could feel a ringing in my ears as everything went cloudy. It must have made Max worried, because he shook me out of it with a yell of my name.

"Alina, what's wrong?" His voice was serious and urgent, and his hands were rubbing up and down my shoulders as if to get blood flow into them.

My fingers trembled as I read the message, my heart pounding in my chest.

"My dad fell," I blurted out, my voice thick with emotion. "I need to get home right away."

Max's expression softened with concern as he reached out to steady me.

"Hey, it's going to be okay," he reassured me, his voice calm and steady.

"You don't understand," I trembled, "he lives alone. He's getting older, and he's had some health issues lately. I just... I need to make sure he's okay."

Understanding dawned on his face. His eyebrows drew together in worry.

"*Shit!*" I cried, my voice trembling with frustration and anxiety. "The train will only get me there in three hours and I don't have a car-"

"I'll drive you." His voice was steady and reassuring. I looked up at him and saw deep concern in his eyes. Why did he seem so concerned? He had never met my dad. He nodded at me steadily and helped me off the couch, grabbing his keys off the counter.

Relief flooded through me at his offer, and without hesitation, I nodded, grateful for his kindness.

"Thank you."

He led me out of his apartment to his car and together we raced through the city to the suburbs, the glow of the mid-afternoon sun casting long shadows across the pavement. He quietly drove as I looked out the window the whole car ride. With each passing moment, my anxiety grew, the fear of what I might find when I reached my father's

Chapter 15

side weighing heavily on my mind.

◆◆◆

The drive felt interminable, my heart pounding with worry the entire way. When we finally pulled up to my father's house, I was out of the car before Max had even fully stopped. I rushed to the front door, fumbling with my keys.

"Papa!" I shouted, bursting inside. "Papa, where are you?"

"*Dapur!*" came his voice, oddly calm and cheerful given the supposed situation.

Confusion mingled with my panic as I hurried toward the kitchen. There, standing in front of the stove, was my father. He looked perfectly fine, not a scratch or bruise on him, stirring a pot of something that smelled delicious.

"What's going on?" I demanded, my voice shaking with a mix of relief and anger. "Marty said you fell!"

Papa turned to me with a sheepish grin.

"Ah, well... that might've been a little fib."

"A fib?!" I cried, my voice rising. "You scared me half to death!"

He held up his hands in a placating gesture.

"I'm sorry, Alina. I just... I missed you, and I was in the mood to cook! I knew you'd come if you thought I needed you."

I stared at him, my emotions warring within me. Relief that he was okay clashed with the anger of being deceived.

"Papa, you can't do things like that. What if something had really happened?"

He sighed, looking genuinely remorseful.

"I know, I know. It was wrong. It's all Marty's fault!"

I gave him a scathing look.

"Okay, okay, don't blame Marty, I made him text you." He admitted, his eyes downcast to the wood floor.

I wanted to stay mad at him, but seeing his remorseful expression, the anger started to fade, and a pit of guilt formed in my stomach at the thought of him having to resort to these means just to get me to come home for dinner.

"Just... don't do it again, okay?"

He nodded and looked back up at me before his gaze shifted to the side, a playful beam slowly taking over his face.

I looked behind me to figure out what he was looking at and saw Max leaning against the door frame, an amused look on his face.

My father's eyes lit up with interest at the sight of him.

"Who's this?" he asked, turning his gaze to me.

Max smiled cheerfully at my dad and stepped forward, holding a hand out. He still had a line of green paint on his forehead and dried paint marks on his clothes. I guess he hadn't paused to clean up before driving me home in a hurry, and my heart warmed at the thought.

"Hi Mr. Bennet. I'm Max. I'm working with your daughter on a rebranding project for GenTech." He greeted politely.

My father's lip quirked in the corner as his eyes drew to Max's forehead and clothes. I held my breath, not sure why I was so nervous all of a sudden. Was this my first time introducing someone to my dad? He had already met Kait and Adam and he knew all my friends growing up, but Max's introduction felt different somehow.

He took Max's hand in a firm grip, and I found myself exhaling in relief.

"Santoso," he corrected with a smile on his face, "Dr. Zaki Santoso, but feel free to call me Zaki."

Max looked over at me with a perplexed look before nodding at my dad and stepping away.

"Max was kind enough to drive me here after your little stunt." I remarked, looking pointedly at my dad.

Chapter 15

"Thank you, Max." My dad responded remorsefully. "But! Now that you're both here, you might as well stay for dinner. There's too much food for just old me."

He gave us both the old man equivalent of puppy dog eyes, and I almost groaned in exasperation.

"Max probably has to head back, especially after wasting all his time driving me, he-"

"Nonsense!" my father interjected before Max could respond. "You're welcome to join us for dinner. It's the least I can do after all the trouble I've caused."

Max glanced at me, and I could see he was trying to gauge my reaction.

"If it's not too much trouble," Max said, looking back at my father.

"No trouble at all!" Papa said with a grin. "Come on in, make yourself at home."

Max nodded, giving me a reassuring smile as he followed my father into the kitchen. I took a deep breath and rolled my shoulders, trying to ease the tension in my shoulders, but just being here had me guarded, and a part of me wanted to escape this house as soon as I could.

There was a reason I always visited my dad at Grahams.

Dinner was a pleasant affair. After my dad showed Max to the bathroom so he could clean up and Max sheepishly did so after realizing the paint still on him, we all sat down to the aroma of my father's cooking filling the air.

My father chatted animatedly with Max, asking him about his art and the project we were working on. Max responded with genuine interest, and I found myself smiling at their easy rapport. Despite the initial chaos, the evening began to take on a pleasant, almost familial atmosphere.

"Alina tells me you're quite the artist," Papa said, passing a dish of fried rice to Max. "I'd love to see some of your work someday."

Max smiled, accepting the dish.

"I'd be happy to show you. Maybe you could come by the studio sometime."

"I'd like that," Papa replied, nodding enthusiastically.

"The studio is just his apartment." I grumbled before shoveling a spoon of fried rice and braised tofu in my mouth.

Max barked a laugh and tried to smother it behind his fist.

"Alina!" Papa scolded. He turned back to Max with a polite enthusiasm. "I'd still love to. I've always loved art."

"Alina actually has been behind most of the creative ideas for the GenTech series. She's got quite an eye for art herself." Max nodded at me.

A blush warmed my cheeks and I shook my head, not sure how to respond.

"Max is being generous. I just threw a few ideas out there."

My dad chuckled, his eyes twinkling.

"Don't sell yourself short, Alina. You've always had a creative streak. Remember that painting you did in high school? The one with your comet?"

I smiled, feeling a nostalgic warmth.

"Yeah, I remember. You hung it in the living room for years."

"And I still have it," Papa said proudly. "It's one of my favorite pieces."

Max looked at me with a raised eyebrow.

"Your comet?"

I nodded, glancing at my father.

"Yeah, the Hale-Bopp comet. It was a school project about significant astronomical events. I chose it because it was sighted the night I was born."

Papa leaned forward, a nostalgic smile on his face.

"Alina was born on the night Hale-Bopp was most visible. I had set up my telescope to watch it, but had to rush to the hospital when her

Chapter 15

mother went into labor. You know her, always early to things. That's why we named her Alina—'light' for the light that seared through the sky that night. She's my *anakku dari bintang*, my child of the stars."

Max listened intently, a soft smile on his face.

"That's a beautiful story."

Papa nodded.

"She's always had a special light in her, just like that comet."

I cleared my throat, eager to change the subject. As the conversation flowed around the table, I felt a warmth spreading through me. Despite the unexpected turn of events, or maybe because of it, the evening had turned into something special.

Max and Papa talked about everything from art to travel to their favorite foods. I chimed in occasionally, but mostly I listened, enjoying the sound of their voices, still reeling from the thought of anything happening to my dad while I was away.

Eventually, the evening began to wind down. I glanced at the clock and realized how late it had gotten.

"We should probably get going," I said, feeling a sudden wave of exhaustion. I missed my dad and his cooking, but just being in this house was draining my energy by the minute.

Dad stood up, stretching.

"It's getting pretty late, and I heard the weather report mentioning icy roads. Why don't you two stay over tonight? There's plenty of room."

"Oh that's okay. Max, if you'd like to leave I'll understand, we've already taken a bunch of your time."

I looked over at him. I wanted to leave, but Max was the driver and if he wanted to stay, I wouldn't leave him here.

Max glanced at me, then back at my dad with a broad smile.

"If it's not too much trouble, that sounds like a good idea."

Dad smiled. "No trouble at all. I'll get the guest room ready for you,

Max. Alina, your old room is just as you left it."

As Dad headed to the guest room to prepare it, Max and I exchanged a glance.

"Thanks again for everything," I said quietly.

"Of course," he replied, his expression serious as he gazed down at me. "I'm glad to be here."

After Dad had finished setting up the guest room, he bid us goodnight and headed to bed. Max and I were left alone in the living room, the house quiet and peaceful around us.

"Do you want a tour?" I asked, standing up. "I can show you around a bit."

"I'd like that," Max said, following me.

We walked through the house I hadn't been to in seven years, and I pointed out various rooms and features. We ended up in the hallway where family photos lined the walls. I kept my eyes averted, awkwardly looking at my fidgeting hands as Max stopped to look at them, his gaze lingering on a particular photo of my parents holding me as a baby.

"So, I've been curious," Max said, turning to me. "Why is your last name Bennet when your dad's is Santoso?"

I sighed, feeling the familiar weight of the story. At this point, all lines had been crossed. I didn't bother trying to create space between us anymore, there was no use. This man drew my innermost thoughts out of me like honey and I was too emotionally wracked from today to filter it.

"My mom's parents didn't approve of their marriage," I started, keeping my eyes on my fingers.

"They married young in college and her parents were the typical white conservative old money types and so they didn't approve of her marrying an immigrant with no money. It didn't even matter to them that he was going to be an astrophysicist and while he tried hard to win over their approval, they never gave it. They actually disowned her and claimed they didn't want anything to do with her or any offspring she produced with him."

I glimpsed up at his face and watched as his grass green eyes widened as he listened. His eyebrows furrowed together and I continued on.

"So, when my sister and I were born, my dad gave me her maiden name in the hopes that if I at least had their name, they would have accepted us. They didn't."

"I'm so sorry." Max murmured.

His hand reached out to my shoulder and he squeezed it gently. I hadn't told anyone this in a long time. Kait was the only person who knew other than family, and when I felt my eyes start to well up with tears, I quickly blinked them away and shakily exhaled.

"Did your mom pass?" He ventured.

"No." My voice grew hard. "She didn't die. She just left."

His gaze widened with disbelief.

A bitter laugh escaped me.

"After years of telling my dad that she didn't need her parents, that we were enough, she left. She packed her bags without a word, and left behind a note explaining that she needed to find herself, whatever that meant. We all knew the real reason. She went back to her cushy life with her parents and we never saw her again. I was seven."

Another shoulder squeeze.

"My dad still thinks she's coming back one day. That's why all her stuff is still here."

I remember the day she left as if it were yesterday, the bitter taste of abandonment still lingering on my tongue. For years, I struggled to make sense of her absence, grappling with feelings of rejection and confusion.

But as time passed, I came to accept that some questions would never have answers, and that closure was a luxury I might never afford. In her absence, my dad took the role of both parents while working and when his money started kicking in after he became more renown, he took more time off of work to raise us.

And when time passed and she still didn't come back, his faith in her wavered, and his brain started trying to cope with it in weird ways. He started using her eucalyptus shampoo, he never talked to other women, and he kept these stupid pictures up of a family that didn't exist anymore after all these years.

"It would have been better if she did die." I said coldly. "At least, that way he could move on instead of being stuck in this limbo she's trapped him in."

Max's hand moved from my shoulder to my arm, pulling me into a gentle hug. He smelled like cinnamon and paint, and a dam of tears broke through me. Fuck, I thought, why did I have to be cursed with the emotional dam of a toddler.

"I'm so sorry you had to go through that," he said softly. "You and your dad both."

For a moment, I allowed myself to lean into him, finding unexpected comfort in his presence. His warmth, his steady heartbeat, and the sincerity in his voice all seemed to ease the tightness in my chest. I hadn't been hugged like this before. He gave the kind of hug that you could easily become addicted to.

I pulled back slightly, meeting his concerned gaze.

My confession must have completely destroyed my filter because for some reason the words came out without any notice, like they had been bottled in for too long and now the pressure was being released.

"My sister left as soon as she turned 18 and I haven't seen her since. I guess that's why I've always avoided relationships," I admitted. "I didn't want to risk the same kind of heartbreak my dad went through both times. I thought it was easier to stay detached, to keep things casual and professional."

Chapter 15

Max nodded in understanding, his eyes never leaving mine. He didn't even try to counter my points. He didn't try to be selfish and convince me to go out with him like other guys would have. It was like he heard me and understood why I was the way I was and he was willing to accept that.

I had spent so many years building walls, convincing myself that it was safer to remain detached, to avoid the kind of pain my father had endured. After my mom left, and then my sister right after, I was scared to give parts of me away that I couldn't afford to lose. I was still scared.

But looking into his eyes, at the way he was comforting me when I had been nothing but cold to him, seeing how he had dropped everything to drive me home without hesitation, I realized that maybe I could take this chance.

Maybe he would hurt me like they did and maybe he would leave, but for some reason, I trusted him and I found myself willing to make an exception. Just this once.

"Ask me again." I whispered softly, watching his face.

He looked at me, puzzled, until realization dawned on him, shock flickering across his face.

"Alina." He rasped hoarsely.

"Ask me again." I repeated. My voice was still quiet in the silent hallway but it sounded more sure this time.

He swallowed and held my arms before giving in.

"Go out with me." His voice brushed against my skin in a soft breath.

I nodded at him, a small smile quirking the corner of my lips.

He kissed my forehead softly, then pulled back to examine my face. I watched as his face brightened in a breathtaking smile, and for one second, I couldn't breathe.

Chapter 16

"You said 'ask me again'?" Kait's voice rattled through my phone's speaker as I charted the projections for the expansion project. It was due in less than three months, and I had barely been able to make any leeway.

"Yep." I responded.

"And he did."

"Yep."

"And you said yes."

"Yep."

"And then?!" She almost squealed through the phone, and I winced as it pierced my hearing.

"We went to bed and he drove me home the next day."

"*We* went to bed?" Her tone took a mischievous quality as she trailed off suggestively, and I groaned.

"Not *together*. This isn't one of your romances with a one bed trope. My dad has three rooms in his house, Kait."

She swore through the phone before continuing on pestering me. Why did I ever tell her things? I should have soft launched it with her

Chapter 16

over the course of three months, but for some reason, I blurted out everything when she called me.

"And then?"

"And then nothing." I shrugged, not that she saw.

"What do you mean nothing? Have you not been on a date yet?! It's been a week!" She cried.

"I've been busy!" I replied, defensively. "Between the two projects I have to juggle, the board keeping a close eye on me, and now my neighbor's cat constantly sneaking its way into my apartment in the dead of night, I've had a lot on my plate. He's been busy too, you know, with the GenTech series and all his other orders."

"Uh huh." She sounded unconvinced.

"He's been texting me and I've told him about my lack of free time and he seems to understand that. Not everyone needs to always be going out to be dating, Kait."

"That's literally the definition of dating." She deadpanned.

"Alina, you can't keep avoiding this," Kait persisted through the phone. "You've got to make time for each other if you want this relationship to go anywhere."

"I know, I know," I sighed, feeling the weight of her words pressing down on me. "But between work and everything else going on, it's not that simple."

"It's never going to be simple," she countered. "But if he's worth it, you'll find a way to make it work."

Before I could respond, my phone pinged with a reminder for my next meeting. I glanced at my calendar and groaned inwardly.

"Speaking of work," I muttered. "I've got to run. I'll talk to you later, okay?"

"Fine," Kait huffed. "But we're not done talking about this."

I chuckled softly before ending the call and quickly gathered my things. As I hurried out of the door, I checked my calendar to confirm the location of my next meeting. A coffee store down the street. I honestly had forgotten what this meeting was for and with whom but I must have been in a rush when I plugged it in.

Arriving at the cozy café, I made my way to the back looking for any possible idea of who I was meant to be meeting. For all I knew, it was probably our business associate from Hudson Tech wanting to discuss a possible collaboration. He did slip me his business card at the auction when I was stuffing my face with crostinis in a corner.

To my surprise, I spotted a familiar head of chocolate brown hair sitting at a table near the window, a cup of coffee in hand and a spare on the table, a warm smile on his face. Why was he here? This coffee shop was nowhere near his studio or any galleries.

Panic struck through me and I felt my fight or flight mode activate at the thought of Max here on a date with someone else. I know I hadn't met up with him in a week and I was too distracted to send more romantic texts but I didn't realize one week was all it took to drive him away.

What if I had been so caught up in my own world that I had neglected our relationship, driving him into the arms of another woman?

My heart started to break in my chest at the thought before he saw me, beamed, and waved me over, looking like a puppy dog with his excitement.

My steps faltered as these thoughts consumed me, my heart heavy with the weight of my insecurities. But then Max caught my eye, his expression softening as he reached out to take my hand. The warmth of his touch sent a jolt of reassurance through me, dispelling my doubts like a ray of sunshine breaking through the clouds.

"Alina, are you okay?" Max's voice was filled with concern as he looked at me, his eyes searching mine for any sign of distress.

I hesitated for a moment, unsure whether to voice my fears or keep

Chapter 16

them buried inside.

"Max, hi. I uh... I thought..." My words trailed off as I struggled to find the right way to express my fears.

But before I could say anything more, Max gently squeezed my hand, his eyes softening with understanding.

"Breathe. You can tell me." He said, his eyes warm as he looked at me.

"It's silly. Stupid really, but the two coffees and you not telling me you were here and me asking you out then neglecting you all week, I just..."

"You thought I was here with someone else," he said quietly.

I felt a lump form in my throat as I nodded, unable to meet his gaze.

Max let out a soft sigh, his thumb brushing gently against the back of my hand.

"Alina, I would never do that to you," he said earnestly.

"I'm sorry." I mumbled, feeling some tension lift from my shoulders.

He had only ever been the nicest man I had ever met, so why was I still struggling with this?

He looked at me sympathetically before nodding and changing the subject, reaching over to take my hand in his.

"I thought I'd surprise you," he said. "I saw you had a 20-minute block in your calendar free at this time, so I put this in while you weren't looking."

"This?" I asked.

"Our first date." He gave me an adorable grin and pulled out my chair for me.

I blinked in surprise as I sat down, my mind struggling to process his words. He had looked in my calendar? This was my twenty-minute meeting I had? How did he even know my schedule? But before I could voice my questions, Max was already continuing.

"I know it's not much," he said, gesturing to the coffee shop around us. "But I thought I'd make the most of these twenty minutes."

I glanced at the clock on the wall and realized we only had about twenty minutes before my next meeting was supposed to start. But the warmth in Max's eyes and the genuine excitement in his voice made it hard to say no.

"Okay," I replied with a smile. "I can spare a few minutes."

Max's smile widened, and he offered me his hand.

"Great! Let's get to it! We only have about," he checked his watch, "18 minutes left!"

"Okay." I laughed, then took a sip of the coffee he had on the table. It was perfect.

"So, what do you do for a living?" He rested his elbow on the table and placed his chin on his palm.

I snorted and gave him a knowing look.

"Max, we already know each other."

"Humor me." He simply said, smiling lazily at me again. Was he ever not smiling? He was honestly the cheeriest man I had ever met. Harper and him would get along well.

I nodded at him, conceding to go along with whatever plan he had.

"I am a Senior Operations Manager at GenTech. And you?" I tilted my head, poking fun at him.

He just rolled with it.

"That's very cool. You must have worked hard to get to that level as young as you are." He had an impressed look on his face. "I'm a freelance artist, but I also work in graphic design. Which is how you know that I'm being honest when I say that I think you're beautiful."

I started and felt the Sahara desert in my cheeks. I didn't get speechless often, but Max always threw me aback with his unflinching candor. How did he always say these things with no reaction, like they were universal truths?

I took a large gulp of my coffee and moved on, not used to being spoken to this way.

"Have you always wanted to be an artist?" I tried.

He gave me a contemplative look and shook his head.

"No, I actually wanted to design rocket ships when I was younger. But it wasn't what I thought it would be."

He cleared his throat and switched gears. "What's something you've always wanted to do?"

I gave it a thought but I knew my answer.

"The Coast Starlight Train."

His dimples deepened as his grin grew wider.

"Not what I expected. What is it?"

"It's this Amtrak route that goes from LA to Seattle. It goes along the coast and you get to see the Cascade Range, Mount Shasta, lush forests, some valleys, and the Pacific shoreline all in one trip."

Just the thought of it made me sigh internally.

Ever since I had read about it when I was younger, it was my dream trip. Once I move up the company some more, hopefully I'll be able to take time off and do it one day.

Max listened intently, his eyes sparkling with genuine interest.

"That sounds incredible. We should do it together someday," he said with a hint of excitement in his voice.

I blinked in surprise, my heart fluttering at the thought.

"Really? You'd want to do that with me?"

"Of course," he replied without hesitation. "I wouldn't go and do it without you, that'd be mean after you were the one who told me about it."

Before I could respond, he glanced at his watch and his eyes widened.

"Twelve minutes left, let's move onto the second portion of the date." He stood up and held a hand out for me with a charming look on his face.

"There's a second portion?"

"Of course. We have a week of dates to make up for."

I hesitated for a moment, glancing at the clock and then back at Max.

"We don't have much time, Max. My next meeting—"

"I know," he interrupted gently. "But trust me, it's worth it."

Something in his eyes convinced me to go along with it.

His hand was still held out to me, and I took it, standing up. It was warm from his hot chocolate mug and large from hours on end painting and drawing and sculpting. Despite the slightly rough feel of it though, it was gentle, and as I tried to let go, he held on tighter, interlacing our fingers.

The fresh air hit me as we stepped outside, and Max led me down the street, his pace brisk but not hurried. My lip quirked at the corner as I stared at our hands like an idiot.

"Section two of our date," he peered down at me with a delighted expression, "a romantic stroll!"

He playfully swung our interlaced hands back and forth as we walked, and a laugh burst out of me.

"A romantic stroll in downtown Chicago? Don't those normally take place in parks or by the beach?"

He turned to me with a mock offended appearance and didn't respond, just swinging our arms as he walked me down the street.

A comfortable silence fell over us and despite the bustling street of downtown Chicago, the walk was nice. Somehow, he managed to make it romantic in the two minutes of walking we did.

When he stopped, we were stood in front of my office building. I looked at him in confusion and glanced at my watch.

"Are we done? There's still ten minutes."

I don't know what it was about what I said that had him grinning even wider from ear to ear, but the way he looked at me made something flutter in my stomach.

Chapter 16

He just wordlessly held the door open, ushered me in, then took me to the elevator. I expected him to press my floor number, but he surprised me when he instead lit up the top floor button.

"Max, what—?" I started to ask, but he held up a hand, stopping me.

"Trust me," he said softly.

He led me inside and up the stairs to the rooftop. As we reached the top, I gasped in surprise. There, spread out before us, was a picnic blanket with some donuts and a pitcher of lemonade. The Chicago skyline served as a breathtaking backdrop.

"Max, this is…" I was at a loss for words, overwhelmed by the effort he had put into this.

"I wanted to make our first date special," he said, his eyes twinkling with excitement. "I asked Kait for your favorite snacks– the strawberry donuts from Doughnut Vault, right? — and I thought the rooftop would be the perfect spot. This way, you can go straight back down to your office after this."

I felt tears prick at the corners of my eyes, touched by his thoughtfulness. Overcome with this golden retriever of a man, I jumped up and kissed him. He made a sound of shock before quickly wrapping his arms around me and leaning into the kiss. His tongue softly brushed against my lips and I let him in, tasting the creamy hot chocolate on his tongue.

When we finally pulled apart, both of us breathless and flushed, Max rested his forehead against mine, his eyes still closed as he savored the lingering sensation of our kiss.

"Max, this is amazing. Thank you," I whispered, my voice thick with emotion.

He smiled dopily at me and then sat down on the blanket, pulling me down next to him.

"We only have a few minutes, so I wanted to make every second count."

I joined him, and we shared a few moments of quiet together, enjoying the view and each other's company. It wasn't a grand, elaborate date, but it was perfect in its simplicity.

"Now," he poured me a glass of lemonade, "what are three things that made you smile today?"

"This donut, the view, and a cute dog I saw on the way to work."

He held a hand to his chest and feigned a look of hurt on his face. "Ouch."

I paused, savoring the way his face turned more and more appalled, before I smiled at him. "And you, I guess."

He smiled, mollified by my answer as he nodded in reassurance.

"Your turn." I said, licking a smattering of powdered sugar off my thumb.

His eyes flashed in heat at the movement, causing a blush to spread across my cheeks before he answered. "Selling a sculpture that had been in the making for a while, that hot chocolate, and a cute girl I saw walking into the coffee shop today."

He smiled at me, and I had to cough to get out the tablespoon of powdered sugar that I had accidentally inhaled in shock from his answer. His expression turned alarmed and he patted my back, lunging for the water jug. This man was going to kill me with sweetness, I could feel it.

As the time ticked away and the conversation flowed, Max looked at me with a soft smile.

"I know you're busy, and I respect that. But I wanted to show you that we can make time for each other, even if it's just for a few minutes."

I reached out and took his hand, feeling a warmth spread through me.

"Thank you. This means more to me than you know."

He leaned in and kissed my forehead gently.

"There's plenty more where that came from," he said with a wink.

Chapter 16

"And next time, we'll have more than twenty minutes."

Chapter 17

As the next two weeks went by, Max surprised me with more 'mini dates', finding ways to show up at my office and apartment and infuse my hectic schedule with moments of us. Each time, he managed to surprise me with something new, each gesture more thoughtful than the last.

One afternoon, he appeared at my office with a small bouquet of wildflowers, the bright petals a welcome contrast to the paperwork strewn across my desk.

"I was painting in the park and saw these. Every girl likes flowers, right?" he said with a warm smile, placing the flowers in a vase he had also brought along.

Another evening, he turned up at my apartment just as I was getting home, holding a picnic basket filled with homemade sandwiches and fresh fruit.

"I know you've been working late, so I thought we could have a quick dinner together," he explained, leading me to the small park near my building, where we ate under a large oak tree.

While I cherished these moments, a nagging guilt began to creep in.

Chapter 17

Max was putting so much effort into meeting with me, and I was too busy to reciprocate. Determined to make it up to him, I decided to dedicate the weekend to him. I worked overtime the entire week to clear my schedule, ensuring I would have the weekend free.

On Friday night, I decided to surprise him with a romantic dinner at my place. I had never been much of a cook, but I wanted to do something special for him. He had mentioned his favorite food once during one of our first meetings, and thank god I remembered. Armed with a recipe for eggplant parmesan and a lot of enthusiasm, I set to work.

Or, at least, tried to. It quickly became apparent that cooking was not one of my strengths. The kitchen turned into a disaster zone and everything that could have gone wrong, went wrong. The eggplant burned, the pasta was overcooked, and I somehow managed to overpepper the sauce.

I didn't even know one could overpepper something.

I thought eggplant parm was meant to be easy. It was always what they ate in date scenes in the movies. Who decided the quintessential date food had to involve three very easy to mess up components?

At one point, smoke filled the kitchen – I don't even know where from – and I had to frantically wave a towel at the smoke detector, hoping it wouldn't go off. I felt my eyes prickle with tears and started crying with frustration that a small chicken parm dish was able to best me this way. All I had wanted to do was make it up to him for how distracted I had been in this relationship. Just as I had given up and laid my head on the counter, the doorbell rang. Max. What the hell was I supposed to do now?

I quickly wiped my tears and took a deep breath before I opened the door to find him standing there with a bouquet of roses, his smile instantly turning into concern as he took in my frazzled appearance and the smoky apartment behind me.

"Alina, what happened?" he asked, stepping inside and gently taking the towel from my hand.

"I wanted to cook you a romantic dinner," I confessed, feeling tears of frustration prick at my eyes. "But everything's gone wrong. The eggplant's burnt to hell, the pasta's a mess, and the sauce is way too peppery."

Max chuckled softly, pulling me into a comforting hug.

"It's okay, Alina. I appreciate the effort, really. How about we order some takeout instead?"

I nodded, feeling a mixture of relief and disappointment. Why was he so nice? A part of me thought that he would leave me after discovering my abysmal cooking skills, but for some reason, he was still here.

"I'm sorry, Max. I just wanted to do something special for you."

"You already did," he said, kissing my temple. "The fact that you went through all this trouble means a lot to me."

"I made hot chocolate," I offered, trying to rectify something in the disaster that was my attempt to do something nice for him.

His eyes lit up. "Really?"

"Yeah," I sniffled, padding over to the stove where the pot was simmering away, ignoring the clutter of the other pots and pans from tonight's failed dinner attempt, "from melting real Belgian chocolate and milk and everything."

I served him up a mug and watched as he eagerly brought it to his mouth and took a sip.

A beat passed.

Then another.

I kept staring at him as I tried to search his face. "Well?"

He gave me a brilliant smile. "It's good!"

Instantly, it felt like my chest felt lighter with relief that one thing went well tonight. "Really?"

Chapter 17

"Mhm," he dove into the mug, taking another long sip, his face encouraging as he smiled at me.

"Yes!" I exclaimed, pumping a fist in the year, unable to help myself. "Wait, now I want to try…" I reached for the ladle, getting a mug from the cabinet, but he jolted to attention and grabbed my hand.

"No! You made it for me, it's all mine."

"Come on, I think I deserve to try the one good thing I made tonight." I shook him off with a soft laugh and reached for the ladle again but he gulped down the rest of the hot chocolate in his mug, stealing the ladle from my hand to refill it, completely draining the pot.

"Do you like it that much?" I laughed.

"Yes. It's delicious. Thank you for making it for me."

This time, I could see the glimmer of panic in his eyes and I narrowed mine at him slowly. "Of course," I said slowly, watching as he cheerfully held his mug with a grateful expression, his hand shaking just the tiniest bit. He was being very shifty right now.

"Max," I started.

"Hmm?"

"Give me your mug."

"No."

"Give me your mug."

"No, I want it all."

"Give me your mug or I will not be kissing you tonight."

His eyebrows raised at my challenge and he hesitated, before reluctantly handing the mug over, hanging his head down.

I took a shallow sip, and almost spat it out. Bitter. This hot chocolate was extremely bitter. It tasted like a piece of charcoal had been dunked in milk and then put into my mouth. He winced at my expression, and the nervous energy that was radiating from him had me on guard.

"Max, this is burnt!"

"Yeah…"

I stared at him, mouth agape. "How did you drink a mug and a half of this? It's assaulting my taste buds right now."

"I wanted to drink it," he said quietly as he shrugged. "You made it for me."

My chest warmed and I could feel my cheeks tinging pink again. I poured the rest of the mug's liquids down the sink, removing the atrocity from society forever, then turned back to him.

"You're sweet. Now help me clean this up, please. Your punishment for lying."

He gave me a salute and a wink, then got to work.

We quickly cleaned up the kitchen together, laughing as we recounted the chaos of my cooking attempt. Max took charge, and soon the mess was under control. We then ordered takeout from a nearby Chinese restaurant and decided to make the most of the evening.

As we waited for the food to arrive, Max suggested we turn the kitchen mishap into a fun cooking lesson.

"Why don't we make dessert together?" he proposed. "Do you like chocolate chip cookies?"

I hesitantly agreed, not wanting to set another thing on fire tonight, and we spent the next hour mixing dough, sneaking bites of chocolate chips, and laughing when some flour got all over his glasses. This man was always covered in some sort of substance. By the time the takeout arrived, the cookies were baking in the oven, filling the apartment with the smell of warm sugar and browned butter.

We sat on the living room floor, the coffee table pushed aside to make space for our impromptu picnic. The boxes of takeout spread out before us looked far more appetizing than my failed attempt at Italian food. We set up the food so we could eat family style and The tension from the week melted away as we shared the food, laughing and chatting like we had all week.

Chapter 17

"You know," Max said between bites of chow mein, "I kind of like this better than a fancy dinner. It's more us."

I smiled, feeling the warmth of his words wrap around me.

"Yeah, I guess it is. Casual, relaxed, and a bit chaotic."

"Hey, chaos can be fun," he cried, holding a hand to his heart.

"Especially when you're with the right person."

He took a moment to look around my apartment as I laughed and a puzzled look crossed over his face.

"Your apartment is a lot... different from mine." He said hesitantly.

I followed his gaze and looked around my apartment. I guess with how welcoming and cluttered his apartment was with colors adorning every wall and handpicked, mismatched furniture, my bare, minimalist apartment did have a completely different feeling. I never really noticed how bland it was here.

My eyes focused on the white marble counters, glass tables, and even the stockroom decor sitting on the TV stand. Why did I have those glass balls? There was no life here. Even my mugs were plain white ceramic compared to his set of unique mugs, clearly picked up from different events in his life.

I sighed and shrugged at him, taking a bite of my egg roll.

"Sorry. I guess I'm just never here enough to actually decorate it."

His eyes widened and he faltered.

"No, it's nice! I just thought it was funny how different our apartments were."

We continued eating, discussing everything from our favorite childhood memories to future travel plans. The conversation flowed effortlessly, the earlier stress of the evening forgotten.

After we finished the main course, Max stood up and made his way to the kitchen. He returned with a tray of freshly baked chocolate chip cookies, their aroma filling the room.

"Ta-da!" he announced, setting the tray down in front of me. "The grand finale."

I picked up a cookie, still warm and gooey, and almost moaned as I took a bite.

"Oh my god."

He grinned and grabbed a cookie for himself.

"We make a pretty good team, don't we?"

I paused. I hadn't been a part of a team in a long time. It was easier but until now, I hadn't realized how lonely it was. Eventually, I responded quietly, "We do."

With cookies in hand, we moved to the couch. Max picked a movie, some old romantic comedy that neither of us had seen before. As the film played, his arm wrapped around my shoulders in a comforting embrace and he dragged me into him. I tensed against him before releasing a breath and relaxing into his side.

"Thanks for turning tonight around," I whispered, keeping my eyes on the screen.

I felt him glance down at me, and when I looked up, his eyes were soft.

"It was never bad to begin with."

He leaned down and pecked my lips, and I closed my eyes at the touch before he pulled away and squeezed me once.

As the movie played, I found myself more focused on Max than the screen. His laughter at the funny parts, the way his eyes sparkled during the romantic scenes, the comfort of his presence, the way he turned to me briefly whenever something funny happened, as if to see if I was enjoying myself—all of it made me appreciate him even more. And all of it made that little voice in the back of my head even more terrified for the day he might leave me.

Chapter 18

The rest of the night passed in a blur for me. During the movie I fell asleep on the couch and when it ended, Max simply put a blanket on me, woke me up to say goodnight, kissed me on the nose, then let himself out, letting the door lock behind him. I remembered half mumbling to him that he could stay but I was too out of it to say much. Still, despite the absolute shit show that was my romantic dinner plans, he had managed to do what he always does, and make me feel better.

True to my word, I had prepared the whole week to dedicate my weekend to him to make up for all the effort he's put in and so I called him to ask him to come to a double date with Kait and Adam that I had set up earlier in the week.

We decided on a quaint, upscale restaurant along the river. Its ambiance was perfect for a night of good food and even better conversation. The soft lighting and cozy booths offered just the right amount of privacy, while the gentle hum of conversation and clinking cutlery provided a comforting backdrop.

As we walked into the restaurant, Kait and Adam were already seated at a table near the window. Kait waved us over enthusiastically, her face lighting up as we approached. Adam just looked down at her, his focus on nothing but her, a soft smile on his face.

"Hey, you two!" Kait greeted us warmly. "We ordered a bottle of wine. I hope that's okay?"

"Absolutely," Max replied with a smile, pulling out my chair for me before taking his seat beside me. "It's great to see you both."

"Wine?" I remarked, staring pointedly at Kait.

She gave me an innocent look and jutted out her bottom lip.

"What about it?"

Adam sighed and took out a thermos from her purse.

"Don't worry about it, we're gonna take her share home for her to sniff later."

Max huffed a laugh and looked questioningly over at me.

I smiled, explaining, "Kait's always been the wine connoisseur. She's missed it during the pregnancy."

Kait smiled sheepishly and grasped her stomach.

"Six-ish months along now."

A bright smile took over Max's face, and he beamed at Kait.

"That's fantastic news! Congratulations to both of you!"

"Thank you," Adam said, smiling proudly as he reached over to squeeze Kait's hand. "We're really excited."

"Any name ideas?" Max questioned, placing his arm on the back of my chair. My breath hitched.

"Well…" Kait started, "I have an idea for one, but Adam doesn't like it."

"I never said I didn't like it!"

Max's fingers started to stroke my shoulder lightly, his touches peppering my skin with goosebumps. He started to trace something but I couldn't make it out.

"You always change the subject when I bring it up!" She returned,

Chapter 18

huffing.

"Yeah, but it's not because I don't *like it*." He looked flabbergasted at her.

"Then why?" I felt Max's nimble fingers find a tendril of my hair and play with it as the couple in front of us quarreled. I turned to look at him and saw he was already smiling softly at me. My heart melted.

He sighed and leaned his face closer to her.

"I like it too much. I picture a little girl with your hair and your eyes and this feeling just comes over me like I want to bite something." He admitted.

Kait's eyes softened and she laughed lightly.

"That's called cuteness aggression, baby."

Adam just shook his head and then shoved his face in Kait's shoulder, clearly embarrassed.

"What's the name?" Max asked, curiously, his gaze finally leaving mine to look at Kait.

"It's freaking 'Lennon', isn't it?" I interjected.

A mischievous smile made its way onto Kait's face and she nodded. I turned to Max.

"In college, whenever Kait told our friends what name she wanted to name her future daughter, they all always made fun of her. It became a running joke in our group – Lennon the Lead Baby, because our apartment was built in the 80s and might have had lead pipes."

Max gave an amused hum.

"I think it's adorable!" Kait said defensively. "Lennon after John Lennon. It's such a good girl's name."

"Hear hear." Adam chirped from Kait's shoulder.

"I think it's cute too!" I agreed, "She just would have to be the coolest girl in class."

Adam straightened up from Kait's shoulder and looked at us miserably.

"Any kid that comes out of Kait is just not going to be the coolest kid in school."

Kait gasped and slapped his arm playfully, opening her mouth to tell him off before a waiter cut her off to set the wine on the table and ask for our orders.

"You know, Max, Alina has told us quite a bit about you," Adam said, a teasing note in his voice. "But I think there's still a lot we don't know." Lies. I hadn't told them almost anything about Max other than what Kait and I discussed before we got together. I narrowed my eyes at him.

Max chuckled, glancing at me before turning back to Kait and Adam.

"Well, I suppose I should fill in the gaps then."

Kait leaned in, curiosity piqued.

"Yes, please do. Start with where you're from. Alina mentioned you're a Texas native, what about your family?"

Max nodded, taking a sip of his wine before speaking. Kait's eyes darted to the wine glass, sorrowfully.

"Yep, I was born and raised in Austin. My parents are both teachers. I have an older brother, Kyle, who's a lawyer. Growing up, our house was always filled with books and lively discussions. My parents were always passionate about making sure we could turn to them for anything. My mom actually gave me my first condom."

"Oh!" Kait said as we all laughed. "Definitely not something my mom did."

"Yeah," Max responded, using his other hand to scratch the back of his neck in embarrassment. God, he was cute. "And I ended up using it too."

"Oh buddy…" Adam looked sympathetically at him.

"Wasn't a great look when she wanted a round two and I brought up how my mom only gave me one."

We all cringed, laughing at his sheepish expression and red cheeks.

Chapter 18

"But seriously, that sounds wonderful," Kait said, her eyes softening. "A supportive family can make all the difference."

"It really does," Max agreed. "I owe a lot to them. They've always been my biggest cheerleaders."

The conversation shifted to Max's art, and he spoke passionately about his work, explaining the inspiration behind some of his favorite pieces. He described how he loved to capture moments of everyday life, finding beauty in the mundane.

"And what about your interests outside of art?" Adam asked. I widened my eyes at the two of them, silently asking them to stop this job style interrogation but they just smirked at me before quickly turning back to them.

Max grinned, unfazed by the interview he was unknowingly going through.

"Well, I love to cook, but I think Alina might have a different opinion after her last attempt." He glanced at me, and we both laughed, the memory of our kitchen disaster still fresh.

"Oh, I've heard all about that," Kait said, giggling. "But honestly, I think it's sweet that you tried."

"It was definitely an experience," I laughed, smiling at Max. "But I'm glad he was there. He really turned it around."

From there, conversation flowed easily as we (sans Kait) sipped our wine. Adam, Kait, and Max hit it off immediately, discussing everything from books to donuts to the perils of cave exploration. I noticed how animated Max became, his eyes sparkling as he shared stories.

Despite conversing with Adam, his arm never left my chair, and he continued playing with my dress strap and hair as he faced Adam, which meant that I kept getting goosebumps, causing Kait to look at me with a knowing expression, annoyingly.

After dinner, we departed and despite Kait living in Max's building, he took a long detour to walk me home. When we landed in front of my teal door, he turned to me and looked down at me with a sweet expression. I felt a mix of anticipation and nervousness.

"I had a great time tonight," I whispered, slipping my hand into his.

"Me too," Max replied, giving my hand a gentle squeeze. "I really like your friends. They're wonderful people."

"They are," I agreed. "And they seem to like you a lot."

His dimples deepened in his cheeks and I couldn't resist. Impulsively, I leaned in and kissed him, my heart racing. His lips were warm and soft against mine, and I felt a rush of fire licking at my stomach. We stood there, wrapped in each other's arms, the world fading away around us. His arms tightened around me, pulling me closer, and I melted into the kiss, feeling something so deep it left me breathless.

His hands slid up to cup my face, his thumbs brushing against my cheeks as he deepened the kiss. I opened my mouth slightly, allowing his tongue to gently explore mine. The taste of wine and the hint of his cologne mingled, creating a heady mix that made my knees weak. I broke off the kiss and frantically unlocked my apartment, letting us in. Something came over him and he made an impatient noise that had my core heated and aching as he picked me up and led us to the couch, settling me on top of him.

I straddled him, my knees sinking into the cushions on either side of his thighs. His hands roamed up and down my back like I was a sculpture he was trying to memorize, and I could feel the heat of his palms through the thin fabric of my dress.

I wrapped my arms around his neck, deepening the kiss. Our tongues danced together, a rhythm that felt both familiar and exhilaratingly new. I could taste the wine on his tongue, and the scent

Chapter 18

of his cinnamon and chocolate flavored musk made me wet and my panties leaking.

If he kept this up, I was soon going to have a very embarrassing wet mark on my dress. Max's hands found the hem of my dress and slipped underneath, his callused yet gentle touch sending sparks of electricity through me.

A soft moan escaped my lips, and Max responded with a low groan that made my heart race and panties soaked. I felt something hard poking against my butt and gasped. My sex was throbbing and it took everything not to hump his leg right there and then. His lips left mine and took the opportunity to trail down my jaw, planting hot, open-mouthed kisses along my neck. I tilted my head back, giving him better access as my fingers tangled in his hair. I loved his hair. It was soft and thick and always messy.

"Max," I breathed, the sound of his name almost a plea.

He paused and looked up at me, his eyes dark with desire.

"Alina, fuck," he murmured, his voice thick with emotion. "You're incredible."

I smiled and leaned down to kiss him again, losing myself in the taste of him. We moved together, a tangle of limbs and heated breaths, each kiss and touch deepening the connection between us.

After a while, we reluctantly pulled away, both of us breathing heavily. I rested my forehead against his, our breaths mingling as we tried to catch our breath.

"Wow," I whispered, a smile tugging at my lips.

"Yeah," Max agreed, his fingers gently tracing patterns on my back. "Wow."

"I want this," I whispered, resting my forehead against his. "But I think we should take it slow. I'm not ready yet."

Max nodded, his gaze tender.

"I understand. This doesn't change anything, we'll take it at your pace."

Relief washed over me, and I smiled, feeling a deep sense of connection to this man.

"Thank you."

He brushed a strand of hair from my face, his touch gentle, and softly kissed my nose three times.

We stayed like that for a while, wrapped in each other's arms, the world outside forgotten. It was perfect.

With one last kiss, we said goodnight, and I watched him walk away, my heart full. As I closed the door behind me, I couldn't help but feel that, despite my earlier reluctance, something had been set in motion, and I couldn't get off this train even if I tried.

Chapter 19

The office was eerily quiet when I walked in, the kind of quiet that made you acutely aware of every footstep and every rustle of paper. My international expansion project was demanding enough, but when I was assigned a third and fourth project because Jenna went on maternity leave, the pressure skyrocketed. When the board decided to make my final report for the expansion project due two months before the final presentation in front of the shareholders, I almost cried.

I took a deep breath, looking at the mountain of files on my desk. Four projects. Deadlines converging like a perfect storm. The responsibility weighed heavily on my shoulders, but there was no room for self-pity. I had to push through. If I was going to run for Jack's position, I had to prove that I could handle the pressure

By the end of the first day, the enormity of the task ahead became painfully clear. My inbox was overflowing with emails requiring immediate attention. Meetings were scheduled back-to-back, leaving little time for actual work. I rolled up my sleeves and dove in, determined to keep everything on track.

The next few days blurred into one long, grueling stretch of work. I spent most nights at the office, my apartment becoming little more than a storage unit for my neglected life. The cafeteria staff learned my coffee schedule by heart. I barely noticed when Max texted, his words a lifeline in the sea of stress.

> *Max: Hey, I know you're swamped. Make sure to eat and take breaks, though.*
>
> *Max: Don't forget to eat. I had some food delivered to your office. Check the reception.*
>
> *Max: I opened my AC vent in my car today and a lizard jumped out at me. Never screamed so hard in my life.*

His texts were always perfectly timed, appearing just when I thought I couldn't handle another minute. I found myself relying on them more than I cared to admit, his steady stream of encouragement keeping me afloat.

I hadn't seen him in a week because of how much time I spent trying to get the three non-art projects together and I was thankful for it. He must have understood the amount of pressure I was under.

True to his word, there were food deliveries at my office and apartment, each one a reminder that even when I didn't see him for days, he was looking out for me.

As the week dragged on, the physical toll of working day and night began to show. My eyes were bloodshot from lack of sleep, and my body ached from sitting hunched over my desk for hours on end. It seemed that every time I finished one task, two more arose on my desk after it. I always thought that going up the chain of command meant less work, but it seemed like the complete opposite.

I had barely spoken to Max, our interactions limited to brief text

Chapter 19

exchanges. He seemed to understand that I needed space, his texts never pressing for more than I could give.

By the sixth day, I was running on fumes. I stared at my computer screen, the words blurring together as I tried to make sense of the latest financial projections. My phone buzzed with another message from Max.

> *Max: So, my friend Emmy just told me that it was wrong of me to throw that lizard out the window on the interstate. I don't really know how to make amends, though. Lmk if I should feel guilty or not.*

I couldn't help the snort that escaped at the texts that this man has been giving me. I leaned back in my chair, closing my eyes for a moment. His words were a balm to my frazzled nerves.

The final night was the hardest. I was down to the wire, racing against time to finalize the expansion project and ensure the other two projects were on track. My mind was a whirlwind of numbers, strategies, and deadlines. I barely noticed when my phone buzzed again.

> *Adam: Where, in tarnation, have you been?*

Ignore.

A few seconds later, another buzz emanated from my phone.

> *Kait: where've you been, pookie? x*

I rolled my tongue in my mouth before responding.

> *Alina: they gave me two more projects and moved up my final*

> *report deadline to tomorrow :(*

Kait: gotcha, remember to eat okay?

I loved her so much. Since we met, she always just *got it*. She knew exactly what I needed and never asked for more than I could give at a time. I sucked my bottom lip and nodded to myself, settling on my response.

> Alina: ...max has been delivering food to me

Kait: AWWWWWWW that's the sweetest thing I've ever heard
Kait: Allie he's a keeper, don't get in your head with him okay?

> Alina: I'm trying not to

I gnawed at my lip as my head rushed with all the possible things that could go wrong and shakily inhaled, on the verge of an anxiety attack, when a buzzing snapped me out of it. Confusion surged in me as I picked up my phone, wondering who it was now.

Adam: You're not serious.
Adam: And here I was trying to be a good friend to you while you respond TO MY WIFE in the room next to me.
Adam: I will never in my life DoorDash you Taco Bell again.

A snicker burst out of me and I shook my head.

> Alina: not your wife yet buddy

Adam: Trust me, I'm trying.

Chapter 20

God, it was freezing. I wrapped my coat tighter around my body as I walked through the streets of Chicago, shivering. It was only November, but there must have been a cold front or something because I could not stop shivering.

After finishing up the international expansion report, and doing the bulk of the other two non-Max related projects, I passed out in bed for 24 hours, a huge load lifted off my shoulders. Now I just had to finish up the three remaining projects and prepare for my final presentation in front of the board and shareholders in two months.

Max gave me space until today, when he sent me a text asking if I wanted to go to the pub with his friends tonight. I had originally hesitated, but ultimately agreed. I couldn't say no when, just a week ago, he spent dinner with my friends.

This afternoon, I had woken up feeling unusually tired, my head pounding and my throat parched and dry, but it was probably from the 24-hour hibernation. My body was screaming for rest but I had rested enough.

When I finally arrived after what felt like forever, I was pleasantly surprised to find that the pub was a cozy, bustling establishment, filled with laughter and the clinking of glasses. Max, Cas, Ezra, Rowan, and a young woman were already gathered at a large table near the back, their faces lighting up as we approached.

"Hey, Alina!" they greeted, their warmth cutting through the chill I couldn't seem to shake.

Max closed the distance and slung his arm around me, guiding me to a seat next to him and pulling me close. He was wearing a beanie, and the combination of his brown locks peeking out the sides of the beanie in curls and his square framed glasses had me pining internally.

"I missed you," he said, kissing my cheek. "Thanks for coming."

"I missed you too," I replied, forcing a smile. Inside, I felt like I was dragging a ton of bricks.

As we settled in, the young woman with shiny black hair and striking blue eyes smiled brightly at me. She looked familiar somehow.

"Hi! I'm Emmy." She greeted cheerily. Mystery solved. This striking woman was the illustrious Emmy Bates, Ezra's sister. I smiled and waved at her politely, the muscles in my face heavy.

"*Hi! I'm Emmy.*" Cas imitated her mockingly into his drink.

She whipped her head to glare at him across the table and reached out to steal his drink, chugging the whole glass in one go as she held eye contact with him. Cas started and glared back at her. She smiled sweetly at him and wiped her lip, then let out a tiny burp.

"Why you little–"

"Enough." Ezra interjected calmly. "I already hear enough about your little pranks on each other all week, just for one night act like adults, will you?"

Their eyes narrowed at each other and they held their glares, waiting for the other to back away first. When that didn't happen, Rowan slapped Cas on the back of the head and he was forced to break away to glare at his friend while Emmy smiled triumphantly and brought her drink to her mouth.

As Max's friends started chatting about their week, I tried to keep up, but my mind was foggy, and my body ached. Max noticed my quietness and placed a hand on my back.

"Are you okay?" he whispered, his brow furrowing with concern.

"Yeah, just a bit tired," I lied, not wanting to ruin the evening.

The conversation flowed around me, but I struggled to stay engaged. My vision blurred at the edges, and I felt lightheaded. Just as I excused myself to go to the bathroom, the world tilted, and I stumbled against the side of the booth.

"Alina!" Max's voice was filled with concern as he caught me before I fell. He held a hand to my forehead and swore. "You're burning up."

His friends gathered around, their faces a mix of worry and confusion.

"I'm fine," I tried to say, but my voice was weak, and my body weight was dragging me down.

"No, you're not," Max said firmly. "We need to get you home."

He turned to his friends, and said something I couldn't hear before carefully reaching around me to grab his wallet and put some money on the table.

He helped me to his car, and I leaned heavily against him, my body trembling. Once we were inside, he drove quickly but carefully, his jaw set in determination.

When we arrived at my apartment, Max insisted on helping me inside. I was too weak to protest, my body aching and my head spinning. He guided me to the couch and kneeled on the carpet to take off my boots before he covered me with a blanket.

"I'll get you some water," he said, disappearing into the kitchen.

I closed my eyes, grateful for the softness of the couch. It felt like a marshmallow against my body. Hmm, when was the last time I had smores? My body was so hot, it felt like it could roast that marshmallow and we could have a smores night. Where's Max? I'll tell him about my brilliant idea when he came back.

When Max returned, he handed me a glass of water and a damp cloth for my forehead. What was I going to tell him again? My brain went foggy.

"Thank you," I whispered, sipping the water slowly.

"You need to rest," he said gently. "You've been overworking yourself."

"I didn't want to miss tonight," I admitted, my voice barely a whisper.

Max's expression softened, and he sat on the ground beside me, taking my hand.

"You should have told me you weren't feeling well. I don't want you to push yourself for my sake."

"I just... didn't want to disappoint you," I confessed, my eyes filling with tears. I was too tired to get angry about my tendency to cry at the slightest emotional turmoil this time.

Max's expression changed from surprise to disbelief as he processed my words. His eyes widened, and his mouth parted slightly in shock. Then, slowly, his eyes filled with a simmering anger, the intensity of his emotions clear on his face.

"You could never disappoint me, Alina," he chastised me carefully, squeezing my hand.

His voice was controlled, but I could sense the hurt and frustration beneath the surface.

"This relationship isn't transactional."

I swallowed, my throat feeling like it had been scratched raw with sandpaper.

"Th-thank you for taking me home. You should go back to your friends now..."

His grip on my hand tightened slightly, not painfully, but firmly enough to command my attention.

Chapter 20

"Alina, listen to me," he said, his voice a low, intense whisper. "Do you really think I would just leave you here like this? That I would abandon you when you're clearly not well? You're my priority, not some night out with friends."

His words hit me like a wave, the weight of his sincerity crashing over me. This was too much for me. Tears spilled over my cheeks, and I felt a sob rise in my throat.

Max's expression softened as he saw my tears. He took a deep breath, trying to calm himself. He raised his hand and I shivered as his thumb gently wiped away my tears.

"I'm sorry if anyone has ever made you feel like you weren't a priority," he said quietly. "But I need you to know that you are to me. You always will be."

I couldn't find the words to respond, my emotions a tangled mess. Who was this man? How could he say these things after I had essentially placed him in a corner all week?

I might have been his priority, but I never treated him as mine, and deep shame and guilt balled up in me.

I didn't deserve him, and I was scared for the day he realized that too. All I could do was nod, hoping he understood the gratitude and relief I felt.

"I wish I was there to take care of you last time," he said gently, caressing my hair. "Get some sleep. You need to rest."

✧✧✧

Over the next day, Max took care of me with unwavering dedication. He moved me to my bed. He stayed by my side, making sure I stayed hydrated and ate small meals. He went to the corner store and got me soup. He brought me medicine and kept the damp cloth on my forehead, checking my temperature regularly. He slept on the couch each night and he even texted Kait and Adam to let them know how I was feeling and that I was being taken care of.

In my feverish state, I drifted in and out of sleep, my dreams a blur of memories and emotions. And each time I woke up, Max was there, his presence a comforting anchor.

One night, as the fever began to break, I woke up to find Max sitting beside me, his eyes heavy with exhaustion but filled with concern.

"Why are you doing this?" I asked, my voice weak.

"Because I care about you," he replied simply, brushing a strand of hair from my face.

"No one took care of me like this when I was little," I murmured, my mind hazy with fever and fatigue.

"What do you mean?" Max asked, his brow furrowing.

I took a shaky breath, the memories surfacing painfully.

"When I was younger, I would get really sick every now and then. My mom was gone, and my dad was always busy trying to provide for us, and my sister was just… absent and I had to take care of myself. I've never had anyone… look after me like this. Not until I met Kait and Adam."

Max's eyes softened with empathy.

"I'm so sorry, Alina. You shouldn't have had to go through that alone."

"It's just how it was," I said with a shrug, though the pain of those lonely days still lingered.

"You don't have to be alone anymore," Max said gently.

He then shifted gears and lightened the subject.

"I didn't take care of you last time when I got you sick, so let's call this me making up for that."

His words were a balm to my weary emotions, and I felt a warmth spread through me that had nothing to do with the fever.

"Thank you, Max," I whispered.

Chapter 20

A question nagged at me and I had to ask.

"Max?"

"Hmm?" He fiddled with a thermometer.

"How come you had to get soup by yourself last time?"

His eyes crinkled in the corners.

"I happened to get sick on the one week all of my friends were out of town."

A sense of bewilderment washed over me.

"How does that even happen?"

He laughed and stroked my arm, tracing a pattern into it.

"Ezra was showcasing a new gadget in China. Rowan was guest teaching a culinary skills class in California. And Emmy and Cas were in Seattle for a conference. And I didn't want to bother them so I didn't tell them."

He was, quite possibly, the most selfless man I had ever met. I examined his grass green eyes and his messy brown hair and couldn't help but marvel at the depth of his character.

At that moment, I realized just how lucky I was to have him in my life.

"You're too good to everyone," I said softly, my voice filled with admiration.

Max chuckled, his eyes softening as he looked at me.

"And you're hopped up on NyQuil."

"I'm grateful for you," I said with a cheesy smile, reaching out to gently caress his cheek.

A warm smile spread across Max's face, and he leaned in to press a tender kiss to my forehead.

"I'm grateful for you too, angel."

The nickname had my heart fluttering in my chest.

"Max?" I started again.

"Alina?" He playfully responded.

"Why'd you leave aerospace engineering?" This cough syrup seemed to completely obliterate my filter.

Max blinked, his expression turning somber as memories seemed to flood back to him. The flicker of surprise in his eyes was quickly replaced by a shadow of pain, and he shifted uncomfortably in his seat.

"It's not something I talk about often," he began, his voice low and hesitant. "But the truth is, I had to leave aerospace engineering because... because of an accident."

My heart skipped a beat, and I reached out to touch his hand, offering silent support as he continued.

"I-I always had a passion for aerospace engineering. I thought working on planes and rocket ships was going to be the coolest thing ever, growing up, and when I graduated from college, I joined my dream company with my dream job."

His eyes left mine and he exhaled shakily.

"We were working on a project, one that was supposed to revolutionize the industry," he explained, his words slow and measured. "But there was a flaw in the design, one that I overlooked. It led to a failure during testing, and... people died."

The weight of his words hung heavy in the air, and I felt a lump form in my throat as I tried to comprehend the magnitude of what he was saying.

I didn't know what to say as he paused, his expression looking tortured, so I placed my hand on his and rubber circles on it, hoping it'd soothe him in some way.

"I couldn't bear the thought of being responsible for so much pain and loss," Max continued, his voice barely a whisper now. "It made me lose any love I had for it. So I walked away."

Tears glistened in his eyes, and I reached out to wrap my arms around him, offering what little comfort I could.

"I'm so sorry, Max," I murmured, my heart aching for the pain he had endured.

He leaned into my embrace, his body trembling slightly with emotion.

"S'not your fault," he mumbled hoarsely.

"How'd you get into art?" I tread carefully.

He was quiet for a second, as if gathering his thoughts before continuing.

"I wanted to create things that brought joy to people's lives, things that inspired them and made them feel something and could never hurt them. I had done a lot of modeling and photoshop in college, so I knew how to work the software. Art has always been one of my passions, and when I sold my first few pieces, they just seemed to skyrocket and suddenly I was this," He paused, his brows scrunching, "'figure' in the art and graphic design world. But I love it. And one day, I'd love to have my own gallery."

"I'm glad you love it." I breathed out, still tasting the acrid taste of the NyQuil on my tongue.

He shrugged, his eyes twinkling with amusement.

"Life's too short to do something you don't love."

His words hung in the air, resonating with a truth I wasn't quite ready to face

"Get some rest. I'll be right here if you need anything." He said, still tracing patterns softly onto my skin.

"Sleep with me." I murmured. It was time I took care of him too.

He observed my face for a minute before nodding and settling in next to me. He reached out and pulled me close, cuddling me into him as he stroked my back, his body bringing a delicious heat to my chilled bones.

I felt my eyes grow heavy with the motion. As I drifted back to sleep, I felt a sense of peace that I hadn't known in a long time. I never thought I'd have someone who cared so deeply for me.

Chapter 21

The next morning, I woke up feeling like a new person, the fever having subsided completely. Max was still by my side asleep, looking a lot better after resting up himself. I spent an hour just looking at him, staring at his relaxed features as he slept.

His impossibly long eyelashes fluttered against his cheeks as he dreamed, and his arms never loosened their hold around me.

He smiled in his sleep.

As Max stirred awake, I couldn't help but smile at him, feeling a surge of affection for this man who had been by my side all weekend.

"Morning, sleepyhead," I whispered to him, reaching out to brush a stray strand of brown hair from his forehead.

Max blinked, his eyes still heavy with sleep, as he stretched lazily.

"Morning," he mumbled, his voice husky with sleep. "How are you feeling?"

"Like a new person," I replied, my smile widening. "Thanks to you."

Max's eyes softened, and he leaned in to press a gentle kiss to my lips.

"You're so much smilier than usual. You didn't chug the cough

Chapter 21

medicine while I was sleeping, did you?" He said with an amused expression on his face.

I laughed softly and leaned in to kiss him again.

That evening, he reluctantly made a move to leave, convinced now that I was better, I would want my alone time. When I made him stay, his eyes lit up and twinkled at me.

"I'll order us a pizza," I offered as he headed to the shower, wanting to make the evening special for him.

When Max returned, the scent of pizza topped with his favorite topping, olives, filling the air, we settled on the floor with the coffee table moved aside, just like our dinner date the week before. We laughed and talked, enjoying each other's company in the comfort of my living room, a movie playing softly in the background.

Now that I was all better and he was all rested up, our laughter filled the room, our conversation flowing easier than before.

As the evening wore on, we shared stories and memories, each revelation bringing us closer together. Max opened up about his childhood, sharing tales of mischief and adventure, while I shared stories of my own upbringing, the good, and the bad.

"There's no way you're freely sharing this information," I teased, nudging him playfully as he recounted a particularly embarrassing childhood memory.

He grinned, his eyes sparkling with amusement.

"Hey, I have plenty of material to work with. Growing up with a big brother guarantees a lifetime of embarrassment."

I laughed, feeling a sense of warmth wash over me.

I had been holding back all this time, afraid I'd fall too deeply for him, only for him to leave. I was afraid of rewriting history.

But this was Max.

This was the Max that took care of me when I was sick. The Max that dropped everything to drive me home when I thought my dad was in trouble. The Max that delivered food to me when I was too busy with work, just to make sure that I was eating properly. The Max that always greeted me with my favorite coffee.

As the night grew late, I found myself drawn to Max in a way I hadn't felt before. His presence was intoxicating, filling me with a sense of warmth and contentment that I had never known.

And then, as if by some unspoken agreement, our laughter faded into a comfortable silence, the air thick with anticipation. I looked into Max's eyes, seeing the same desire reflected back at me, and in that moment, I knew.

With a trembling hand, I reached out to touch his cheek, my heart pounding in my chest. Max's breath caught in his throat, his eyes darkening with desire as he leaned in closer, his lips hovering just inches from mine.

And then, without another word, our lips met in a searing kiss. In that moment, as our lips touched, it felt like the entire world fell away.

The soft brush of his lips against mine sent shivers down my spine, igniting a fire in my core that had never been lit before. His hands found their way to my waist, pulling me closer, as if he wanted to touch as much of me as possible.

His tongue brushed against my bottom lip and I let him in, feeling his agile tongue stroke softly against mine. I responded eagerly, tangling my fingers in his hair as I deepened the kiss, losing myself in the taste and feel of him. Cinnamon and chocolate.

The scent caused a Pavlovian response in my underwear, and I rocked my hip against him softly. He growled low in his mouth before pulling back to throw his glasses onto the coffee table, confidently sweeping me up in his arms and setting us on the couch, holding himself above me as he hungrily kissed me.

Despite the desperation in his kiss, he was still gentle. His talented hand made its way down my body and stroked my thigh lazily, the

Chapter 21

sensation causing an insane wetness to gush to my folds. I leaned up and felt his hardness against my inner thigh and whimpered as I roamed my hands across his chest, surprised at the lean muscle I felt. Just as I ground my hips against his and moved to take off his shirt, he threw himself against the couch, panting.

"I'm sorry." He rushed out, still panting. "You're not ready."

He readjusted my clothes to cover my body, his hands shaking slightly as he tried to get his breathing in order, like it was taking everything in him not to continue.

In that moment, I knew that I was all in, ready to give myself completely to this incredible man who had stolen my heart with a sneeze in an elevator.

"Max?" I said, still panting.

He took his head from his hands and gazed at me. "Yes?"

"Don't hurt me." I breathed.

"I would never." He responded without hesitation, his voice genuine in the quiet of the room.

I tucked that information away and nodded, inhaling deeply.

"I'm ready."

Chapter 22

Max held my cheek, his eyes searching mine for any semblance of doubt before he nodded to himself in affirmation. His arms made their way to my hips and he lifted himself off the couch, taking me with him. On instinct, I wrapped my legs around his narrow waist as he carefully carried us to my bedroom and laid me gently on the bed.

I felt my head sink into the plush pillows of the bed and watched as he ran his eyes down my body before settling on my face, his gaze dark and sinful. This was a whole different side of him I hadn't seen before. For some reason, it was making my panties drenched.

I felt the bed shift as Max climbed between my legs. I suddenly felt his cool breath wash over me as he whispered into my neck.

"You're so beautiful, I'm the luckiest man alive." He trailed his fingers down the side of my neck, I couldn't help the shiver that went through me when he skimmed the side of my breast.

I kept my eyes closed so I didn't have to be hit by his green orbs. I was convinced they would kill me, searing with their intensity.

"You were meant for me." He softly bit my ear lobe. "That first time I saw you in that elevator, I wanted to ask you out right then and there."

Chapter 22

He chuckled darkly against my skin.

"Even dying with fever and on the verge of hallucinating, all I could think about was how beautiful you were."

His compliments had me whimpering and I pushed up against him, latching my lips onto his neck and running my hands over his hard body through his shirt. I felt him smile against my neck before nipping at it, sending shocks down my body.

I gasped when his hand grasped my left breast that was covered with my oversized sleep shirt but I still felt the flames of his touch prickle my skin.

"Max." I mumbled, hoarsely. My core was burning and I felt like I couldn't breathe with how much I was panting against him.

"Hmm?" He hummed against my skin, dipping his nose down to nuzzle the crevice of my breasts. My breathing grew even shakier and I clutched at the bottom of his shirt, desperately wrangling it away from his body.

"I- I need this off. Now."

He lifted his head from my breasts and gave me a tender smile, nodding as he leaned back onto his heels. I lifted myself off the bed and swallowed, taking his shirt in my hands and lifting it off his body as he helped me.

My eyes widened as I examined his lean body and I felt myself salivating as I directed my gaze at his tapered v, his strong but subtle set of abs being illuminated softly by my dim bedside lamp– not an 8 pack by any means, and definitely not a washboard, but just the perfect amount, at least, the perfect amount for me. I felt my eyes darken with lust as I looked at the small mattering of hair leading down into his waistband, before he took my face in his hands again and kissed me searingly.

I licked his lip with my tongue and felt his mouth open slightly, letting me in. It was as if all the pent-up emotions and unspoken desires between us were finally being released, flooding over us in a tidal wave of passion and intensity.

With each tender caress of his lips, I felt myself falling deeper and deeper into him, the boundaries between us blurring until there was nothing left but the overwhelming sensation of us being together.

I tore away from his lips to frantically take my sleep shirt off, and was distracted by the design in my hand. Oh God, it was my Winnie the Pooh sleep shirt. Who wears their oversized, ratty old cartoon sleep shirt the first time they initiate sex with someone?

My eyes darted to my closet thinking of the sexy set of lingerie, Kait had sneakily shoved in there and I cringed, embarrassed and looked up shyly at him but he just smiled at me with amusement, his eyes still smoldering with desire.

He took the offending desire gently from my hand, placing open-mouthed kisses on my wrist, and placed it gently on the bedside table.

He trailed his kisses up my arm then down my torso, nipping, licking, suckling every part of me, laying me down onto the bed as he made his way down. I felt his lean body against me and clutched at his hair in pleasure, feeling my nipples pebble under his lips and my sex leaking into my panties with anticipation. When he got to my plaid sleep shorts – seriously, why couldn't I have changed before this? —, he looked up at me and fidgeted with the hem of them, waiting for my response. I nodded eagerly.

The corner of his lip quirked and he more firmly grabbed the waistband of my sleep shorts and panties, patting the side of my hip for me to lift my hips. Once he removed the rest of my clothing, I laid naked under his burning gaze and felt a heat rush up all over my body. Before I could even try to shy away from his eyes, he dove in and sucked my clit into his mouth.

"Fuck," I moaned, a fiery heat blazing up my body. My back arched and I gasped as he pushed two fingers inside me. It had been so long

Chapter 22

since I last did this that I felt full at just those two digits. What was I going to do when it was his cock? I squeezed against his fingers and grounded my hips against his mouth, panting as he licked and nipped at my sweet spot.

When his tongue flicked against my throbbing clit, I saw stars and had to grip his soft hair to avoid screaming. A whine escaped my mouth as he worked me like an instrument and as the pleasure built and built in my core, his tongue and fingers became more determined, sucking harder and moving more intensely inside me.

I ground my hips more desperately against him and chased my release, feeling it coming closer and closer within my reach.

Just as I thought I wouldn't find it, his spare hand reached up and tweaked my nipple, and the dam burst within me. I squeezed his fingers mercilessly and threw my forearm over my mouth, muffling my moans through the most intense orgasm I had ever experienced.

He kept licking my folds and moving his fingers against me and I rode out my orgasm and when I finally came down, shaking on the bed beneath him, he detached from my sex and hovered above me, his leather cord dangling and brushing against my breasts as I hungrily sucked in air.

His face was glistening as he gave me a brilliant smile and leaned down to suck my bottom lip into his. I tentatively brushed the back of his neck with my nails and he groaned lowly before breaking away to stand at the foot of the bed to take off his chinos. He gazed hungrily at me as he took them and his boxers off in one swift movement, and I inhaled sharply, nervous prickles spreading under my skin.

He was beautiful, I realized. His body was hard but lean and mattered in hair in all the typical places. I swallowed as my eyes trailed down the soft hair leading down onto his manhood. He was... larger than average. Thick. And throbbing. The head of his cock pulsated at the tip and I licked the corner of my lip as I saw it drip with pre-cum.

Never, in my life, have I had the desire to put a cock in my mouth. I always thought they were disgusting. But this man was changing me in ways I never expected. Suddenly, I was hungry for it. I needed it now.

I started to crawl forward to the foot of the bed to taste him but was stopped when he gently placed his strong hands on my arms and shook his head, laying me back down onto the bed.

"I wanna–" I started, embarrassed at the whiny tone my voice had taken.

"I know. But I just want to enjoy you tonight." He brushed my hair out of my face and kissed my forehead, then reached around me and grabbed a pillow. My brows furrowed in confusion but I let him take control as he smiled at me reassuringly and gently lifted my hips to tuck the pillow under me.

The new angle had my pussy raised towards the corner of the ceiling and was unnatural but surprisingly comfortable. He trailed his fingers up and down the side of my body again, causing shivers to go through me and put a condom on from my bedside table before he settled himself at the apex of my thighs, reaching his face down to kiss me passionately.

My muscles went rock hard from anticipation.

I curled my legs around his waist and clawed lightly at his back as he ground himself into me.

"Please." I breathed. I had never wanted this this much. The last time I did this, the guy just took me to his place, did his thing, then fell asleep. The guy before that did the same thing. For the past few years, I thought I just didn't like sex. But I didn't realize it could be like this, until him.

"I wanna make sure you're ready." He murmured huskily into my neck, moving down to suck my nipple into his mouth. I cried out and tried to lift my breast closer to him, but couldn't because of the raised

Chapter 22

position he had my hips in.

"I-I," I shuddered against him as he lightly bit my nipple before swirling his tongue around it to soothe the ache. "I need you."

Finally, he leisurely lifted his head from my breast. His eyes, dark and alluring, shone with satisfaction and he came back up to kiss me, slipping his tongue between my lips. I moaned into his mouth and returned the kiss, stroking my tongue against his.

He reached down and grabbed his cock, rubbing the tip over my folds, and sending me to heaven. I groaned and shifted, trying to get him closer, and felt as he sunk into me.

He rocked his hips slowly, carefully, easing into me an inch, then two, before he pushed himself all the way into me. I was so drenched, he slipped in easily. A whimper escaped the back of my throat at the intrusion, and I squeezed around him, shifting my hips to relieve the burning.

"Fuck, Alina." He gasped, his breathing getting heavier.

Time seemed to stand still as he thrusted into me, each moment stretching out into eternity as he explored the depths of my pleasure.

"It's," I gasped. "I feel so full."

"You feel so good around me." He moaned and reached down to rub circles around my throbbing clit.

I threw my head back, overcome with the sensations, and screwed my eyes shut, crying out. The raised position he had set me up in had the head of his cock rubbing against some secret part of me I didn't know existed. Every rock of his hips sent sparks flying from my core to my stomach, building and building.

He leaned back and watched my pussy wrapping around him, his cock disappearing behind my slick folds as he thrusted. He growled with pleasure at the sight and placed a strong hand surely against my stomach. Oh god. He thrusted into me harder and I saw stars behind my eyelids.

"Your pussy looks so beautiful, taking me in like this." His velvety voice washed over me.

"Max, I-I," I panted. "I can't."

"You can."

"It's too much."

"It's a good thing you've always been an overachiever, then," He responded casually, showing me no mercy.

I gasped and cried out as the pleasure crescendoed in me. Between his thumb circling my clit, the hand pressing down against my stomach, heightening the intensity of everything, and his large cock filling me over and over, it was all too much, and he caught my moan between his lips as my orgasm exploded within me. I felt myself squeezing around him and making a mess on the bed, triggering his own release.

He groaned loudly in pleasure as he spilled into his condom and peppered kisses all across my face as my body shook beneath him. My lips. My cheeks. My nose. My eyelids. My forehead. He took his time, as if savoring every touch of my skin against his.

He didn't stop until I caught my breath, completely spent beneath him, my eyes struggling to stay open. I kissed his jaw and laid back, too tired to do anything else but close my eyes. He didn't even know it, but he has ruined me for all men.

My vagina ached with a soreness which I'm sure was him imprinting his cock in me, marking it as his forever. I felt him kiss my temple again before he got off me and gently removed the pillow from under my hips, covering my shivering, damp body with the covers.

I heard a rattling in my bathroom as he removed his condom before he came back to bed and pulled me into him, spooning me in his embrace. I felt his fingers pat my waist three times before he started tracing patterns into it. The warmth made me sigh in pleasure, and I swiftly fell asleep in his arms.

Chapter 23

The next morning, I woke up to the faint sound of clinking dishes and the aroma of something cooking. Blinking sleep from my eyes, I rolled over to find Max's side of the bed empty. The events of the previous night came flooding back, and a contented smile spread across my face.

I wasn't expecting to have sex with him this soon, and I definitely wasn't expecting it to be as good as it was. He made me feel things I had never felt before, and butterflies raced in my stomach when I thought of how he took control last night. I was in control almost all the time at work, delegating, managing, organizing, and it felt amazing to just lay back and let him take the reins off my hands.

Finding my oversize sleep shirt neatly folded on the chair, I put it on and made my way to the kitchen.

Max stood at the stove, wearing nothing but his boxers and a frilly cooking apron that I had never worn and was just for display, his back to me as he expertly flipped something in a pan. The sight of him, so at ease in my space, domestically wearing this pink frilly apron Adam had gotten me as a joke, when just last night he was making me see

God had a blush warming my cheeks.

"Good morning," I greeted, my voice still thick with sleep.

He turned, a playful grin spreading across his face.

"Morning! I hope you're hungry."

I walked over and peered into the pan, smiling as he wrapped his arms around me from behind and placed his chin on my head.

"What are you making?"

"Fried rice," he said, laughing. "Speaking of, the only thing I could find in your fridge was a carton of eggs and rice. Literally nothing else. What the fuck is up with that?"

His chin bounced against my head with laughter.

A burning heat made its way up my neck and I responded, embarrassed.

"You've seen me cook."

"Aww, baby," he cooed, turning me in his arms and smiling brightly.

"Last night was incredible." He said.

"It was." I agreed. "Thank you."

He barked a laugh, throwing his head back. His chocolate locks flopped in the air as he did so, and my breathing deepened when I saw how it highlighted the strong veins in his neck.

"You don't have to thank someone for having sex with you, Alina." He teased.

I blushed and shrugged before turning to the stove, pursing my lips as I looked at the food.

His gaze didn't waver and I felt his eye bore into the side of my face. Before I knew it, his fingers were grasping my chin and turning me towards him.

"Thank you for last night, Alina. It was everything." He asserted, his voice low in the quiet din of my apartment.

He turned back to the stove, expertly scrambling the eggs.

"How about you grab some plates? Breakfast is almost ready."

Chapter 23

We ate in comfortable silence for a few moments, just enjoying each other's company. I questioned the fresh bouquet of pink, orange, yellow, and white daisies in the center of my dining table that wasn't there last night and he shrugged, giving me an impish look.

When we finished, Max quickly helped me put the dishes in the dishwasher before we separated to get ready for work. Annoyingly, my heart twisted in my chest when I watched him leave and I had to shake my head to stop staring at the door behind him so I could get ready for the day.

✧✧✧

Feeling rejuvenated after Max had nursed me to health all weekend, I returned to work with a new energy. Just as always, the sound of typing, the murmurs of the water cooler conversations, and the buttery scent of Kelsey's popcorn had me relaxed and ready to finish out the new projects. As I settled into my desk, a buzzing drew my attention to my phone.

It was another photo from Harper, this time posing with a sycamore tree. She looked even happier, her eyes shining with brightness under her beanie. I was so happy for her. This cabin in the woods seemed to cure her heartache, and I hoped she would stay there as long as she needed. Just as I was about to put my phone down, something caught my eye.

The angle of the photo was different. Up until now, it had always been clear that the phone was on the ground against an opposing tree, catching her at a weird upwards angle that sometimes had me seeing up her nose. But this photo, it was more face-on, capturing her full, radiant smile. I pocketed that information for another time and put my phone away.

However, as I tried to dive back into my work, I found myself strangely unmotivated. I thought that after a weekend of rest – the first weekend of rest I've had in months – I would be getting more work done than ever today, but every time I held my fingers to my keyboard, my brain went blank. My usual drive was missing, and it left me confused.

I shook my head, trying to focus, but my thoughts kept drifting back to the weekend with Max.

Just as I was starting to make some progress on my emails, Jack appeared at my desk. He was holding two cups of coffee and had that familiar smirk on his face.

"Morning, Alina. Brought you your usual," he said, placing a cup in front of me.

"Thanks, Jack," I replied, taking a grateful sip.

Black.

My face screwed up slightly before I plastered a content smile on my face.

I had gotten so used to Max making sure I had my favorite that I had forgotten that, up until now, I only drank black in work settings. "How was your weekend?" I asked.

"Oh, you know, the usual. Went to see a movie, did some hiking, took the mister out on a kayaking date." He wriggled his eyebrows at me, which made me snort into my cup.

"Saw you finished your expansion report. It looks great!" He remarked. "I'm sorry the board moved up your deadline again, hopefully things will get better with someone new stepping up to my position soon." He tilted his gaze at me.

"It was fine." I waved away. "Just preparing for the final shareholder presentation next month."

"You've got it." He clicked his teeth and winked at me before turning serious. "I heard you were under the weather this weekend. Twice in one quarter, you must have been livid."

Chapter 23

I nodded, feeling a blush creep up my cheeks as I thought about Max.

"Yeah, I was. But I had a good friend taking care of me."

Jack raised an eyebrow, intrigued. "A good friend, huh? Anyone I know?"

"Just a friend," I said quickly, trying to keep my tone casual and not reveal too much. "No one from around here."

Jack's eyes narrowed slightly, clearly not buying my vague response, but he let it go with a knowing expression.

"Well, I'm glad you're feeling better. We've got a lot to catch up on."

"Of course," I said, trying to sound enthusiastic. "I'm ready to dive in, just need to grab my notebook," I replied, trying to focus on the tasks at hand, my mind wandering to a certain brunette artist with a perpetual smile.

Chapter 24

The next two days were a blur of meetings, appointments, and project research. As Jack and I had walked to the conference room, my mind kept drifting back to the weekend. The way Max had held me, the tenderness in his eyes, the way he felt, and sounded, and smelled... It had been hard to focus on spreadsheets and project updates when all I wanted to do was relive those moments over and over again.

I had sat down at the conference table, nodding politely as my colleagues trickled in. The meeting began, and I did my best to pay attention, taking notes and contributing when necessary. But my mind was elsewhere the whole time, no matter how hard I tried to focus. It was like I had never had a crush before, which, reflecting back, I don't think I ever did.

"Alina, what do you think?" My boss's voice had jolted me back to the present. I had looked up, realizing everyone was waiting for my input.

"Uh, sorry, could you repeat the question?" I had asked, feeling my cheeks flush.

"We were discussing the marketing strategy for the new campaign,"

Chapter 24

Jack had said, giving me a bemused look. "Do you have any thoughts?"

I took a deep breath, trying to gather my scattered thoughts, and gave a half-hearted suggestion.

Jack had nodded, seeming pleased with my response.

"Good idea, Alina. Let's explore that further."

The meeting had continued, and I forced myself to stay present, contributing ideas and taking detailed notes. But I couldn't stop my mind from wandering to Max. It was getting a little annoying how my brain kept taking me off track during an important phase of my career. I'd have to get this sorted out somehow soon.

Wednesday 6pm arrived, the date and time he had blocked off in my calendar, and I felt a mix of excitement and nerves. As I walked over to his studio with a bounce in my step, I couldn't help but wonder why I was so jittery. I had spent the entire weekend with Max. He took care of me. We had sex. This was how relationships went, as far as I knew. So why did the thought of seeing him again, just two days later, make my heart race?

When I finally did arrive at his studio, I knocked and waited, my heart pounding. The door swung open, and there he was, his brown hair a mess on his head and his clothes covered in all different colors of paint, bringing a small smile to my face. I hope he never changes.

"Hi," he greeted me with a warm smile, his eyes lighting up as he saw me, taking me into his arms in a strong hug. He shoved his face into my neck and hair and inhaled deeply, humming with pleasure as he stroked my back with his hands.

A laugh broke out of me and I hugged him back, relieved at how easy this still was. "Hey yourself."

He held me for a few more seconds before giving me one final squeeze and stepping back, kissing me sweetly and opening the door to me with a radiant smile on his face. Immediately, I felt a cold wave hit me at the lack of his warmth, and I sighed internally at the detachment.

I pulled a crinkled up brown paper bag from my purse, wincing at the crumpled up texture of it that came from wanting to keep the contents of it warm on the walk over for the ten-minute detour it took.

His lip quirked as he inspected it. "What's this?"

"A croissant."

A look of amusement spread across his face. "And why are you giving me a croissant?"

Because I feel like our relationship has been one-sided which is my fault, and I'm trying to make up for it.

"Because," I shrugged, "you like them. And they're half off today."

He chuckled, shaking his head as he took the wrinkled up bag from me. "Always thinking about the deals, aren't you?" He pulled the croissant out, inspecting it with a discerning eye before taking a bite. His eyes closed in appreciation, a small moan escaping his lips. "Perfect. You know me too well."

I watched him enjoy the pastry, feeling a warmth spread through my chest.

"So," he said between bites, "ready to see the next three pieces?"

I stepped inside, taking in the familiar yet still somewhat surreal sight of his studio apartment. The artwork, the scattered brushes, the faint scent of paint—it all felt so intimate and personal. He closed the door behind me, and I felt his presence, comforting as always.

He led me to the back of the apartment where his studio was and sat me down in front of three covered pieces.

"No coffee?" I remarked. He usually always had a cup of my favorite coffee ready for me when I arrived, and today, I noticed the distinct lack of its presence.

He shot me a scathing look. "It's 6:30 pm."

"I'm sorry, is it your bedtime, Adult-Man-who-drinks-Hot-

Chapter 24

Chocolate-at-29-years-of-age?" I retorted. I always had coffee late at night. How else was I supposed to get as far as I did in my field?

"You're mean tonight," he mused impishly, "are you already going through caffeine withdrawals?"

I slapped his arm, offended, and he leaned down and kissed me softly, taking my breath away. I closed my eyes and sighed into the kiss, feeling my body turn to jelly, and felt him smiling against my lips. I decided then that I really liked kisses. I hadn't experienced a lot of them before Max, but now each one was like a treat I tried to savor.

Max pulled away with a grin and uncovered the three pieces with a flourish.

"Ta-da!"

I stilled. The first painting was a futuristic cityscape, illuminated with vibrant lights and clean energy sources. Wind turbines dotted the skyline, and solar panels glistened on every rooftop. The entire scene exuded a sense of innovation and progress, perfectly encapsulating GenTech's commitment to a sustainable future.

The second one was a striking depiction of a thriving, green ecosystem. Trees, plants, and animals coexisted harmoniously, and the entire scene was teeming with life. In the background, a sleek GenTech building stood, seamlessly integrated into the landscape.

The third one, it took my breath away. It was an abstract representation of data and technology, with swirling lines and interconnected nodes forming intricate patterns.

"It's beautiful," I breathed, reaching out to touch the first canvas lightly. "The colors are so vivid, and the way you've captured the city's energy… It's incredible, Max. And this one too, it's like a Modern Eden. Oh my god, and this one! It's like… I don't even know. The closest I could say is it's like you've captured the essence of innovation"

He beamed, clearly pleased with my reaction.

"That's what I was aiming for."

I turned to him, my heart swelling with pride and admiration.

"You're amazing, you know that?"

He blushed, rubbing the back of his neck sheepishly.

"Thanks, Lina. I'm happy you like them. Hopefully the rest of GenTech does too."

He sat down next to me and we spent the next hour discussing the paintings in detail, analyzing the techniques, the inspiration, and the messages behind them. We also researched other tech company logos to see what facets of a logo have become identifiable with tech.

It was easy to get lost in our conversation, to forget everything else and just focus on the art and each other. I kept forgetting what I was saying at some points, when he'd lean over and stroke my arm or thigh lightly, but we still managed to have a strong discussion.

Eventually, Max stood up and walked over to a corner of the studio, pulling out a smaller, covered painting.

"I um- I actually have one more thing to show you," he said, a nervous glint in his eye.

I raised an eyebrow, curious.

"Another painting?" I jumped and gasped. "Did you finish the series!?"

He shook his head, a smile playing on his lips.

"This one's a bit different. It's a gift. For you."

My heart skipped a beat as he pulled off the cover, revealing a stunning painting of a comet streaking across a starry night sky. The comet was rendered in exquisite detail, its two tails – one white, one blue – illuminating the darkness. In the corner of the painting, a hill overlooked the night sky and when I inspected it closer, I saw a little gray telescope propped on the hill.

"Max," I whispered, feeling tears prick at the corners of my eyes. "It's beautiful. But why?"

He stepped closer, his expression tender as he shrugged bashfully.

Chapter 24

"Your dad said you were born the night Hale-Bopp was at its brightest. I wanted to create something special for you, something you could hang in your apartment to make it more you, since, you know, your apartment is bland and boring... and all creative juices go there to die."

I scoffed at his remark, playfully smacking his arm. Leave it to him to give me a heartfelt gift but avoid the moment getting too fluffy with an insult. No one had ever given me a gift like this, and I felt a ball form in my throat when I looked at my dad's little telescope in the painting.

"Thank you," I managed to say. "I um– I don't know what to say..."

Max smiled and wrapped his arms around me, pulling me into a warm embrace.

"You're welcome, beautiful. I'm glad you like it."

After a few minutes, Max gently pulled away, a mischievous glint returning to his eyes.

"And now, for the final surprise of the evening."

I blinked, confused.

"There's more? Max, you're gonna kill me." I deadpanned.

He snorted then nodded at me, grinning.

"You hungry?"

Chapter 25

Two minutes after Max asked if I was hungry, there was a knock on the door. On the other side stood his group of friends, all huddled in the tiny hallway, holding bags of food and hollering at him.

"Hey, chef! Are you gonna let us in or what?" Rowan shouted, balancing multiple takeout bags, the logo hidden.

Max opened the door wide, laughing as they all spilled into the studio apartment. "Come on in, everyone. Make yourselves at home."

"Hey Alina." They all chorused. Ezra just gave me a nod of his head. Bewildered, I turned to Max and he laughed at my expression, his eyes twinkling.

"I know you felt bad about last time so I invited them over."

There was no need to be surprised. This was just how he was, thoughtful and caring. I tried not to smile, but failed, taking his hand and walking over. The group were all setting up the plates and food on his coffee table as he didn't seem to have a dining table and judging by the methodical nature they moved furniture around and took plates from his cabinets, I could tell they had all done this plenty of times before.

Chapter 25

Emmy and Cas were already at each other's throats again, how, I had no idea. They just got here.

"You KNOW my tower was better, dipshit," Emmy declared, glaring at him. "Don't think I didn't see *my* Italianate domes in *your* final design."

Cas rolled his eyes dramatically.

"Please, Emmy. Those domes were practically begging to be included. I improved on them, made them more… structurally sound."

"Oh, please. You wouldn't know structural soundness if it hit you in the face."

Rowan, ignoring their bickering, set the food on the table and turned to me with a nervous smile.

"Hey, Alina. Brought some food from Alegria. Hope you like it."

"Thanks, Rowan. I'm sure it's amazing," I replied, trying to reassure him. He always seemed so confident in his element, but tonight he looked a bit anxious.

Ezra, as usual, was quiet and grumpy. He gave a curt nod in my direction before plopping down on the couch, arms crossed, observing the chaos with a furrowed brow.

Max noticed my nervousness and squeezed my hand.

"They're excited to see you again," he whispered. "They were really worried about you last time. They were *not* disappointed."

I nodded at him, a grateful expression on my face. He kissed my temple and sat me down on the floor with the rest of the group, bringing one of my legs over his, and plating up my food.

As everyone settled in, the atmosphere became lighter and more cheerful. The conversation flowed easily, filled with laughter and funny stories from their university days.

"Remember that time Max tried to impress that girl in his architecture elective by building a Sydney Opera House replica with toothpicks?" Emmy started, her eyes sparkling with mischief.

Cas chimed in, "Yeah, and it collapsed right in front of her! I've never seen anyone turn so red."

Max groaned, covering his face with his hands.

"I thought we agreed never to bring that up again. You guys were the ones that made me take that architecture class. This is your fault."

Cas laughed. "Too late. We're bringing out all the embarrassing stories tonight."

They continued sharing tales, passing around a case of beers, and I found myself laughing along, feeling more at ease.

Ezra was distant as usual, piping in now and then, but Rowan seemed withdrawn tonight, and his leg hadn't stopped shaking under the table the whole time. It seemed I wasn't the only one picking up on it, though.

"Rowan, genuinely, what the fuck is up with you tonight?" Cas started.

Emmy slapped him across the head, to which he glared at her, pointing his plastic fork in her direction.

"What was that for?!"

Emmy rolled her eyes. "Be nice, Cas. Rowan looks like he's about to have a meltdown."

Rowan threw his hands up and scoffed.

Ezra chimed in gruffly. "They're right. You're quiet. What's wrong?"

Rowan groaned and shoved his head in his hands, mumbling something indiscernible into them.

"What?" Max cringed and asked.

Rowan lifted his head and glowered at Max, his expression a mixture of frustration and anxiety.

"I've got a food critic coming next week. I'm just nervous about it."

Emmy's eyes widened in realization. "Oh, Rowan, why?! Your food's delish and Alegria is doing super well."

"No one I know has ever been able to get a reservation," I nodded.

Chapter 25

"And this meal really is so good, even takeout-ed."

Emmy nodded in agreement. "You've had tons of food critics stop by before and they've never fazed you. What's up?"

Rowan smiled slightly at me then answered, his shoulders slumping. "It's different. She's a part of Bread and Butter magazine. Every restaurant she's ever featured has been booming in business and on track to win a Michelin. I'm just nervous she won't like my food."

Max placed a comforting hand on Rowan's shoulder.

"Hey, don't worry about it. Your food is amazing. You've got nothing to be nervous about."

Cas nodded in agreement. "Yeah, man. You're a culinary genius. You've got this."

Ezra, surprisingly, offered a rare smile. "We'll be there to support you every step of the way."

Rowan managed a weak smile.

"Thanks, guys. I appreciate it. Hopefully she agrees."

"So, Emmy," Cas shifted gears and said with a sly grin, "how's the wedding binder now? Found anyone desperate enough to marry you yet?"

I laughed at the thought of this beautiful woman with jet black hair and striking blue eyes being a last resort for anyone.

Max smiled at my reaction and placed a hand on the exposed skin where my work pants met my sock, stroking it lightly. He had been doing that a lot lately, tracing patterns into my skin while his attention was elsewhere.

Emmy threw a piece of plantain at him.

"Oh, shut up, Cas. I'll have you know I have plenty of suitors. I'm just... waiting for the right one."

Rowan laughed. "Right, and how many have run for the hills after one date?"

"At least they didn't hide in the kitchen like you did that one time,"

Emmy shot back.

I couldn't help but laugh at their antics. It was clear they all had a deep bond. It made me think of me, Kait, and Adam and my heart warmed in my chest just thinking about them.

The evening passed in a blur of laughter, conversation, beer, board games, and delicious food. Max's friends were warm and welcoming, and I found myself relaxing and enjoying their company.

They taught me how to play a card game they had been playing for years and in return, I taught them how to open a beer bottle on a can of soup. We shared stories, jokes, and experiences, and by the end of the night, I felt like I had passed some sort of test they were proctoring.

When they all eventually left, Max wrapped his arm around my waist, pulling me close and kissing my hair.

"They like you" he whispered in my ear. "Thank you for staying."

I smiled, blushing, and leaned into his embrace.

Chapter 26

The mall was a kaleidoscope of activity, with the chatter of shoppers blending seamlessly with the occasional bursts of laughter from groups of friends. Emmy and I navigated through the bustling crowds, the festive atmosphere of the mall almost infectious. I had wanted to get something for Max, since he had done so much for me recently, but nothing seemed right.

Thankfully, Emmy had given me her phone number at dinner yesterday and she was more than happy to come to the mall with me, despite having only met one and a half times.

"Thanks for coming again, I really appreciate the help," I said, glancing over at her as we passed a boutique filled with vintage clothing. "You've known Max for a long time. What would he appreciate the most?"

Emmy smiled thoughtfully, her eyes twinkling with amusement. "The guy's a puppy dog. He loves anything unique and heartfelt, you know. He's always been one for personal touches. Maybe something related to his art, or his mystery novel addiction, or even something 'Texas'?"

"I keep forgetting he's from Texas. He doesn't give 'Texas' at all."

She laughed, the sound contagious and light-hearted. "Yeah, he's definitely more of a Midwest guy now, but he still has a soft spot for his roots. A little reminder of home might mean a lot to him."

I nodded, considering her suggestion as we continued our search. We wandered into a store that specialized in quirky home decor items, filled with everything from abstract sculptures to hand-painted vases. I picked up a few items, but nothing seemed quite right.

My eyes darted to a ceramic cow in the corner with the most giant udders I had ever seen, for some reason wearing a cowboy hat and smoking a cigar.

"What about that?" I said with a poker face, picking it up.

Emmy, who had been crouched down to look at an orange vase, looked up and immediately recoiled, a look of disgust on her face. "Dear god, no."

I groaned gutturally in defeat. This was way too hard. Being in a relationship took so much time, I don't even know how Max had all the time to plan those dates before when he's fully a renowned artist.

"Let's get some fries, we'll think better after the carbs," Emmy suggested, her crystal blue eyes lighting up at the prospect. "Ooh! And then we can walk by the chicken teriyaki sample guy a bunch for protein."

I chuckled at the eagerness in her face and nodded, putting down the bovine atrocity, before we left the store.

The food court was a whirlwind of scents and sounds, a mix of sizzling grills, bubbling fryers, and kids running around the playpen in the center. With our fries and chicken teriyaki sampled secured, we finally found a table as far away from the chicken teriyaki man as possible. He had started recognizing us after the fourth pass and was now giving us the stink-eye from across the court.

As I took a bite of a perfectly crisp, slightly unsalted fry, Emmy

Chapter 26

looked at me thoughtfully. "So, do you have any other ideas for Max? Maybe something completely outside the box?"

"I don't know," I said, shaking my head. "I feel like everything I pick is either too impersonal or just not right."

"Don't stress too much. The perfect gift will come to you when you least expect it," she said, popping a piece of chicken into her mouth.

Before I could respond, a woman brushed past our table, her hand lightly grazing Emmy's purse, causing it to fall off her chair with a thud.

"Oh, I am so sorry about that," she said, bending down to grab it and dusting it off.

I froze, my fry halfway to my mouth as I stared at the table. That voice.

Emmy gave her a bright smile as the woman placed the bag on the table. "That's okay! Thanks for getting it."

"Of course, it was the least I could do after knocking it off. I'm not a heathen," the woman laughed softly as she looked at Emmy with a polite smile. "It's a lovely purse, where did you get it?"

That voice. It was so familiar, but it couldn't be. There was no way.

"I actually got it at a yard sale about two years ago. Sorry, that probably isn't very helpful."

"No, it's better I don't look for one like it. It probably doesn't suit a woman of my age."

They laughed together and I tensed in my seat at the familiar sound that had been haunting me for years.

It had to be her.

I turned to look at her, my heart pounding in my chest. The woman had blonde hair streaked with gray, and though I could only see the side of her aged face, there was no mistaking it.

"Mom?" The word slipped out before I could stop it.

The woman paused and turned to me, her eyes widening in surprise. For a moment, she looked blank, and then realization dawned. Her face paled. "Alina?"

I couldn't believe it. After all these years, here she was, standing in front of me in the middle of a bustling food court. My emotions were a tangled mess I couldn't even decipher and I found myself frozen in my seat.

"Yes, it's me," I said, my voice shaking. "I can't believe it's you."

She didn't say anything as she started fidgeting, her hands wringing together causing the many bracelets on her wrists to clink together quietly. She glanced nervously around the food court, her brown eyes darting as if looking for someone. I followed her gaze and spotted a little girl, maybe ten years old, with blonde hair set in pigtails playing with an older woman at a nearby table. The girl was laughing, her eyes lighting up with joy as she played with her grandmother.

I turned back to my mom, my stomach twisting in knots. "Who is she?" I asked, my voice barely above a whisper. But I already knew. I just needed to hear it from her.

My mom's face fell, and she glanced back at the girl, then at me. "My daughter," she said quietly.

The words hit me like a punch to the gut. "Your daughter?" I echoed, feeling the world tilt beneath me. "You have another child?"

"Yes," she admitted, her voice filled with a mixture of guilt and fear. "Her name is Lily. She's ten."

I felt tears prick at the corners of my eyes. "And the woman playing with her?" I asked, my voice breaking.

She hesitated, a flare of panic rushing through her eyes. Finally, after a few seconds, her shoulders dropped and she looked down. "Her grandmother."

"From which side?"

She didn't answer.

Chapter 26

I clenched my jaw, my eyes hardening. "From. Which. Side?"

She sighed. "Mine."

I nodded, sucking my lip between my teeth, gnawing at it as I looked at this woman who couldn't even bring herself to look at me. I always pondered what would happen if I ever saw the woman who left me seventeen years ago again. It was always a toss up between screaming at her for all the pain she caused us, and jumping into her arms, crying for how I had missed her. But as I stared deadly at this woman who didn't seem to want anything to do with me, I realized that I didn't have anything to say to her. Not at this moment.

When a beat passed and I realized she wasn't going to say anything after that, I scoffed in disbelief, packed up my purse, and walked away.

"Alina, wait!" my mom called after me, but I didn't turn around. I couldn't. My chest felt tight, and I needed to get out of there.

Emmy followed me, her hand gently touching my arm. "Alina, are you okay?"

I shook my head, trying to hold back the tears. "I need some air," I managed to say, pushing through the crowds to find an exit.

We stepped outside into the fresh air, the cool breeze a stark contrast to the stifling atmosphere inside the mall. I took a deep breath, trying to steady myself.

"I know we barely know each other, but do you want to talk about it?" Emmy asked softly, her eyes filled with concern.

I shook my head again, wrapping my arms around myself. "I can't. Not right now. I'm sorry."

She nodded, respecting my need for space. "Okay. I'm here for you, whenever you're ready."

I appreciated her understanding, but right now, all I could feel was the overwhelming rush of emotions. Anger, hurt, betrayal, confusion—they all swirled inside me, leaving me feeling raw and exposed.

We stood there for a few moments in silence, Emmy's presence surprisingly comforting next to me. I was surprised she stayed. We were just barely close acquaintances now, but she didn't make a move to leave once, even after I told her she could go if she needed to. It made sense, though, that she was friends with Max. I took another deep breath, trying to focus on the present, on the feel of the cool air on my skin, the distant sounds of traffic.

Chapter 27

After the events of the mall, Emmy and I had agreed to just call it a day. I stumbled through the front door of my apartment, my mind a chaotic mess of swirling emotions. The silence in the house felt heavy, almost suffocating, amplifying my sense of isolation. Sinking into the couch, I stared blankly at the empty walls as my mind screamed at me for how I had handled the situation.

For years, I had dreamed of the day I could finally tell her off, pouring out all the rage from the years after she had left. But after seeing she had no trouble moving on, my mind just went still. And when I saw the woman who was meant to be a grandmother to me, the one who had never met me before because of her own racism, playing with her and smiling fondly at the little blonde girl, my mind went numb.

Before I had time to process much, the doorbell rang, startling me from my daze. I hesitated for a moment, then stood up, dragging myself to the door. As I opened it, Max stood there, his face etched with worry.

"Hey," he said softly, stepping inside as I moved aside. "Emmy told me what happened. Are you okay?"

I forced a nod, but the weight of the day was too much for me. I didn't trust myself to speak, so I just walked back to the couch and slumped down, feeling utterly defeated. Max sat beside me, his presence both comforting and aggravating. I knew he was here to help, but right now, I didn't want to deal with anyone.

"Do you want to talk about it?" Max asked gently.

I shook my head, not trusting myself to maintain composure. "No."

Max studied me for a moment, his concern evident. "Are you sure? If you need space, I understand and I'll respect it, but sometimes it helps to—"

His thoughtful response made my heart ache even more. It was exactly what I needed, but I couldn't help the flood of frustration that washed over me.

"No, Max." I snapped, frustration leaking into my voice. "I don't want to talk about it. I just need to be alone."

Max's face tightened with concern and frustration. "Alina, this isn't helping. You can't just shut me out like this. I want to be here for you."

"I said no!" I shouted, my voice rising. "I don't want to talk about this with you. I don't want to talk about this with anyone. I just need some *space*."

I don't even know why I'm shouting. All I knew was that I needed to let this anger out before it swallowed me.

Max's expression hardened. "Shutting me out isn't going to solve anything. If you need space, that's fine, but don't push me away like this. It's not fair."

The rawness of his words hit me hard. I turned away from him, feeling overwhelmed. "It's not about fairness," I said, the frustration seeping through my voice, "Seeing my mom today... it- it just brought up all these things I've been trying to ignore. I can't keep doing this. I can't keep dragging you into my mess."

Max's frustration boiled over. "What do you mean, 'dragging me

Chapter 27

into your mess'? I'm here because I care about you!"

And that's when the dam broke.

"I don't want to be the reason you're unhappy!" I screamed, angry tears running down my face, my brain foggy and numb to everything. "I thought I could handle this, but I'm just messing everything up! I'm not built for this!"

Max's face was a mix of hurt and determination. He took a deep breath, trying to steady his voice. "Alina, listen to me. I know you're not upset with me, not really. This is about what happened today. Your mom was obviously a trigger of some sort, and you're taking it out on me right now, which I can handle. But I don't want you to say anything you're going to regret, later."

My breath hitched, and I looked away, feeling the weight of his words as a pit of guilt formed at the bottom of my stomach, threatening to drag me to the ground. I was expecting him to yell back at me. I could handle him yelling back at me. But the kind tone he was taking had my shoulders slumping in dejection.

"You don't understand," I said quietly, my voice cracking. "Seeing her today just brought everything back—the pain, the fears, the reason I've always kept people at a distance."

"I *don't* understand," Max said softly but firmly. "I probably never will. But I know that you're not being yourself right now, and I'm not leaving this place until you've gotten all of this out."

I felt a wave of guilt and sorrow wash over me.

"I'm sorry," I whispered, my voice strained. "I didn't mean to push you away. I'm just… I don't know how to deal with all of this."

Max's expression softened, and he reached out to gently take my hand. "That's okay. I know you didn't mean to. You can deal with this however you need to, just don't take it out on yourself, because you don't deserve that either."

I finally broke down, my body shaking with silent sobs as I buried my face in his shoulder. Max moved closer, his arms wrapping around me in a comforting embrace. He pulled me into his lap, his warmth and steady presence providing a stark contrast to the emotional storm inside me. And that was how we spent the rest of the day: Him holding me in his arms as I let out all the pain and grief and anger I had suppressed for this woman all these years.

Chapter 28

The London House was alive with the hum of conversation and clinking glasses, the air thick with anticipation as GenTech's end-of-year cocktail party unfolded. Stepping through the doors, I was immediately greeted by the opulent surroundings—a sea of elegantly dressed guests mingling beneath glittering fairy lights. Being winter in Chicago, the rooftop was covered in heaters, and I shivered as I felt the waves of heat warm my skin.

I stood at the entrance, my heart racing with excitement and nerves, dressed in a sleek black cocktail dress that hugged my curves, and matched my wavy black hair.

A pair of daisy earrings Kait had gotten me after seeing Max's daisies adorned my ears, and I decided to go drastic tonight with a bold red lip, ready for another night of networking and schmoozing.

Déjà vu prickled in me at the similar scene to the yearly charity auction, except this time, Max was standing across the room talking to some of my coworkers, dapper in a tailored suit, his usual messy locks tamed for the occasion.

He had been invited due to his work with GenTech as our contracted artist, and a flicker of pride warmed my chest at the sight of him chatting so effortlessly with my colleagues.

I quickly darted my eyes to his wrist, checking for something, and smiled to myself at the ever present pink friendship bracelet gracing it. It didn't quite go with the rest of his outfit, but knowing the reason behind its presence was special, and I loved that I knew these things about him that no one else in this room did.

After that night on the couch, I had felt closer to him than I ever thought I would. Him seeing me at my worst and staying rigid as I tried to push him away unlocked some hidden feelings that I didn't realize I had for him.

We had agreed to come separately to avoid people knowing about our relationship. I really did not want to face having to go through any misogynistic comments about unprofessionalism on the cusp of a possible promotion.

He seemed to agree when I brought it up to him. Despite his polished appearance, I found myself missing the colorful splashes of paint that normally adorned his clothes and skin.

As I watched Max laugh and engage with my coworkers, he suddenly glanced my way, our eyes locking across the room. I felt my heart skip a beat and my cheeks warmed all of a sudden. When did I start getting these autonomous reactions when it came to him? I cursed my body internally for betraying my normally stoic character.

His smile widened, and he excused himself from the conversation, making his way over to me with purposeful strides.

"Hey there, beautiful," he said lowly, his voice soft and warm, meant only for me.

"Hey yourself," I murmured, unable to keep the smile off my face. God, my cheeks have been getting the workout of their life ever since he came into mine. "You look incredibly handsome tonight."

He chuckled, brushing a hand through his neatly styled hair.

Chapter 28

"Thanks, though I have to admit, I miss my usual getup. This suit feels too stiff." He shifted, rolling his shoulders and winced.

I laughed, feeling the tension of the evening melt away.

"I know what you mean. You look great, but I prefer you with your paint-splattered clothes and messy hair."

"Well, it's only for tonight," he promised, his eyes twinkling. "Wanna get cheeseburgers later?"

I stifled a laugh behind my hand before nodding at him with a smile.

As we looked around at the event, Jack approached us with a warm smile, his middle-aged frame showing through his sleek tuxedo.

"Alina, Max, I've been looking forward to this moment all year," he said, gesturing toward the center of the room where seven large pieces were covered on display.

A wave of shock flared through me at the sight of them. I didn't know they were going to be the centerpiece of the cocktail party. Judging my Max's unfazed appearance, it seemed he knew.

"I snuck a peek earlier. Your work is truly remarkable."

Jack then turned toward the crowd, tapping a spoon against his glass to get everyone's attention. The room quieted down, all eyes turning to him.

"Ladies and gentlemen, thank you all for joining us tonight to celebrate another successful year at GenTech. This probably will be my last address to most of you, since I'll be leaving in about a month." He paused, looking around. It was silent.

"Sad! I know!" He deadpanned, causing a wave of laughter to erupt from the crowd. "Anyway, tonight is not about me, so if you need a farewell speech or anything, you're not getting one." He was standing in front of us now, next to the paintings in the center of the rooftop.

"As you know, we are not just about technological innovation, but also about fostering creativity and sustainability. Tonight, I am thrilled to unveil a series of paintings that will soon be gracing our office walls, reflecting the very core of our values. Not only that, I will also be unveiling GenTech's newest logo, a symbol of the extensive rebranding we have undertaken this past fall. And, if you look at midnight, you will find that our website has also been relaunched and updated to fit the rebranding. "

Heat flared in my cheeks. I normally loved any chance to get recognized for my work, but for some reason, I was feeling some embarrassment at the attention. Something stroked gently at my arm, hidden behind Jack's frame, and I felt myself exhale as Max's pinky wrapped around mine.

Jack paused, letting the anticipation build, his everlasting mischievous smile on his old face.

"These pieces are the work of two incredibly talented individuals, our own Alina Bennett and the brilliant artist from our FOK auction, Max Reynolds. Their collaboration has resulted in something truly special, and I can't wait for you all to see it."

With a flourish, Jack pulled the covers off the paintings one by one, leaving the logo in the center for last. Emotion built in my stomach, and I gripped Max's pinky tighter with mine as the crowd began murmuring in admiration.

I felt a surge of pride as I gazed at the paintings and our new and improved logo. Each piece was a testament to our creativity and vision, and I couldn't help but feel a sense of accomplishment. They also sparked the beginning of our rocky relationship, and as I looked at each painting, my smile deepened. I saw Max turn to me with a secretive smile and knew he was thinking the same thing.

Jack continued, "These paintings are more than just decorations; they are a representation of who we are and what we stand for at GenTech. I'm honored to be leaving at a time when we can safely let the new generation take the reins. They're gonna do great things."

He tipped his flute at me and winked and I felt a ball form in my

Chapter 28

throat. This felt like the end of something. It felt final and I didn't know how to process that.

The room erupted in applause, and I felt a warm flush of pride. Max squeezed my hand, his eyes sparkling with shared joy. Jack gave us a nod of approval before stepping away to mingle with other guests.

Max turned to me, a proud smile on his face. "We did it," he whispered.

"We did," I echoed, feeling a deep sense of connection with him at that moment.

We both smiled at each other warmly before being pulled away by the masses of people who suddenly had a lot of opinions about art and graphic design.

✧✧✧

As the night wore on, I found myself engrossed in conversation with members of the GenTech board, discussing my upcoming expansion presentation. Normally, I would have relished the opportunity to network and make connections – I wouldn't even have taken a drink before I made my way around the room, which dimmed my excitement for these events over time – but tonight, all I wanted to do was enjoy the night with Max.

Max, ever the social butterfly, was engaged in animated conversations with some guests, making them laugh with his charm and wit. Yet, I could see him glancing at me frequently, and it made me feel warm all over.

Max sensed my distraction and left his conversation, coming over to pull me away from the board to a secluded corner of the room.

"You know, this feels strangely familiar," he remarked with a playful smile.

I laughed, remembering the awkward encounter that had marked the beginning of our friendship.

"Hmm. I don't know… I definitely like you more now than I did then," I teased.

"Come on. You always liked me."

"I definitely did not." I snorted, quickly bringing my drink to my lips when I saw his offended expression.

"Wha-Bu-But," he stammered, "we just had that whole push and pull thing going on."

"It was just a push thing on my end. I don't know where you got the pulling from."

He jutted his lower lip. "I thought that was all just foreplay."

I stared at him incredulously.

"You thought getting me sick in an elevator, then my complete ignoring of you for days was foreplay?"

"Well- like those boys in school who pulled on little girls' pigtails because they liked them."

I snickered and patted his upper arm. "Oh, honey."

His pouting stopped abruptly when his eyes zeroed in on a server walking by with a tray in their hands. Without missing a beat, his hand darted out and grabbed a caprese crostini off the tray and he handed it to me, wordlessly.

I looked at the little toast snack in my hand, then back at him, puzzled.

"What's this for?"

"You like those, don't you?"

"Yes… but how'd you know that?" I don't recall ever eating one in front of him.

A mischievous glint sparkled in his eyes as he leaned in closer.

"I snuck a peek at you at the auction while you were talking to Jack. You shoved one of these in your mouth, trying not to let anyone see, and your cheeks blew up like a chipmunk. It was adorable."

Chapter 28

Warmth filled my chest, and whatever was fluttering around in my stomach was giving me heartburn.

"You saw that?"

"Of course I did. I noticed everything about you that night. You were the most interesting person in the room."

He tucked a stray hair behind my ear. "It's also how I noticed that you get mean when you're hungry. Eat up."

A blush crept up my neck as I nibbled on the crostini.

"Well, you built a weak Sydney Opera House replica for a girl you just met."

He laughed heartily and tugged a lock of my hair.

"Come on," he gestured his head at the elevator, "do you want to leave so I can get some food in you?"

I turned my eyes to survey the crowd. I still had so many more people I had to talk to. Connections I had to maintain with small talk and excruciatingly long stories about the newest golf course and Christmas holiday plans and questions on what I was planning on doing if I decided to have kids one day. As if my partner couldn't pick up a baby and a mop.

Still, my connections have gotten me this far, and I should go and expand my network more.

But, I turned back to his soft expression and murmured, "Let's go."

Chapter 29

"I just don't think dinosaur meat would taste anything like chicken."

"The chicken is the dinosaur's closest living relative. I'm just saying it would only make sense!"

"Chicken and duck taste completely different, and they're both birds." I mumbled around a bite of my cheeseburger, groaning at the taste of the grilled meat, soft bread, and melty cheese in my mouth.

We had gotten Billy Goats on the way to his apartment and were now chomping down on them as we walked down the Chicago streets, the moonlight illuminating the walkways beneath us.

I had planned to go home after the party and food, but Max had insisted we go to his place since he 'wasn't a psychopath and actually had viable food in the fridge for breakfast'. My eggs and rice worked for me, but his hopeful face wore me down.

His eyes flared with heat at my groan before he shook his head.

"You don't know for sure that dinosaurs *don't* taste like chicken."

"I'm sorry, did you not go to an esteemed college for a STEM degree? What kind of scientific argument is that?"

He threw a fry at my head. I opened my mouth at him, ready for the

Chapter 29

next one.

A short laugh escaped him and he pushed me to the side playfully before grabbing my hand and pulling me back to him. He tucked me under his arm and looked forward, taking a big bite of his burger.

"They didn't teach me about the texture and flavor profile of extinct animals in my aerospace engineering degree."

I looked up at him with a mildly amused expression. Wearing my heels every day, I was never more than an inch shorter than him.

"Let's just agree to disagree."

He nodded and took a triumphant bite of his burger.

"Fine, but I'm telling you, if they ever clone a dinosaur, I'm the first in line to find out."

I rolled my eyes, laughing.

"If they ever manage to successfully bring back an extinct species, I don't think they're gonna let you cook it for your own curiosity."

He grinned down at me, mischief twinkling in his eyes.

"Hey, never say never. Science is always advancing. And who knows? Maybe one day, we'll be at Alegria, and Rowan will be cooking us Dino burgers in the back."

I shook my head, leaning against him as we continued our walk.

"Only you would come up with something as ridiculous as that."

He squeezed my shoulder affectionately. "That's why you like me."

My heart skipped a beat at his words, and I glanced up at him, warmth flooding through me.

"Yeah," I admitted softly. "That's one of the reasons."

Eventually, we reached Max's apartment building, and he led me inside, up the stairs, and into his cozy space, taking my empty burger wrapper and throwing it away. The familiar scent of paint and coffee greeted us as we entered.

"Welcome to my humble abode," he said with a flourish, tossing his keys onto the counter.

I smiled, taking in the organized chaos of his apartment. Canvases were propped against the walls, paint splatters adorned the floor, and his easel stood proudly in the corner. Despite the mess, it felt cozy and lived-in and I loved it.

"Make yourself at home," he said, heading to the kitchen to grab us some drinks.

I sighed in relief as I slipped off my heels, immediately feeling the throbbing in my feet. I tried to hide my discomfort, but Max noticed as he returned with two glasses of wine.

"Are you okay?" he asked, concern etching his features.

I forced a smile. "Yeah, just a little sore from wearing these all day."

He frowned, setting down the glasses and coming over to me.

"Sit down," he commanded gently, guiding me to the couch. "Let me take a look."

I obeyed, sinking into the cushions. He knelt down, taking my foot gently in his nimble hands and rubbing it with a concentrated look on his face. I tried to tug my foot away but he stopped me with one look and took it back.

I winced at first, but the pain quickly turned into soothing relief under his skilled fingers.

"You really need to stop wearing these torture devices every day," he scolded, his voice soft but firm.

I chuckled, leaning back and closing my eyes as he continued to massage my foot.

"They make me more confident. People respect me more when I wear them."

He shook his head, moving to my other foot.

"You've tailored your entire life to fit your work, from the black coffee to the shoes. You don't need to hurt yourself to gain respect, Lina. Everyone already respects you."

Maybe it was the casual way he said it, or the truth that laced

Chapter 29

his words, but his words struck a chord in me, and I shrugged halfheartedly, a pit forming at the bottom of my stomach.

"I guess old habits die hard."

He slowed his massaging my foot and looked up at me, his eyes filled with tenderness.

"I love your feet. I love every cute toe you have. Even this weird triangular nub."

He pinched my pinky toe. I chuckled with soft laughter. I had told him the story of how I jammed it kicking a wall when I was 5 because my dad had been unlucky enough to inform me that Santa was already married to someone else. He had burst into laughter heartily for a long time.

His tender eyes looked back at mine. "I hate that you torture them like this."

He leaned down and pressed a gentle kiss to the arch of my foot. Something burned in my chest again. I thought it was heartburn from the cheeseburgers, but watching him take care of me again, without expecting anything in return, seeing how much of me he's figured out and likes anyway, made the burning in my chest even stronger.

Warmth flooded my chest at his words and actions, and I realized the burning wasn't heartburn at all. The sincerity in his eyes, the warmth of his touch—it all became too much. My emotions surged, and before I could second-guess myself, the words spilled out.

"I think I love you." I blurted out.

What the fuck.

There was no turning back now, I guess.

Max's eyes widened in surprise, and for a moment, I wondered if I had said too much too soon. But then a slow, radiant smile spread across his face, and he leaned in closer, cupping my cheek with his hand. I was so hopped up on adrenaline and shock that it didn't even occur to me his hand was just on my foot. I wouldn't have cared anyway.

"You *think* you love me?" His eyes danced with mirth behind his soft expression.

I swallowed and pursed my lips.

"Mhm."

"Alina." His tone was serious.

I turned beet red. This was not how I was planning for tonight to go.

After a couple of seconds of silence with his unwavering gaze upon me, I exhaled shakily and breathed, "I love you."

"I love you too," he murmured, his voice thick with emotion.

I felt a rush of happiness and relief as he pulled me into a kiss, our lips meeting in a tender embrace. His lips were softer than ever and somehow, despite the burger we just chowed down, he tasted like chocolate. His arms wrapped around me and pulled me onto his lap, pulling me closer.

The world seemed to melt away as we lost ourselves in each other, the warmth of his body grounding me in the moment.

When we finally pulled away, breathless and smiling, Max brushed a strand of hair behind my ear, letting his hand land on the back of my neck. My head tickled as he played with the baby hairs there.

"You have no idea how long I've been waiting to hear you say that."

"I'm scared." I whispered.

"Of what?" He continued stroking my hair, his eyes warm and shining as he looked at me.

"It's more real now." I turned my eyes to his canvases in a corner. "What if you realize you deserve better than me and you leave me one day like everyone else has?"

My voice was quiet. Almost too quiet for him to hear. But I had to tell him, so he could leave now if he wanted to and save me the pain later.

Chapter 29

Max's grip on my hand tightened, and he gently tilted my chin back so I was looking directly into his eyes.

"Alina, listen to me," he said softly but firmly. "I'm not going anywhere. I'm here because I want to be with you. I know exactly who you are, and I love you. I'm not going to leave you."

I searched his eyes, looking for any hint of doubt, but all I saw was sincerity and love. I bit my lip, trying to hold back the tears that were threatening to spill over.

"You promise?" I whispered, my voice breaking.

He leaned in and pressed a soft kiss to my forehead.

"I promise," he murmured against my skin. "You're stuck with me now."

"Even if I don't try dinosaur meat with you?"

I felt his body shaking under me with laughter.

"Even if you don't try dinosaur meat with me."

He looked at me for a moment, his eyes softening behind his amused grin.

"I love you." His eyes were sincere.

I smiled and leaned down, pressing my lips to his.

Chapter 30

What started off as a simple kiss quickly escalated to more. Max's hand moved from my cheek to the nape of my neck, his fingers tangling in my hair as he drew me closer. Our breaths mingled, and I could feel the warmth radiating from his skin. His eyes, dark and filled with emotion, locked onto mine.

A smile overcame his lips and he pulled my lips back to his, devouring them between his soft lips. His hand tightened in my hair as he deepened the kiss, his mouth moving against mine with a hunger that made my heart race. I responded eagerly, parting my lips to allow him in. His tongue brushed against mine, and a moan escaped my throat, swallowed by his fervent kiss.

The kiss grew more urgent, our mouths moving in a dance of passion and need. I lost myself in the sensation of him—his taste, his touch, the way he made me feel like I was the only woman in the world. His lips trailed from my mouth to my jaw, then down to the sensitive skin of my neck, leaving a trail of fire in their wake.

I felt an aching warmth below and ground my hips against him, desperately seeking release. Sparks of pleasure emanated up my body

Chapter 30

from the friction of his suit pants on my clit, and a breathy moan made its way out my lips. A burning knot of need was blazing deep in my belly.

He gripped my hips as he groaned lowly at my rubbing against him, and I felt something hard poking at my thigh through my dress.

Wanting to touch him, I reached my hand low between us and felt him through his suit pants, sighing when he gripped my hips tighter. Our tongues met once again in the heat, and I felt my clit throbbing at the lack of contact.

"Max," I gasped, my fingers digging into his shoulders.

He responded with a low growl, his teeth grazing my earlobe. "Alina," he murmured, his voice thick with desire. "I need you."

I pulled him back to my lips, our kiss reigniting with even more fervor. His hands roamed over my body, exploring every curve and dip, and I felt like I was melting under his touch. My own hands were just as eager, tugging at his shirt, desperate to feel his skin against mine.

We broke apart for a moment, both of us breathing heavily. His forehead rested against mine, and he looked at me with such intensity that it took my breath away.

"Are you sure?" he asked, his voice hoarse.

I nodded, unable to form words. Instead, I pulled him back to me, our lips meeting once more in a kiss that spoke of all the things we couldn't say. We got up and he quickly pulled my dress over my head before ripping off his suit.

I laid on the couch, ready for him to climb over me but he shook his head and pulled me up with a hand before sitting on the couch and pulling me on top of him, his grip firm and unyielding.

"I want you in control tonight." He said. His tone had an air of finality in it that had me shivering and I nodded before pressing my lips roughly against his. And as I kissed him, I fumbled for him, found his rigid, throbbing cock, and instinctively started to stroke him hard and fast. He arched up against me with an almost pained grunt.

I loved how gentle he was with me, but I needed this to be hard tonight. I needed to feel the way he ached for me, and I wanted to be reminded of it when I tried to walk tomorrow morning.

I felt myself spreading my juices all over his thighs and when I looked down to see the evidence of it, he did too. His eyes darkened with some sort of pride and he slammed his lips into mine, trailing open-mouthed kisses down my neck. I was panting with need as he bit and suckled in the crevice where my neck met my shoulder, and I ground against him, feeling the velvety flesh of his cock rubbing deliciously against my slit.

All words left me when he took a nipple into his mouth and bit it gently.

I threw my head back, giving him better access to my breasts and he took advantage of it. He nuzzled my breasts, biting, sucking, licking at them as I rocked my hips back and forth against him. I needed him now, I decided.

I hovered above him and grabbed his dick with a shaky hand, trying to position it into me but was stopped by his own hand, causing my eyes to snap to his in exasperation.

"Condom." He sounded out. He was breathing heavily against me, as if stopping me took a lot of effort.

"IUD." I replied, looking back down and trying to get him in me.

His fingers gripped my chin and brought me back to him.

"Are you sure?"

"Yes." I was sure. Of course, I was sure. I loved him. And I need him now.

He nodded and I took that as my cue to position him again before sinking onto him. A low moan emanated from both of us, and I pressed my head to the crook of his neck, breathing slowly and trying to adjust

Chapter 30

to him inside me. I forgot how big he was last time. He wasn't a monster by any means but he definitely was well-endowed and I could feel him stretching me delightfully.

He peppered kisses on my breasts as he waited patiently, and a soft laugh came out my lips. He was a boob man. Max Reynolds was a boob man. Both times we've had sex now, he's paid an inordinate amount of attention to my breasts and it filled me with a sickening delight. My nipples hardened between his lips.

When I finally felt the tightness ebbing away, I started rocking my hips against him lightly. His fingers gripped my butt cheeks hard and I knew if he pulled away, he would have left pale marks for the blood to rush back in.

I rode him harder and a curse fell from his lips.

"Fuck," he breathed, letting his eyes fall closed, thrusting up to meet mine.

The sight of him in so much pleasure lit a fire within me, and suddenly all I wanted was to see him come undone in front of me. I ground my hips harder against his, finding a fast rhythm, and felt him come to the hilt every time he thrusted up into me. His eyes opened and I swallowed, seeing them flare with heat before he engulfed my moans in a kiss.

If every time was going to be like this, I don't know how I was ever going to leave this apartment.

When we both gasped for air, his hand made its way down our bodies and landed at where we connected, rubbing his thumb against my clit roughly. A whimper fell from my lips and my eyes clenched shut from the pleasure as I felt the burning pressure in my belly build and build.

I started to moan loudly as my thighs began to shake; then shuddered and bucked hard against him as the first waves of my orgasm struck me. My legs clamped down on his thighs and I writhed, crying out.

"Fuck, you're so beautiful when you come." He murmured, still rubbing circles around my clit as I came undone on him.

My hips stopped moving from all the pleasure flooding my body but he compensated and started thrusting harder up into me, almost balls deep. Just as I came down from my first orgasm, I felt my stomach tighten again.

"Wha-" I started, my breathing growing heavier as I tried to suck air into my lungs.

His eyes filled with wonder and he examined my body, the way my chest was heaving against his, my legs shaking.

"Breathe, angel," He whispered, "you're having a second one."

Shock ran through me, and I clenched my eyes shut again as the mountain of pressure built and built in my stomach. He was so deep, rubbing against my G-spot, and I could feel waves of pleasure go through me with every circle he rubbed against my clit.

"I'm... I'm..."

A strangled moan wrenched through me and I arched over hard, falling in against him, unable to control the way my legs shook around him as a titanic orgasm broke over me.

"That's it," he grunted, rocking my hips against him with his hands.

I need him to come. I couldn't do this much more. But my body was starting to feel like jello and I wasn't sure how much longer I could last. With all the energy I could muster, I leaned down and bit his nipple as I squeezed hard around him, milking his pleasure as much as I could.

He buried his head in my neck, groaned my name, and spilled into me, coming deep inside me. We stayed there for a few minutes, just trying to catch our breaths while sneaking soft kisses and rubbing our faces together. He liked kissing my eyelashes.

When his breathing eased, he gripped my butt, lifting the both of us off the couch, and walked us to his bed, him still inside me. He laid me down on the right side, the side I preferred, and reluctantly pulled out of me.

Chapter 30

He went to walk to the bathroom before his body did a double take and his hypnotized gaze locked in on my sex. A hunger flared in his eyes again and I held my body up on my elbows to see what caught his attention.

A steady trickle of his seed leaked out of me, and my pussy looked raw and pink and puffy. A blush spread all over my body, up my chest and into my cheeks, and I looked at him shyly. He just reached a long finger out and rubbed at my pussy lightly, mixing our juices together. A shudder ran down my body and I jerked from the pleasure.

"So beautiful." He rumbled, his voice so low it was like it was just for him.

I pulled him up and kissed him hard. It was like my body had started to grow addicted to his touch and craved it constantly.

He cleaned me up, laid himself next to me, pulled me in, and fell asleep with one hand holding my breast gently, a finger tracing a similar pattern against my skin.

I loved him.

Max

I have loved Alina Bennet since the day I met her in that elevator. I loved the way she rushed in – she was always in a rush. I loved the flustered look on her face when she realized she wasn't alone in the stuffy space. I even loved the way her eyebrows furrowed together in annoyance when I smiled dopily at her. For a second, I thought my fever had me hallucinating an angel. A very grumpy angel.

Then, when we got paired together at her boss's behest, and she did everything in her power to stay away, I grew amused with her. With the way she would correct herself when she started smiling at me more. The way she would get extremely animated when discussing art, despite referring to herself as the complete opposite of an art connoisseur. The way she huffed and puffed and rolled her eyes at me when she thought I wasn't looking at her.

I was always looking at her.

It wasn't that she wasn't like other girls. She was. But she was *the* girl. As we grew closer and she let me in more, I knew. I knew that she was *the* girl for me. And I was willing to wait. I would have waited forever if she needed me to. But somehow, she found me worthy of placing her trust in me. And it made my heart so fucking huge, I thought it was gonna burst in my chest.

Five nights ago, when she finally said she loved me, it felt like everything had fallen into place. I had been prepared for her never to say it. With all that she's been through, I wouldn't have blamed her for keeping that last bit of her to herself. But hearing those words from her, it was better than everything else I've ever thought was good.

I woke up to the soft light of the morning sun streaming through the blinds, casting a golden glow over the room. The light highlighted the soft curves and delicate features of Alina's face, making her look even more ethereal than usual. I laid there for a moment, just watching her sleep, feeling an overwhelming sense of contentment wash over me.

Her dark black hair fanned out across the pillow, the strands catching the sunlight and creating a slightly reddish hue that I wanted to put to a canvas immediately. I reached out to gently brush a lock away from her face, careful not to wake her.

Her skin was smooth and flawless, a warm olive that seemed to glow in the morning light. Her eyelashes, long and dark, cast small shadows on her lightly freckled cheeks, and her lips were slightly parted in the soft rhythm of sleep.

I traced the curve of her cheek with my gaze, moving down to the elegant line of her jaw and the graceful slope of her neck. Her normally harsh expression was smoothed out with sleep, and it made her look younger.

Unable to help myself, I leaned down and kissed her lightly freckled shoulder softly, my lips barely brushing her skin.

She stirred slowly, a soft murmur escaping her lips as she began to wake up. Her eyes that kissed in the corners fluttered open, and for a moment, she looked disoriented. Then her gaze found mine, and a slow, sleepy smile spread across her face.

I loved the moment between sleep and waking up. It was when she was at her most unguarded state.

"Morning," she whispered, her voice still husky with sleep.

"Morning, beautiful," I replied, unable to keep the smile from my face.

Her sleepy smile turned into a frown. "Were you... watching me sleep?"

"Mhm." I nodded.

She looked deeply disturbed.

"Like a psychopath?" Her voice was clearer now.

"Like a romantic." I corrected.

"Just- no." She shook her head, her brows furrowed, and placed her slender hand over my lower face.

I grinned and licked her finger, and her face crumpled in indignation as she yanked her hand away and wiped it on my hair.

She gave me the stink eye.

I kissed her, a chaste but passionate morning kiss.

She smiled at me sleepily again.

She rolled her eyes playfully, but there was a soft blush creeping up her cheeks. "You're such a sap."

"Only for you," I said, leaning in to press a soft kiss to her forehead.

She hummed in contentment, her eyes closing briefly.

"I could get used to waking up like this."

"Me too," I admitted. "In fact, I think I might insist on it."

She laughed softly, the sound like music to my ears.

"Oh, you insist, do you?"

"Absolutely," I said, pretending to be serious. "It's non-negotiable."

She pushed herself up on one elbow, looking down at me with a mischievous glint in her eye.

"And what if I refuse?"

I shrugged, grinning up at her. "Then I guess I'll just have to make it worth your while to stay."

Her eyebrows shot up in mock surprise. "Is that a challenge?"

"Consider it a promise," I replied, pulling her down for a kiss.

When we finally pulled apart, she was laughing, her eyes shining with happiness.

"You're impossible, you know that?"

"I've been told," I said, brushing my thumb over her cheek. "But you love me anyway."

She paused. She still looked conflicted every time I told her I loved her since the first time, 5 days ago, but I didn't hold it against her. She loved me. She just didn't know how to say it.

"I do," she finally agreed, her expression softening.

And I felt my heart soar.

We stayed like that for a while, just enjoying the moment, the quiet intimacy of the morning.

"Breakfast? I got brand-new groceries just for you since you're a rice and egg hater," she suggested after a while, her stomach growling softly.

"*No.*" I groaned, laying my head on her belly. I felt her slim fingers curl into my hair and I blew a raspberry on her bare belly, smiling internally at the giggle she emitted. "Let's just stay like this forever."

"I have to go to work later." She said gently.

"No you don't. It's the holidays." My voice was muffled by her stomach, and I could feel it shaking with laughter under me.

"Yes I do," she insisted, "I have my final presentation less than three weeks from now."

"Do your work here."

"I can't."

"Do your work here or *you're* cooking breakfast. I want to make New Year's resolutions with you."

Her fingers in my hair stopped their exploration for one moment. Two. Then continued again.

"So we've come to blackmail, is that it?" Her voice had a teasing quality to it, and I felt my blood rush to my nether regions.

I nodded against her stomach and tilted my head to face the side again, listening to the soothing sounds of her stomach.

"And then we watch Love Actually tonight." I added.

She barked a laugh. "Isn't that a Christmas movie?"

"You were in work mode on Christmas. I barely saw you."

Her fingernails scratched lightly at my scalp, and a groan let loose from my lips. At this rate, she was gonna give me my second erection this morning.

Not that I would mind it, though. I was intoxicated with her.

"Okay," she conceded, "But we have to get up now."

"Sounds good," I said, reluctantly letting her go. "Let's go."

She laughed, swinging her legs over the side of the bed. "I'm only agreeing because I'm starving and I don't trust myself not to burn the apartment down. Plus, I switched out my cheap eggs for your fancy, humane, pasture-raised ones – even though they cost like an extra five dollar – just for you, and I want to see if they're worth it taste-wise."

Smiling to myself at her little act of service, I watched her as she stood up, admiring the way the sunlight played on her skin, the way she moved with an effortless grace.

Over the years, I had seen my friends fall in and out of love, while I had always kept it casual. Despite my protests, Cas was always regaling me with stories of his most recent one-night stand, but every now and then when I did indulge in one, it always left me feeling empty and unfulfilled. I guessed it just wasn't for me.

It seemed Cas was feeling the same way recently because I hadn't heard a debrief from him in a while.

But this was different. I loved her, more than I ever thought it was possible to love someone, and I knew I would spend the rest of my life making sure she knew that.

Max

✧✧✧

After breakfast, Alina let me cuddle her on the couch while we watched the morning news. *Just five minutes,* she had said. But over thirty minutes had passed and she hadn't moved at all from her position next to me, her legs swung over my lap and her body leaning into my side. It filled me with a warmth I had grown to associate with her.

"Do you talk to your brother often?" Her gaze was still forward, focused on the TV.

I cocked my head, wondering what brought this on.

"Sometimes," I stroked her socked foot on my lap in thought, "Not enough."

"How come?"

"Well we used to talk a lot more, we were actually super close growing up, but Kyle became a lawyer and stayed in Texas and I moved up here. We still call once a week but I haven't seen him in a while."

"Maybe you should visit him more," she suggested, her voice soft but earnest.

"I will."

And I meant it. She had mentioned briefly that she hadn't seen her sister since she left her and her dad over ten years ago, and I was sure that's what was running through her head right now.

I knew she was close to her cousin Harper and viewed her as a sister of sorts, but I'm sure the pain still lingered.

I squeezed her foot gently, offering silent support.

"So, what's the deal with Ezra?" She turned her face to me, a twinkle in her eye.

I loved when she let her guard down and let herself be playful. Her eyes shined, and her dimple deepened in her cheek adorably.

"What do you mean?" I responded impishly.

"Why's he always so grumpy and quiet?"

I chuckled under my breath. "Is that how you see him?"

She nodded.

"He… he just doesn't like being around a lot of people. It takes a second for him to warm up."

At her curious gaze, I added, "He likes *you*, though."

She chuffed. "It's just him and Emmy are so different. He's so quiet and she's the most animated person in the room from what I've seen. Other than being basically twins, I never would have guessed they were siblings."

Following her line of thoughts, I sighed deeply. Emmy and Ezra were just completely different, but the reasoning behind it always made me hurt for my best friend.

"He doesn't love to talk about it, but when they were kids, their parents died. Mugging."

Her mouth fell open and I pecked her chin.

"He had to grow up fast and with the foster system being what it is, he took it upon himself to raise Emmy. And Emmy took it upon herself to always try to make him smile."

Her eyes dawned in understanding. "So that's why he's so serious."

"He really does warm up around people he's close with, he just can't help but be on the lookout whenever he's surrounded by strangers. Until us, Emmy was the only one he was himself around. But we wore him down."

I smiled as I thought about the rough first few days in our college house as roommates and how far our friendship has lasted since. We had an unbreakable bond, all four of us (five, sometimes including Emmy), and I wouldn't change it for the world.

"And Emmy and Cas?" She ventured, her voice trailing off.

I rolled my eyes and sniggered.

"Those two have been at each other's throats since the day they met. It only got worse when they both decided to become independent architects in the same city."

"But there's nothing going on there?"

"They both think there's nothing going on there." I started, "But Cas wouldn't let anyone other than Emmy mess with him the amount she does. That girl once sent a stripper dressed in a banana costume to a date he was on and had her give Cas a lap dance in front of his date and everyone in the restaurant."

"Oh god." Alina winced.

"Yeah. It got worse later when he retaliated by sending his cop friend a perfect description of *her* date as a joke and getting him arrested right before dessert in front of her."

She laughed that rich, somewhat raspy laugh of hers, covering her face with her sweater sleeves. A smile quirked at the corner of my lips and I pulled her closer into me.

She nestled deeper into my side, her head resting comfortably on my shoulder.

"I can't imagine living in a prank war like that."

"Yeah, it keeps things interesting," I admitted. "But I wouldn't trade it for anything. They're family."

We sat in comfortable silence for a few moments, the news droning on in the background. I could feel Alina's body relax against mine, her head nestling further into the crook of my shoulder.

It was easy, talking to her. I went my whole life thinking that I wouldn't be good enough for anyone. That my mistakes and past meant that I deserved to be alone.

But it was different with her. Everything was different with her.

I smiled down at her as she chuffed at the human interest piece rattling on the TV.

Her skin glowed in the sunlight, and I found myself lightly stroking her calf, tracing the same pattern on her skin I had been tracing for months now.

I love you.

Chapter 32

Oh god, this was it. I didn't think it would come this soon. Sure, in college, Kait and I were always joking about her lack of protection usage and how we'd have to raise an apartment baby, but this was real. My best friend was a mother.

When I got the text from Adam, Max was in the middle of an important Zoom for one of his clients, so he insisted I take his car and go without him.

Driving in Downtown Chicago was not an experience I would recommend to anyone. Did people in this day and age not know how to drive? I almost got into five car accidents on the way over.

Frantic, I rushed to the maternity wing and double-checked my phone for the room number. I hurried through the hospital corridors, my heart racing with anticipation.

When I reached Kait's room, I paused for a moment outside the door, taking a deep breath to steady myself before pushing it open quietly.

The sight that greeted me was one of pure joy. Kait was sitting up in bed, looking exhausted but radiant. Her dark blonde hair was slightly tousled, and there were dark circles under her eyes, but she had a serene, glowing smile on her face. Adam was sitting beside her, beaming with pride, holding a tiny, bundled-up pink blob in his large arms.

"Allie!" Kait exclaimed, her face lighting up even more as she saw me. "You're here!"

I rushed to her side, feeling tears of happiness welling up in my eyes.

"Of course I'm here. How are you feeling?"

"Tired, but so incredibly happy," she replied, her eyes shimmering with tears. "How was Christmas with you and Max?" She wiggled her eyebrows.

"*Kait!*" I yawped in vexation.

"I'm kidding. We'll talk about that later." She laughed hoarsely, her voice still raw from labor. "Meet our little girl."

Adam stood from his chair and placed the little pink bundle gently in my arms. His eyes were red and puffy and I smiled, feeling tears prickling behind my eyes at the sight of my large friend in this emotional state.

"Meet–" he hiccuped.

"Lennon Mae Flynn." Kait said wistfully, a proud smile on her face.

I felt my heart twist and looked down at the tiny newborn in my arms. She was perfect, with delicate features and a head full of dark hair. Her eyes were closed, and she had a peaceful expression, as if the world outside was too big and new to disturb her slumber.

"She's beautiful," I whispered, feeling a lump form in my throat.

"I told you she would be with a stunning fox as her mom." Kait remarked.

"And dad," Adam chimed in, his voice breaking.

"Lennon Mae," I repeated softly, smiling down at the baby. "Welcome to the world, Lennon. You've got the best parents anyone could ask for."

Chapter 32

We spent the next few minutes in a blissful silence, just marveling at the new life in our midst. The room was filled with a sense of peace and love that was almost tangible. I felt incredibly honored to be a part of this moment, to share in their joy.

After a while, I handed Lennon back to Kait and took a seat beside her bed. "How was it?" I asked, keeping my voice low so as not to disturb the baby.

Kait chuckled softly. "It was intense. But Adam was amazing, and the doctors and nurses were wonderful. And now that she's here, it was all worth it."

"So worth it," Adam said genuinely as he held up his right wrist and my eyes widened at the splint covering it.

"Holy shit, what the hell happened to you?"

He looked down sheepishly. "I gave my hand to Kait in support during a contraction."

She glowered at him.

He coughed and the tips of his ears reddened. "I mean- I fell on it because I was so enraptured with Kait's angelic beauty as she was pushing."

She nodded, satisfied.

I laughed quietly behind the back of my hand, making sure not to wake the baby.

"So you sprained it?"

"Yeah, she," Kait glared at him again and he cleared his throat, "*I* sprained it, the doctors had to pull me aside and splint me up and everything."

"Oh, honey." I gave him a hug, feeling his splint scratch against my back as he reciprocated it. That was gonna be annoying for him. He wore an ankle splint for two weeks in college and moaned the whole time about it.

When he pulled away, his eyes locked in on his daughter. "I think we were both running on pure adrenaline. But when she finally arrived and we heard her cry, it was the most incredible sound in the world."

I sat down in the chair, feeling a warm, contented glow spread through me. "I'm so happy for you both. Lennon is so lucky to have you as parents."

Kait reached out and squeezed my hand again. "And she's lucky to have you as her godmother. Thank you for being here, Alina. It means the world to us."

I felt tears prick at my eyes again and blinked them back. "There's nowhere else I'd rather be."

Uncomfortable with the mushiness of it all, Kait sucked her teeth and the sound echoed through the quiet hospital room.

"Leave it to you to give birth on New Year's Day." I laughed.

"It was the easiest birthday to remember." She deadpanned.

"You didn't induce."

"Yeah."

Adam took over. "Lenny Mae just knows what's up. She's gonna be a little genius, I can feel it."

He leaned over and stroked his daughter's cheek, an adoring smile on his face. Kait looked up at him with a peaceful smile on her face, and I took a photo discreetly, unable to resist. They'd want this one day.

We spent the next few hours talking and sharing stories, the room filled with laughter and love. I learned all about the birth, every little detail that Kait and Adam wanted to share. It was a beautiful, intimate, slightly gross experience that I would remember forever. At one point, Max had texted me to check in.

Max: How are Kait, Adam, and the baby?

Alina: they're great

Chapter 32

I sent him a photo of sleeping Lennon Mae with Kait's enthusiastic approval.

Alina: Lennon Mae Flynn :)

Max: Oh I think I'd fight a shark for her she's so cute.

Alina: i know, i love her so much already

Max: Send my best wishes to Kait and Adam, don't worry about the car, I love you

Alina: thank you <3

Max: Alina

Alina: love you too

As the evening approached, the room was bathed in the soft, golden light of the setting sun. Lennon stirred in Kait's arms, her tiny face scrunching up as she let out a small, sleepy sigh. It was a sound that melted my heart and filled me with an overwhelming sense of love and protectiveness. Kait tried asking about Max but it was clear the exhaustion of birth was finally catching up with her and she fell asleep halfway through her question.

Adam quirked a brow at me, taking Lennon from her arms so she wouldn't fall off.

"Kait sprained my wrist." He quipped.

"Oh really?" Sarcasm oozed from my voice and he shook his head at me, chortling.

He looked at his fiancée with love in his eyes, then settled his gaze on the infant in his arms in awe.

"I just can't believe we made her."

"Me neither."

"How did she even fall in love with me? I was an ass."

"Yeah," I replied, "but you ended up pretty good."

"I can't wait to marry her." His voice was soft and wistful, a hint of a smile playing at the corners of his lips as he gazed at her from across the room.

He hummed under his breath and looked back down at little Lennon Mae. She cooed and opened her eyes blearily at him, a drop of spittle going down her chin. He carefully wiped it away with a cloth.

"It's weird to think that our trio just became your trio." I admitted, letting the sadness wash over me. Others would have said this was something I should have kept to myself. But we were always honest with each other – it was why our friendship was as deep as it was, even now, after all these years.

He looked down at me with a knowing look.

"Don't be silly." He admonished. "We'll always be a trio. We're just two different coaster sets on the same table now."

I laughed a watery laugh and smiled down at the baby in Kait's arms, reminded of all the memories the three of us made together in college. Reminded of the day Kait and Adam had met, of how nervous she was before her first date with him, of how I spent hours picking out an outfit for her and waiting for her to come home to debrief the date at 2am.

A part of me wished that we never had to grow up, that we could have stayed like that forever. No one ever told you how different adulting was in the real world compared to college. We weren't surrounded by a city of kids our age anymore. I can't walk across the hall to debrief a night out with Kait like we used to every Sunday morning.

Chapter 32

We haven't run through the streets hollering with bags of partially opened Taco Bell, hearing people on their balconies cheering us on since we graduated. And we haven't talked to a lot of people we were friends with since graduation.

I loved our lives now and wouldn't change it for the world, but it felt like when we graduated, we had left behind a part of ourselves in that apartment that we could never get back. But, I knew now that if you found someone you wanted to keep in your life, you had to hold on tightly to them, and I would never stop holding on tightly to Kait and Adam, and now baby Lennon.

Chapter 33

"Alina, Kelsey accidentally set the microwave on fire with her popcorn again."

Dan's head popped into my office quickly with the statement, his words rushed as if he was trying to get this over with.

I sighed and pinched the bridge of my nose. Wasn't it already January? Why was Kelsey the intern still here microwaving popcorn every day instead of at school? The firm had already been closed for a week after the holidays, and I had missed it. Until I came back to this again.

After closing out the office art decor project with Max, a huge weight lifted off of my shoulders, but now I had 5 days before my final presentation on my international expansion project in front of the shareholders as well two other projects I had to finalize and I felt like I was drowning.

"How long was it on fire?"

"About 10 seconds. Carla put it out with a pot of coffee."

"Did it set off the fire alarm?" I asked patiently.

"No." Thank god. The last thing I needed was to handle the fire

Chapter 33

department coming in and creating a scene for a 10-second fire.

"Okay, thanks Dan. Could you please tell the office that microwave popcorn is banned from the office?"

After three different popcorn related fires, it was time. I hated doing this, it felt like an infringement on their rights and I loved popcorn as much as the next girl, but at this point, it was just a hazard. I took a stretch break then went straight back to work, figuring out my graphic visuals and double-checking my KPIs.

The days blended into nights as work consumed my life. My desk became a fortress of paperwork, and my computer screen a maze of spreadsheets. Late nights bled into early mornings, and exhaustion settled deep into my bones. I hadn't even seen Kait since she gave birth a few days ago and I felt myself desperately needing to shove my nose in Lennon's hair and inhale her comforting scent.

It was during one of these late nights that Max's text came through, breaking the monotony of my solitary struggle.

Max: One sentence check in: I ate a frozen Orange Chicken meal tonight, and was deeply disappointed at the lack of chicken. It was like all breading.

Alina: That was two sentences.

Max: ... You're two sentences.

Alina: Question: Are you a middle school boy?

Max: Real question: Are you or were you ever a boy scout?

My lips turned upwards in the corners and while I still felt overwhelmed, I felt slightly better. Despite our strained communications, Max seemed to understand when I needed encouragement the most.

We hadn't spent much together since the office reopened and I dedicated all my time to this presentation, but he didn't seem upset by it. He seemed quite busy himself, in fact, with a new client from Minnesota contracting him to create a piece for their gallery.

Like last time I got caught up in work, he has continuously been sending food deliveries to my office and home, making sure I eat. It kind of became our love language in a way.

Each time I had a bite of an egg roll or pasta dish, I thought about him and picked up the phone to call him for a minute.

As the days blurred together, my routine became a relentless cycle of meetings, reports, and sleepless nights – it had been difficult to sleep when a large bulk of my project required communications with China, India, and Spain.

Each project demanded more than I thought I could give, yet somehow, I pushed forward.

One particularly challenging night, I found myself in the office well past midnight, surrounded by towers of paperwork that seemed to mock my efforts. The silence of the empty office pressed in on me, a stark reminder of how important it was that I get this promotion. It was everything I had been working towards for years.

Then, like clockwork, there was a knock on my door. I glanced up, half-expecting another urgent request or last-minute change in plans. Instead, it was Max standing there, holding a bag that emitted the familiar aroma of takeout.

"Hey," he said softly, offering me a tired smile. "Thought you might need a break. Alegria okay?"

I blinked back surprise, momentarily at a loss for words. "Yeah, thanks," I managed to say, taking the bag from him. "I appreciate it. I'm so close to finishing, I'm sorry I've not been the most attentive."

Chapter 33

Max nodded, his expression softening behind his tortoiseshell frames. "It's okay, I know you. You've been pushing yourself hard. Don't forget to take care of yourself, too."

I gave him a hug and embraced him as he kissed me.

"Maybe I can help?" He offered, looking around my office and scratching the back of his head.

I laughed breezily. "It's okay. I have to do this on my own."

"It's okay to accept help sometimes, angel."

"I know," I swallowed, "I'm just... used to doing it on my own."

"Okay. I love you." He murmured.

"You too." I breathed. He looked like he wanted to say more but he just smiled at me and with that, he left, leaving me to eat while I worked.

The days passed in a blur of dry runs and late-night strategy sessions. Each project brought its own challenges, testing my resolve and resilience. But with Max, Kait, Adam, and Jack's support, I found the strength to keep pushing forward, even when I wanted to quit a few times.

As the day of my final presentation approached, I couldn't help but feel a sense of pride. Despite the setbacks and obstacles, I had made it through. And as I stood before the shareholders, presenting my vision for international expansion, I knew that I had given it everything I had.

The applause that followed was a validation of months of hard work and dedication. I couldn't have been more prepared, and it showed in that boardroom today. The meticulous research, the endless late nights, and the relentless drive to exceed expectations all culminated in this moment of triumph.

Several members of the board and shareholders came up to me personally to congratulate me on my work. Their smiles and firm handshakes were tangible acknowledgments of my success. It seemed like everything I had been striving for was within my grasp.

But amidst the celebration and relief, a shadow lingered in the back of my mind. I had worked day and night for months on end to make this project and presentation the best it could be, and I delivered it perfectly.

So why did it feel empty?

I should have been elated, basking in the glow of my achievements. Instead, I felt an unsettling hollowness. The faces of the shareholders, filled with approval, began to blur as I grappled with this unexpected emptiness. As I left the boardroom, the congratulations still ringing in my ears, I felt a pang of regret. I had achieved almost everything I wanted, yet it seemed like something fundamental was missing.

It was probably just tiredness, a sign I needed to go home to Max. I missed him.

Chapter 34

I dragged myself through the front door, the weight of the day pressing down on me like a suffocating blanket. The apartment was dark except for the soft glow of the kitchen light. The smell of cooking hung in the air and I furrowed my brows in confusion before realizing the only person it could be.

"Max?" I called out, dropping my bag by the door and kicking off my presentation heels. My feet throbbed, and my mind buzzed with the residue of the past week of near zero sleep, countless meetings, late night calls, and the final presentation.

"In here," came his voice from the bathroom.

I walked in to find him walking over to the small dining table, a soft smile laced with an inch of worry etched on his face. He glanced at me as I entered, his eyes searching mine for something I wasn't sure about.

"Hey," he said softly, standing up and walking over to me. He wrapped his arms around me, pulling me close. "How did it go?"

I melted into his embrace for a moment, savoring the comfort, before the exhaustion and stress resurfaced. "It was… a lot," I admitted, pulling back a little. "The presentation went well, but I feel weird, I don't know."

He nodded, his expression understanding and easy as always. "I made us dinner," he said, gesturing to the bowls of chicken curry soup noodles on the table. "Thought you might need a break."

My brow quirked at the familiar scent of my dad's homemade recipe. Were they in contact?

"Thank you," I murmured, feeling a wave of gratitude. He was always thinking of me, always trying to make things easier. He gave me a brilliant smile and as we sat down to eat, a silence filled the space between us. Normally, we had a good streak of comfortable silences, but this one was different. Something seemed to be on his mind.

As I ate my food, my exhaustion making the food tasteless, I noticed Max watching me, his gaze heavy with something I couldn't quite read.

"What is it?" I asked, trying to keep my voice steady.

"Nothing." His eyes shifted to his bowl, making me miss his usual easy going demeanor.

"No, tell me."

"It's really nothing." He insisted.

Despite how tired I felt and how hard it was to keep my eyes open and my body upright, I leaned over and placed my hand on his leg.

"Max," I whispered, "what is it?"

He took a deep breath, setting down his fork. "I got a call today," he began, his tone careful. "From the gallery in Minnesota. They offered me a permanent position. They want me to move there and head up their new exhibit."

My heart dropped to my stomach.

"Minnesota?" I repeated, my voice a little too sharp.

"Yes," he said, his eyes never leaving mine. "It's a huge opportunity, Alina. A chance to really make a name for myself in the art world."

Chapter 34

I nodded, trying to process the information through the fog of exhaustion and stress.

"That's... that's great, Max," I said, forcing a smile. "You deserve it."

"I turned it down."

A spark of relief flooded through me, but my exhaustion had my defenses up. This was a great opportunity for him. He had always dreamed of heading his own gallery, of having his art recognized on a larger scale. I knew how much it meant to him, how hard he had worked for this moment.

And yet, as much as I wanted to be happy for him, a part of me felt a gnawing fear. I would just... hold him back.

In time, he'd grow to resent me, and he'd leave me, and I'd be alone again. The thought of losing him, of watching him grow distant and unhappy because he had sacrificed his dream for me, was unbearable. I could already see the future playing out in my mind: the silent dinners, the forced smiles, the inevitable fights. The fear of being abandoned, of not being enough to keep him happy, loomed large. It was easier to push him away now, to create distance before the hurt became too deep.

"Why?" I asked, my voice hard.

He jerked back, looking stunned.

"Why'd I turn it down?"

I nodded almost imperceptibly.

He stood up, running his hands through his messy brown hair in exasperation.

"What do you mean? For us, Alina, for our future!"

He wasn't yelling, but he had never spoken so harshly to me before, it was like he was.

"What about *your* future?" I stood as well, the food forgotten on the table. "You *need* to take that job."

He flinched back, his eyes filling with pain. "What do you mean *'my* future'? It's our future, Alina, *I love you!*"

I walked over to him and looked up at him, fire in my eyes. The fog of exhaustion took a step back but I still felt it in my eyes.

"This is a great opportunity, Max. It's your *dream*. I've worked so hard for so long, sacrificed everything that I had, working towards *my dream* for years and now that it's close, I *still* may not even get it! You're basically being handed yours on a silver platter, and you're not even gonna take it?!"

"Because I can have more than one dream, Alina, and I want to pursue my dream with you!"

"You deserve better than me!" I cried out. "You're sweet and you're kind and you're funny and you prioritize me when I can't even let you help me on a project I'm wrapped up in. I am a barely functional adult woman with mommy issues and a career that will never stop. You. Deserve. Better. Than. Me."

His expression softened as he took a step closer to me, his hands reaching out but stopping just short of touching me. "I don't want better. I want you."

I shook my head, stepping back and wrapping my arms around myself as if trying to shield my heart from the truth of his words. "I can't be the reason you give up on your dreams."

He took a deep breath, his body shuddering as he tried to collect himself and his eyes locked onto mine.

"I feel like you're always looking for an out, Alina. Every time things get serious, you pull away."

"That's not true," I protested, but the words felt hollow even to me.

"It is true," he insisted. "You have these walls up, and no matter how hard I try, I can't get through to you."

I felt tears prickling at the corners of my eyes. "I'm just... I'm scared, Max. I've worked so hard to get to where I am, and I don't want to lose it."

Chapter 34

"And I understand that," he said gently. "But what about us? What about what we have?"

"I don't know," I whispered, my voice breaking. "I don't know how to balance it all." And that was the truth of the matter, the truth I had been trying so hard to deny the past few months. I didn't know how to balance this. It was entirely new terrain to me and I was drowning.

He reached out, taking my hands in his. "I'm not asking you to choose between your career and me, Alina. I'm asking you to let me in, to trust me."

"I do trust you," I said, but even as the words left my mouth, I knew they weren't entirely true.

He shook his head, a sad smile tugging at his lips. "No, you don't. Not completely."

The silence between us was thick with unspoken words and unresolved emotions. Finally, Max knelt in front of me, resting his forehead on my stomach. His vulnerability broke something inside me, but I couldn't let go of my fear.

"Please, Alina," he murmured, his voice filled with anguish. "Put me out of my misery. Tell me what you want."

I stood there, my hands trembling as I gently pushed him away. "I don't know, Max," I whispered, tears streaming down my face. "I'm scared. I don't know how to be what you need."

He looked up at me, his eyes filled with a mix of love and pain, shiny from the tears welling in them. "I don't need you to be perfect, Alina. I just need you to be here. With me."

"I can't," I choked out, the words tearing at my heart. "I can't do this right now. You need to take the job."

For a moment, he just looked at me pleadingly, as if telling me I could still take back my words. When I didn't, he stood up slowly, the hurt in his eyes cutting deeper than any words could.

"I love you, Alina," he said, his voice trembling. "But I can't keep fighting for us alone."

I choked back a sob and pressed my lips together, looking at the floor.

We stood there in silence, the distance between us growing with each passing second. Finally, he turned and walked towards the door, pausing for a moment before looking back at me.

"This isn't me leaving. This is you pushing me away."

With that, he left, the sound of the door closing echoing through the empty apartment. I sank to the floor, the weight of my decisions crashing down around me. The silence was deafening, and for the first time, I felt truly alone.

Chapter 35

It has been a week since Max and I's argument, and I haven't seen or heard from him since. Not that I expected to after the way I treated him. I sat in my darkened apartment, the only light casting a soft glow from the laptop screen in front of me. The document I'd been working on blurred as exhaustion tugged at the edges of my consciousness.

Time had become an elusive concept, days melding into nights as I threw myself into work, trying desperately to drown out the ache of what happened between us.

I barely remembered what happened. It was like I had blacked out. Everything happened so fast, and there was a pain in my chest and stomach that followed me all week. Regardless, this was for the best. He was better off without me. Now he could feel free to follow his dreams instead of having me tie him down.

Closing my laptop with a heavy sigh, I leaned back in my chair and rubbed my temples. The silence in the apartment was palpable, a constant reminder of Max's absence. The constant chatter and noises of the office would have been helpful, but I couldn't get myself to leave my apartment and see the paintings we had worked on together on display everywhere, and so I had been working from home the past few days, trying to get myself together.

I pushed my head side to side to crack my neck and let my gaze drift around the room, landing on the framed painting of a familiar comet hanging by the sofa. The pain twisted in my chest and I stood up, unable to bear the weight of memories that surrounded me.

Everywhere I looked, there were traces of him: the fresh flowers he had placed all over my apartment, the cozy throw blankets he had picked out for our movie nights, the canvases he had left behind at my place in preparation for a painting night together. Each item whispered of his thoughtfulness, his love, and the void he had left behind.

I had barely slept all of last week in preparation for the presentation that would secure my standing for a promotion, but despite being home now and having the burden lifted off my shoulders, I still couldn't sleep. I couldn't remember the last time I slept for anything more than three hours in a row. All I could think about was him and his last words to me.

This isn't me leaving. This is you pushing me away.

Those ten words were pounding around in my head, forcing me to relive that one moment over and over.

With a frustrated groan, I paced the room, my footsteps echoing in the empty space. Reflecting on our relationship brought a mix of emotions—love, longing, regret, and a deep sadness. I realized how much I missed him, how much I valued his unwavering support and understanding, even when I couldn't give him the same in return.

A buzzing on the table drew my attention to my phone and gave me a break from my wallowing.

Kait: are you okay? what happened? i haven't seen or heard from you in days x

Chapter 35

With a sigh, I set my phone down, ignoring the text, laid on the couch, the same couch he nursed me back to health on, and let the sadness swallow me.

In the following days, I threw myself even deeper into my work. It was a distraction, a way to numb the pain that threatened to overwhelm me whenever I allowed myself a moment of stillness.

The days blurred together, punctuated only by fleeting moments of reflection when memories of Max would flood my mind. Each passing day seemed to reinforce the conviction that he was better off without me.

But no matter how busy I kept myself, reminders of Max were everywhere. I had to put the painting and blankets in the closet and throw away the wilting flowers because of the heaviness that filled my heart every time I looked at them. Now my apartment just looked the way it did before he entered my life: bare and unlived in.

As the days stretched into a lonely haze, even working from home became a struggle. The familiar rhythms of my job, once a source of comfort, now felt unfulfilling and like I was just going through the motions.

I retreated deeper into isolation, avoiding the office where reminders of Max lurked around every corner—the conference table he had spilled hot chocolate on, the paintings we had worked tirelessly on together, the rooftop he had taken me to for our first date.

One afternoon, there was a knock on my apartment door, pulling me out of a haze of spreadsheets and unanswered emails. My heart pounded, a hint of relief or exhilaration flaring inside me as I hesitated.

Was it him? He could have been in Minnesota already for all I knew, but a tiny part of me that I wanted to die hoped it was him. A beat passed and I smoothed down my hair as I crossed the room to open it.

"Alina," Jack greeted me with a concerned smile, holding a small bouquet of flowers in his hand. "I hope I'm not intruding."

"Jack." I stated, staring at the sight of my boss standing in my door frame, a welcoming but worried expression on his face. I felt my expression falter before I managed a weak smile, stepping aside to let him in. "No, not at all. Please, come in."

Shit. I was wearing my pajamas and my boss and mentor was in my apartment. A grimace crossed my face and I glanced at my bedroom, wondering if it was worth it to change into more appropriate attire and freshen up.

He entered, glancing around the dimly lit apartment. "It's been a while since you've been in the office," he observed gently, placing the flowers on the table. "And I've noticed you've been working from home more than usual."

I nodded, sinking onto the couch opposite him. "I... I just needed a change of scenery, I guess."

"Your final presentation went extremely well. I can't tell you who won yet but I can tell you that I'm incredibly proud of you."

The encouraging words made a small genuine smile grace my lips.

"Thank you, Jack." I said, tiredly, unable to muster the enthusiasm I should have.

Jack studied me intently, his brow furrowing with concern. It made the wrinkles on his face from age deepen in his skin, and a flicker of sadness passed through me at the thought of my mentor aging.

"The change of scenery... it's more than that, isn't it?" He pried.

"No," I insisted, "I–"

"Don't lie to me, girl." Jack's stern eyes bore into mine.

I sighed, the weight of the past weeks pressing down on me. "Yeah, it's... it's been tough."

He leaned forward, his voice gentle. "Is it about Max?"

My head snapped up and I felt my body jerk back in shock.

"You knew?"

He blew a raspberry and waved me away with a wrinkled hand. "Of

Chapter 35

course I knew."

"Wha- How?" I asked, flabbergasted.

He rolled his pale blue eyes at me. "I could sense something the night of the auction. But I really knew for sure when you and him poorly pretended you weren't together at the end of year party only to be seen canoodling in a corner then leaving together. You were not subtle."

"Right," I muttered, feeling a mix of embarrassment and gratitude for Jack's perceptiveness.

"I'm sorry, Jack," I said, my voice wavering. "I didn't mean for it to be so obvious. I didn't want it to reflect poorly on you."

He waved off my apology with a dismissive gesture. "There's no need to apologize, Alina. Relationships are never easy, especially when they end."

I nodded, my gaze falling to my hands where they clenched in my lap. "I miss him," I admitted quietly, the ache in my chest threatening to spill over into tears once more.

I had never been so personal with Jack before– with anyone from the office before. But this whole past week felt like I was grieving something and I needed to tell someone to get it off my chest.

Jack sighed and rubbed a hand over his face before looking at me very seriously. "I don't know what happened, but that boy looked at you like you hung the moon. I think anything that might have been broken here, can be fixed again."

I shook my head and tried to blink the tears away.

"Relationships are complex," Jack offered, his tone understanding. "Sometimes, you can't anticipate what your partner needs, all you have to do is be there for them."

He reached out, placing a hand on my shoulder. "Take all the time you need," he said sincerely. "But don't shut yourself off completely. Sometimes, facing our pain is the first step towards healing. They'll be announcing the new DOO next week."

Jack stood up, giving my shoulder a reassuring squeeze before heading towards the door. "Even once I retire, if you ever need to talk, my door is open."

"I know," I nodded gratefully, the weight of his words settling over me like a comforting blanket.

With a final nod, Jack left, closing the door softly behind him, and the emptiness swallowed me again.

Chapter 36

Two days later, I was cocooned in the familiar dimness of my apartment, ready to spend another night laying on the couch, watching Love Actually, when a notification and buzzing lit up my phone like a beacon in the dark.

Kait: Dolphin

Oh, god. 'Dolphin' was a code we had created in college for when one of us was ever in trouble. We had emphasized never to use it unless we needed help right away, but not to the level where we needed the police involved.

The urgency in her message propelled me into motion, casting aside my melancholy thoughts momentarily to check her location. I didn't hesitate, grabbing my keys and slipping on a pair of shoes before I hurried out the door.

I hailed a cab and directed the driver to Kait's building, the journey filled with nervous energy and unanswered questions swirling in my mind. What could be so urgent that Kait needed me there? Was she in trouble? Oh God, was it Lennon Mae? What happened? My thoughts raced as the city lights blurred past, the cab eventually pulling up outside her apartment building.

As I stepped into the crisp evening air, I couldn't help but glance up at the building, a pang of sadness tightening my chest. I had forgotten that Kait's apartment was also his. Somewhere up there, Max's apartment loomed, and just thinking about it made my stomach twist.

Pushing aside the swell of emotions, I focused on Kait's plea for help and hurried up the stairs to Kait's floor, my heart pounding with a mixture of worry and anticipation.

The hallway was dimly lit, casting long shadows that seemed to dance with my anxiety. When I reached Kait's door, I paused for a moment, steeling myself before knocking firmly.

The door swung open, revealing Kait's beaming face framed by tousled dark blonde curls. "Alina!" she exclaimed, relief evident in her eyes as she pulled me into a tight hug. "I'm so glad you're here."

"Kait, what's going on?" I asked, stepping inside as she closed the door behind me. The cozy familiarity of her apartment enveloped me with its clutter and baby furniture everywhere, a stark contrast to the bare, lonely apartment I had been living in the past few days.

"What's wrong is you haven't seen me or my baby in over a week." She looked at me, pointedly.

"Kait, you know we only use 'dolphin' when it's an emergency." My voice raised slightly in anger.

"It *was* an emergency. I was worried about you," Kait admitted, her expression softening as she settled onto the couch. "You've been MIA for weeks, and I had to resort to desperate measures to get you out of your cave."

I sighed, plopping onto the couch next to her, feeling the stray baby blankets and pacifiers around me.

Chapter 36

"What happened?" She looked at me, concern in her eyes.

"Max and I broke up."

It still hurt to say it. I sniffed and wiped my eye with my sleeve, annoyed at the tears that kept surfacing when I thought about him.

Kait padded over to the kitchen and brought out a bottle of wine and two glasses.

She poured the wine and I took it wordlessly. Just as she lifted it to her face and I thought she was going to sniff it like she did the past nine months, she surprised me by taking a large swig.

"Kait, you're breastfeeding."

"I pumped a lot earlier. My tatas are producing like crazy."

"Where's Lennon?"

"With Adam's mom for the night. I needed a mental health day."

"So you called me over here to see her and she's not even here?"

"Yep."

"Okay then." I conceded.

"Okay then." She repeated, a comforting smile on her face.

We clinked our glasses and got to talking and I told her everything.

◇◇◇

As we sipped our wine, the tension in my shoulders began to ease. Kait was right—being here with her, surrounded by love and friendship, was exactly what I needed. The hours passed in a blur of laughter and shared memories, the heaviness in my heart momentarily forgotten.

Three hours later and a few more glasses down, just as we were settling into a buzzed, sleepy silence, the doorbell rang, startling us both. Kait jumped up with a grin. "Yes!" she exclaimed, practically skipping to the door.

I watched curiously as Kait opened the door, expecting to see Adam's familiar face. Instead, a comically large bag with a familiar logo on it sat on the doormat. My confusion must have been evident because Kait turned to me with a mischievous grin.

"Adam's at a conference, but he knew we needed a pick-me-up," Kait explained, picking up the food and shutting the door.

A rush of warmth spread through me at Adam's gesture. Even from miles away, he knew how to make us smile. We settled back onto the couch, unpacking the feast spread out before us.

"Classic Adam," I chuckled, recalling the countless times he had surprised us with late-night Taco Bell Doordashes when we were too drunk to order ourselves after a night out during our college days. We would FaceTime him, completely drunk out of our minds, and he'd place an order for us because our college apartment was too far away from the closest Taco Bell.

Kait nodded, her expression thoughtful as she bit into a chalupa. "Speaking of Adam," she began casually, "he used to struggle with commitment and communication too, you remember that right?"

"How could I forget?" I mumbled around the cheese, chicken, and tortilla in my mouth, moaning at the orgasmic flavors of the classic chicken quesadilla me and Kait always split. "You were always talking about it when y'all were in that situationship for six months before dating."

"Anyway!" She glared at me. "The only reason we're here right now with this beautiful baby is because he almost lost me at one point. I left, and he realized his fears of commitment were more about his fears of abandonment. And then he realized that his fear of losing me was so much worse than his fear of me leaving."

I swallowed my bite, my throat suddenly dry.

She continued on. "I told him what I needed from him and while it took him a while, he worked on it and eventually was able to give me it. Then, he worked on it some more, and he was able to better communicate with me what he needed from this."

Chapter 36

"It took work and it was hard," She gave me a sad smile. "But it's work that is worth it."

Silence settled between us, the only sound the gentle hum of the city outside my window. I thought back to the moments Max and I had shared—late nights discussing art, lazy Sundays curled up on the couch, the quiet comfort of his presence. It felt like a lifetime ago, yet the memories were still vivid, still raw with emotion.

"Do you regret it?" Kait's voice broke through my reverie, pulling me back to the present.

"Regret what?" I asked, my brow furrowing in confusion.

"Walking away," she clarified, her gaze unwavering.

I hesitated, the question weighing heavily on my heart. "I don't know," I finally admitted. "Part of me feels like I made the right decision, for him... for us. But another part..." My voice trailed off, unsure of how to articulate the conflicting emotions swirling inside me.

Kait nodded, understanding spreading on her face. "You did what you thought was best," Kait said quietly. "That's all anyone can ask of you."

I sighed, contemplating her words. "I just wish things hadn't ended the way they did," I confessed, swirling the wine in my glass absentmindedly.

"Sometimes, things fall apart so they can grow and fall back together better than before," Kait quoted gently, her gaze meeting mine with unwavering support.

We sat in silence for a minute, sipping our wines and basking in each other's company. I looked around at their apartment and smiled to myself as I looked at a travel crib in the corner, a mess of baby blankets on the couch, a formula mixer on the kitchen counter, and a series of baby locks on every cabinet and door in the room.

"Dude, you're a mother. Genuinely, what happened?"

"You see, when a mommy and a daddy love each other very much–" I threw a stray pacifier at her and laughed softly at her outraged expression.

"I don't know," she said wistfully, "all I know is that I would do anything for her. I'd eat you for her if I had to."

"I'd gladly let you barbecue me for her if it came to it, but let's hope it doesn't." I hugged her and she swung her legs over my lap, tucking into my side.

We talked late into the night, sharing stories and secrets, laughter and tears. Kait listened without judgment as I poured out my heart, recounting the highs and lows of my relationship with Max. In her presence, I felt a weight lifting off my shoulders—a sense of clarity and acceptance settling in.

It was too late to try to reconcile things. Even if I stalked him down in Minnesota, if he moved there, he was better off without me. I hurt him so much, and I didn't want to hurt him more.

As the hours slipped away, the remnants of Taco Bell scattered across the coffee table, I felt a sense of peace wash over me. It helped, talking about it. And it helped knowing that even if Max and I didn't reconcile, I had my people and I wouldn't be alone.

Chapter 37

"Kelsey's internship ended while you were gone and she's headed back to school." Dan's head poked into my office, a wary smile on his face.

"Did she get a return offer?" I asked.

He nodded, his expression telling me she already accepted it.

"Great to hear, hopefully she doesn't renege later on." I smiled at him then turned back to my work. The girl was a popcorn eating hazard, but she did great work and she had a friendly aura she brought to the office.

After debriefing with Kait and getting lifted out of my funk, I found myself ready to go back to work in person. It was time to re-enter society and with the promotion announcement later today, it was good for me to come back to work. Hopefully, it'd provide a distraction from the constant dull ache in my chest.

As I settled into my desk, emails and reports awaited my attention. I delved into them with a focused determination, pushing aside lingering thoughts of Max and the conversation with Kait from the previous night.

The office hummed with activity around me, colleagues chatting animatedly about projects and upcoming deadlines. It was a familiar backdrop, grounding me in the routine of my professional life.

Carla and Shay had already welcomed me back earlier this morning, and a few colleagues had wished me good luck on the announcement later today.

Walking into the office itself was a struggle for me this morning, seeing the colorful six pieces we had developed together adorning the walls made me lose all air in my lungs for a moment, but it was nice to be back, even if all I wanted to do was go home and bask in the solitude.

Just as I was about to dive into a particularly complex spreadsheet denoting our San Francisco office figures, a knock on my door interrupted my concentration.

"Come in." I said steadily. It was probably Jack, looking to get some sweet words wishing he could stay and praising all he had done for the company, the way he had been pestering everyone in the office for the past few days.

"I already told you I was gonna miss you," I hollered, eyes on my spreadsheet, "stop fishing for compliments, old man."

A throat cleared at my door and I froze. Startled, I looked up to see Emmy standing there, her usual easy going expression grave.

"E-Emmy." I stood, my hair raising on my arms. What was she doing here? I wasn't prepared to see anyone from Max's life ever again. I assumed they all had shunned me for the way things went down. It was a shame too, I was really starting to love them, and I could feel Ezra warming up to me over time.

Emmy hesitated for a moment before taking a seat opposite me in front of my desk. I sat down too, unsure what to say. Her usually confident demeanor seemed subdued, her sharp blue eyes searching mine with an intensity that made me uneasy.

"I need to talk to you," she said finally, her voice low yet firm. "About

Chapter 37

Max."

My heart skipped a beat at the mention of his name. I swallowed, uncomfortable with the situation, and nodded.

"What did you do to him?" Her eyes were accusatory and her tone bewildered. This wasn't the warm, carefree Emmy I knew. This was a protector, standing guard over her wounded friend, ready to attack at all costs.

"I don't," my words caught in my throat and I shook my head, "I let him go. I let him be free to chase his dream without me holding him back."

My voice was steady, as steady as I could make it anyway.

"You broke him." Her eyes shone with wetness and her voice was filled with quiet rage. "He let you in, we all let you in, and you cut him off like he was *nothing*! How could you do that?"

"*I HAD TO!*" My voice raised, breaking softly at my words. "Don't you get it? I was scared. Scared of holding him back, scared of being the reason he didn't reach his full potential. I thought... I thought I was doing the right thing by stepping away."

Emmy's eyes narrowed, her jaw tightening.

"You thought you were doing the right thing? By breaking his heart? By leaving without giving him a chance to decide what he wanted? You didn't even give him a choice, Alina. The boys had to console him for days. He just stopped talking to anyone, to any of us."

Tears pricked my eyes, but I blinked them back, determined to keep my composure. "He deserves someone who can support him fully, who doesn't drag him down with their own issues. Someone who can be there for him without reservations."

"You don't get it, do you?" Emmy leaned forward, her voice dropping to a fierce whisper. "Max loved you. He wanted to be with you, despite everything. He chose you. And you just... pushed him away."

Her words hit me like a punch to the gut, the reality of my actions settling heavily on my shoulders. "He's better off without me," I whispered, my voice barely audible. "Now he's in Minnesota, heading his own gallery like he always dreamed. He's free of me."

Surprise flared in her eyes, but she remained steely.

"Do you love him? Did you ever love him?" She asked calmly.

My eyes snapped to hers and I felt a fire rise in me. "*Of course* I love him. I loved him so much, I didn't know how to handle it."

"Max loves deeply." She nodded. "He's the happiest guy I know, and for whatever reason, he chose you. I have never seen him as happy as he was with you. So you need to fix this, now, because he hasn't been the same since whatever happened between you two, and we need our best friend back."

Her words hit me like a punch to the gut, the reality of my actions settling heavily on my shoulders. "I didn't know," I whispered, my voice barely audible. "I didn't know he felt that way. I thought I was sparing him."

"You weren't sparing him anything," Emmy replied, her tone softer now, but no less intense. "You were sparing yourself. From the fear, from the potential hurt. But in doing so, you hurt him more than you can imagine."

I looked down at my hands, unable to meet her gaze. The enormity of my mistake loomed over me, suffocating in its weight. "I… I thought I was doing the right thing," I repeated weakly, the words sounding hollow even to my own ears.

"You need to talk to him," Emmy said firmly, standing up. "He's still here. He hasn't left for Minnesota. He's not leaving for Minnesota. You owe him that much, Alina. You owe it to both of you."

"He's still here?" I asked quietly, unable to mask the hope that flickered in my voice. "What about the job?"

Emmy nodded, her expression softening with empathy. "They offered it to him again. He didn't take it. He's still here. But he's

Chapter 37

hurting, Alina. He's hurting more than you know."

The weight of her words settled heavily on my shoulders. Guilt and regret churned within me, mixing with the lingering ache of losing Max.

I hadn't meant to hurt him, but my fear had clouded my judgment, driving me to make decisions I now regretted.

"I don't know everything," Emmy continued gently, "but it sounds to me like you were scared of him leaving you down the line, so you left him first."

Her words hit me like a punch to the gut. She was right. Fear of abandonment, fear of being left alone again—it had clouded my judgment, pushing me to break things off with Max before he could potentially hurt me. I thought I was protecting myself, but I wasn't. In doing so, I had hurt us both, and I had to make it right.

Tears welled up in my eyes, threatening to spill over. "I didn't mean to," I whispered hoarsely, my voice cracking with emotion. "I love him, Emmy. I still do."

Emmy reached across the table, her hand resting gently on mine. "I know you do," she said softly. "And I think he knows it too. But he needs to hear it from you, Alina. He needs closure, and so do you."

Closure. The word echoed in my mind, stirring a tumultuous mix of hope and fear. Could there be a chance for us to talk, to find a way back to each other? Or was it too late, the damage irreparable?

"I don't know if I can face him," I admitted, my voice trembling. "I'm scared of what he'll say, of how much I've hurt him."

Emmy squeezed my hand reassuringly. "You won't know until you try," she said gently. "Just talk to him, Alina. Give yourselves a chance to heal."

Her words resonated with me, stirring a resolve within me that had been buried beneath layers of pain and regret. Taking a deep breath, I nodded slowly, steeling myself for the conversation I knew I needed to have. But, I felt a spark of hope blooming within me. Maybe I could fix this, fix us. Fuck the promotion announcement, all I wanted was to take the day off and run over to his place. But first, there were things I had to do.

Chapter 38

It had been a week since Emmy's visit to my office. Her words had echoed in my mind, pushing me to confront the fear that had driven me away from Max. Every day this week I wanted to rush over to his place to see him, explain myself, and beg for forgiveness. And every day, I had to stop myself from giving into my urges. I had hurt him. Badly. This had to be perfect.

As the afternoon sun dipped lower in the sky, signaling the end of the workday, I found myself standing outside Max's apartment building. My heart pounded in my chest, each beat echoing the uncertainty and longing that filled me. The familiar surroundings brought back a flood of memories, reminding me of the love I had walked away from.

Summoning all the courage I could muster, I climbed the stairs to his floor, each step heavier than the last. When I reached his door, I hesitated for a moment, my hand hovering over the doorbell. Should I have sent a text? What if he didn't want to see me? What if he had moved on?

With a steadying breath, I pressed the doorbell, the sound echoing through the quiet hallway. Moments passed, each second stretching into eternity, until finally, the door swung open.

My breath hitched and I had to restrain myself from jumping into his arms.

There he stood, Max, his expression a mix of surprise and apprehension. His eyes met mine, and for a moment, the world fell away, leaving only the two of us standing there, face to face. I had resigned myself to the fact I might never see him again, but seeing him now, I have no idea how I went three weeks without him.

His brown hair was messier than normal, slightly longer around his face. He had a short scruff on his usual clean-shaven face that I wanted to run my fingers over. He wasn't wearing his glasses, and all he wore were gray sweatpants and a gray sweatshirt with the Riverview University emblem on it. But all thoughts in my head vanished the moment I looked into his eyes.

He looked different—exhausted, with dark circles under his eyes and a weariness that hadn't been there before. His usually bright, cheerful expression was absent, replaced by a somber, guarded look. A pang went through my heart at the thought of him in pain because of me, and I saw now why Emmy was so insistent I come.

Finally, he spoke, his voice raspy and tired.

"Alina," he said softly, his voice barely above a whisper. "I didn't expect to see you."

"I needed to talk to you," I replied, my voice trembling despite my efforts to steady it. "Can we... Can we talk?"

He hesitated, uncertainty flickering in his eyes. Then, with a silent nod, he stepped aside, wordlessly inviting me into his apartment. I followed him inside, the familiar space enveloping me with its warmth and familiarity. It felt like coming home, and yet, everything had changed between us.

He gestured for me to sit on the couch, then went to his coffee maker, fiddling with it in silence. Two minutes passed without us speaking,

Chapter 38

and when he came back, he had a mug in his hands that he handed to me mutely before sitting down himself.

I looked at the mug in my hands and almost cried at the sight of the familiar drink. Black coffee. Two creams. One sugar. And a dash of cinnamon.

The warmth of the drink in my hands gave me the smallest comfort, and it had me pressing my lips together to stop myself from crying before we even talked.

We settled on opposite ends of the couch, the silence between us heavy with unspoken words and unfinished emotions. Max's gaze never left mine, his eyes searching for answers that I wasn't sure I could give.

"I'm sorry, Max," I began, my voice raw with emotion. "I'm sorry for hurting you, for pushing you away, for not letting you in fully."

He listened quietly, his expression unreadable. The weight of his silence pressed down on me, urging me to continue, to lay bare the truth that had been buried beneath layers of pain.

"I was scared," I admitted finally, tears streaming down my cheeks. "Scared of losing you, scared of being left alone again. And I let that fear drive me to make a decision that I now regret more than anything."

His hand reached out as if to comfort me before it halted midair as if it had happened without his thinking. He took it back, then looked at me, his eyes filled with a mixture of pain and anger.

"Why, Alina? Why did you push me away? You just… gave up on us."

"I thought I was doing the right thing," I said, my voice breaking.

Max's expression hardened. "By saying we had no future? You didn't even give me a choice, Alina. We could have figured it out together."

Tears welled up in my eyes as I nodded. "I know, I was wrong. I was so scared of losing you that I pushed you away first. I was afraid that my issues would drag you down. All through our relationship, you were kind and sweet and prioritized me even when I didn't deserve it, while I couldn't even make time for you unless you blocked it off in my calendar. I don't even know how to show you affection the way you show me. You deserved someone better than me. You still do."

He shook his head, his eyes filled with frustration. "You don't get it, do you? I chose you because I love you. You're everything I need. There's no 'deserving' anyone in this, Alina, love doesn't have to be earned. And I'm sorry your past ever made you think it did."

I choked back a sob and nodded. His words hit me hard and for a second, I was scared there was no coming back from this. From what I did to us.

Max's eyes softened with understanding, a flicker of pain crossing his features. "I loved you, Alina," he said quietly. "I still do. But love isn't enough if we can't trust each other, if we can't be honest about our fears and insecurities. If you don't stop looking for an out every time this gets too deep."

"I know," I whispered, my voice choking with emotion. "I'll try harder, I promise. I'll talk to you more about what's bothering me when it's bothering me and I'll talk to someone about my issues."

"I could accept that it was hard for you to say 'I love you' to me and I could accept that you were struggling with balancing it all, but you told me we didn't have a future, Alina."

His voice was pained and when I looked into his eyes, I saw them glistening with unshed tears.

"I was wrong to say that. I do. I do see a future with you, Max. I want to spend the *rest of my life* with you. Please." My voice was pleading.

His brows furrowed and he looked down at his hands, a contemplative look on his face.

Silence descended upon us once more, the air heavy with the weight of our shared regrets and unspoken truths. The distance between us felt insurmountable, yet there was a glimmer of hope in Max's eyes—a hope that maybe, just maybe, we could find a way back to each other.

Chapter 38

Finally, he broke the silence and softly murmured. "Did you get the promotion?"

I looked at the coffee in my hands and saw the mug was shaking almost imperceptibly. I looked back at the side of his face as he stared at his hands, trying to figure out how to fix this.

"Yes."

"Congratulations," the smallest smile graced his lips, "I knew you'd get it, you always were–"

"I turned it down." The words escaped my mouth before I could think.

He stiffened and turned to look at me, confusion clouding on his face.

"You turned it down? It was your dream job, why would you do that?" I inhaled deeply. It was time.

I reached into my bag and pulled out a binder about an inch thick, gently placing it in his hands.

"Because of this."

His hands trembled just barely as he took the binder from me, his eyes narrowing in confusion. He opened it, and I watched as his eyes scanned the first few pages. His brows furrowed in concentration, and then, as realization dawned, his eyes widened in disbelief.

"Alina, what is this?" he asked, his voice a mixture of surprise and confusion.

I took a deep breath, feeling a mix of nerves and dread. This could all go wrong very quickly. It might be too late for us. But I wanted to try. I needed to prove to him how serious I was about us. If this didn't go the way I had hoped, I'd have to crawl into a hole and die of embarrassment.

"It's a business plan," I explained.

"For a gallery." He interjected.

"Our gallery." I corrected him softly. "I've spent the past week working on it. I've found the perfect location. It's a plot of land that used to be a Whole Foods so it's got a good amount of foot traffic and it has a solid demographic and is right next to a park so it has a lot of natural light. And Cas and Emmy are already fighting over the design of the building. It's perfect for a gallery."

Max flipped through the pages, his expression shifting from confusion to awe. He paused at a sketch of the proposed layout, his fingers tracing the lines on the paper. "You did all this?" he murmured, almost to himself.

I nodded, my heart pounding. "I *do* see a future with you. I'm sorry I ever said I didn't. Do you- do you like it?"

He closed the binder and set it aside, his gaze locking onto mine. "Of course I like it. Alina, I don't know what to say. This is incredible, but..."

"But?" I prompted, my heart sinking slightly.

"What about your job? You love your job."

"I don't." My voice was shaky, and my hands were trembling again. "I don't love it. It was just all I had. All I could dedicate my energy to."

I sucked my bottom lip before admitting to him softly, "The most fun I ever had on that job was working on the rebranding with you."

He looked at me, hesitation in his eyes.

I reached out, my hand resting gently on his. "I know I hurt you, and I will regret that for the rest of my life. But I want to make it right. I want to show you that I'm committed to us, to our future. I'm not looking for an out anymore. I'm looking for a way back to you."

Max looked down at our hands, his thumb brushing over my knuckles. Silence stretched between us, the weight of our past mistakes and future hopes hanging in the balance. Finally, he looked up, his eyes searching mine.

"Are you sure about this?" he asked quietly. "Are you really ready to build a future together?"

Chapter 38

I nodded, my voice unwavering. "Yes, Max. I'm sure. I want to be with you. I want to build something beautiful with you. Please, give us a chance."

He closed his eyes for a moment, taking a deep breath. When he opened them again, there was a glimmer of hope in his gaze. "Okay," he said softly. "Let's try. But it's going to take time, Alina. We need to rebuild trust, and it's not going to be easy."

"I know," I replied, squeezing his hand gently. "I'm willing to put in the work. Whatever it takes, Max."

He nodded, a small smile tugging at the corners of his lips. "Alright then. Let's do this together."

And seeing the look on his face, I didn't regret turning down the promotion once.

Chapter 39

A moment of silence enveloped us, filled with the unspoken emotions that had simmered between us for weeks. Slowly, I placed my mug on the table and moved closer, closing the distance between us. His breath hitched slightly as I reached out, cupping his cheek with my hand. His skin was warm under my touch, and I could feel the slight stubble of his unshaven face.

"I missed you so much," I whispered, my voice trembling.

"I missed you too," he replied, his voice equally unsteady. His eyes softened, and I could see the walls he had built around his heart begin to crumble.

Our faces were inches apart now, and I could feel the magnetic pull between us, drawing us closer. My heart raced in anticipation, a mix of excitement and nervousness coursing through me.

We smiled at each other for a moment, and then it was like the last three weeks built something up that had to be released immediately because before I knew it, he was tossing the business plan on the coffee table and pressing his lips to mine.

The kiss was gentle at first, a tentative exploration of familiar

Chapter 39

territory. It felt like coming home, like finding a piece of myself that had been missing. His hand moved to the back of my neck, pulling me closer as the kiss deepened. Every doubt, every fear, every regret melted away in that moment.

Then, he placed his hands on my waist and pulled me closer into him, slipping his tongue between my lips and kissing me more fervently. Needing air, I gasped and he took that opportunity to move his attention to my neck.

"I missed you so much." He reiterated, murmuring against my neck. "I couldn't pick up a paintbrush the whole three weeks we were apart." His hands roamed up the sides of my body and clutched me to him.

"I missed you too." I breathed shakily. "I was lost without you."

His lips moved back to mine and I melted next to him. My hands fervently took his shirt off as he helped me and I stood up, pulling him to the bedroom, kissing the whole way there.

We stripped each other of our clothes, and seeing his wondrous expression as he looked at my naked body had my heart soaring in my chest. My hand palmed his free cock and he moaned into my mouth at the feeling of his smooth, velvety dick in my hands.

Our lips separated and slowly, I knelt to the ground in front of him, keeping our eyes locked together. A rush of pleasure ran through me at the sight of his eyes darkening above me and I gulped as I knelt face to face with his member. I had never enjoyed doing this for men – it felt too degrading for me – but right now, I found myself licking my lips with excitement at the thought of pleasuring him in this way.

My hand steadily raised and grasped his dick, pumping once, twice. A groan escaped his lips and he closed his eyes, tilting his head back.

A small drop of pre-cum leaked from his head and I darted my tongue out to lick it, tasting the salty, musky scent of him on my tongue. Encouraged by how he sucked in a breath, I put him in my mouth and sucked.

My head bobbed back and forth as I tried to fit more of him between my lips. He smelled… clean, and already I was feeling my juices leaking into my underwear. I ran my tongue down the underside of his cock and lurched forward, my nose making contact with his hips. He groaned, lowering his head and wrapping his long fingers around my hair, pushing and pulling me gently against his cock.

The tip of his cock brushed against the back of my throat and I gagged around him, water rushing to my eyes. He was a lot bigger than the men I had done this with before. I felt him let go of me but I gripped his thighs and sucked him deeper, moaning around his shaft.

"You're so beautiful." His voice was filled in awe. I looked up at him through my eyelashes and saw him staring at me, a warm expression on his face.

I moaned around him and swallowed, letting my throat tighten around his cock, and beamed with pride internally at the swear he let loose. Just as I was about to attempt to deep throat him, his grip tightened on my hair and he pulled me up, slamming his lips onto mine.

I sighed into his mouth, my breathing heavy, and enjoyed the soft feel of his lips moving against mine.

"When I cum, I want it to be inside you." He whispered, panting against me.

I nodded, placing a peck on his jaw and without waiting a second, a pleased sound escaped him as he pushed me roughly onto the bed and climbed on top of me. Kissing his way up my neck, he stopped for a moment to just look at me, as if marveling at the fact that I was here. My nipples hardened against his chest as he gazed across my body.

His hand reached down, stroking lazily at my folds and satisfied with what he felt, his eyes brightened in confirmation and he took my lips in his again. He buried himself inside me with one swift motion, and I choked at the fullness inside me as he stretched my inner walls.

Chapter 39

A sharp yelp escaped me and I shuddered against him as he rocked his hips against mine, slowly at first then harder and harder until the sound of our hips slamming against each other echoed through the room.

"I love you." He panted, pressing a kiss to my forehead as he thrust deeper and deeper into me.

I cried out as his cock hit my G-spot, sending sparks of electricity down my clit to my toes. "I love you too."

The words fell out easily. I thought I'd always have trouble saying them to him but now I just wanted to shout it to everyone I knew.

A large hand reached up as he thrusted rhythmically into me and wrapped itself gently around my neck. He didn't squeeze or create any marks, he just held me there as if to hold me to him and it made me whimper in pleasure.

He began to slam himself into me, an almost-painful sensation of over-fullness of my belly... and then I felt him groan, shudder under me, sucking my nipple into his mouth as he began to throb deep inside me.

"Max," I gasped, when I could. It felt like my heart was about to burst.

"Cum with me." He grunted, bringing a hand to my clit and rubbing circles around it.

The pressure in my stomach built and built until I couldn't take it anymore. The pressure burst in me and I bit down on his shoulder to muffle my sobs as waves and waves of my orgasm flowed through me, making me see white.

My pussy squeezed hard around his cock and had him making a low sound that rattled in his throat as he shuddered against me, unraveling. He held me tightly against him and I couldn't speak. All I felt was his hot cum spraying deep inside me, painting my pussy wall white.

The shockwaves of pure pleasure rolled over us as we held each other.

And then, the post-orgasmic descent came and we were catching our breaths together, his firm cock still buried deep in my aching, throbbing pussy, his lips on my nipple. He held himself up and murmured sweet nothings in my ear, and I felt the last piece of me I had been keeping hidden for myself all these months surrendering itself to him.

Chapter 40

The soft light of dawn filtered through the curtains, casting a gentle glow over the room. Max and I lay tangled in the sheets, our naked bodies close as he held me.

Max's fingers traced lazy patterns on my back, his touch soothing and intimate. I felt a contentment I hadn't known in a long time, and I couldn't help but smile.

"What are you thinking about?" Max asked, his voice a soft murmur in the quiet room.

"Just how perfect this is," I replied, my fingers idly playing with a strand of his hair. "How much I love you."

He smiled brilliantly at me. "I love you too. You were all I thought about those three weeks." he said, his hand gently cupping my cheek.

My hand made its way to his scruff and I saw his nose crinkle adorably.

"I'm gonna shave it asap, don't worry. I know I look ridiculous right now."

I stroked the stubbly hair on his jaw and smiled at him. "I kinda like it. It's doing something for me, not gonna lie."

Brushing Off Business

He snickered and grabbed my hand in his, stroking my wrist with his thumb.

"You preferred the beast over the prince growing up, didn't you?"

A laugh made its way out my throat. "He was hot!"

"I can't believe it. My cool, powerful, sexy girlfriend is into beastiality. Whatever should I do?" He sighed dramatically and fell back against the bed.

"I do not! This is slander, expect a cease and desist in the morning."

I smacked his face with a pillow lightly and huffed as a playful expression made its way onto his face and he wrapped me up in his arms mercilessly, peppering kisses all over my face.

We lay in silence for a while, simply enjoying each other's presence. I glanced around the room, my eyes landing on an open sketchbook on his bedside table. Curiosity got the better of me, and I reached over to pick it up.

"What has the great Max Reynolds been drawing lately?" I announced jokingly before my body froze at what I saw.

It was me. The sketchbook was filled with drawings of me—pages and pages of my face, some of my body. Each one captured a different aspect of me, a different mood or moment. Some pages used pencil, some used charcoal, one was even made with what looked like watercolors. It was both flattering and overwhelming to see myself through his eyes.

"I missed you. I couldn't draw anything else." He breathed, his gaze unwavering.

My heart warmed, and it felt like I was falling. I cleared my throat and smiled at him, trying to keep my emotions in check. I could not cry right now.

"Don't draw me too much, or you're gonna get tired of looking at me," I joked wryly, flipping through the pages.

He smiled at me then. That lazy, lopsided smile I've started to get

Chapter 40

addicted to.

"I never get tired of looking at you"

He said it like it was objective truth. A fact of life. He rested his cheek on his palm and looked at me some more, that lazy smile never leaving his face.

A blush bloomed on my cheeks and I pressed a kiss to his cheek, trying to show more affection like I promised.

"You know, Emmy came to my office."

His eyebrows rose in surprise. "Really?"

"Mhm. A week ago. She shook some sense into me and made me realize what I needed to do."

He winced. "Was she harsh on you?"

"Yes. But I needed it."

"She can be pretty scary when she's defensive. More so than Ezra, honestly."

An amused hum bubbled up as I looked at him seriously. "You have some great friends."

He smiled and a flicker of pride illuminated his eyes. "I do. You do too."

"I do."

He leaned in and kissed me sweetly over the sketchbook and I felt myself melt into him.

I set the sketchbook aside and scooted closer to him, feeling the warmth of his body against mine. His hand made its way to the side of my rib, just under my armpit, and his fingers began tracing that familiar pattern on my skin, sending shivers down my spine. The sensation was comforting, yet it piqued my curiosity. I didn't notice it at first, but every time he stroked my skin like this, it was always the same motion, over and over again.

"Max," I murmured, looking up at him, "what is it that you keep tracing on my skin? It feels familiar."

He looked at me, a glint of amusement and affection in his eyes. Without a word, he sat up against the headboard and gently pulled me onto his lap, positioning me so I could see his hand clearly. He rested his chin on my shoulder and traced the pattern slowly on my left thigh in front of me. I watched intently, curiosity blooming within me.

A sharp intake of breath escaped me as realization struck.

I turned my body to face him, taking his face in my hand.

"But you've been tracing that since November," I said, a mixture of surprise and realization in my voice.

"I know," he replied softly, his green eyes locking onto mine with a depth of emotion that made my heart swell.

A lump formed in my throat as I processed his words. I cupped his face in my hands, my fingers gently caressing his jawline. "Max," I whispered, my voice trembling with emotion.

A beat passed as we stared at each other, our faces inches apart.

Finally, I broke the silence, my voice barely above a whisper. "What do you see for our future?"

He looked at me, his expression thoughtful yet tender. "I see us building something beautiful together. I see us in our gallery," his finger wrapped around a tendril of my hair, the black curl wrapping around his finger, "the soft glow of sunlight turning your hair that reddish black color as you talk to clients. I see me cooking our meals, since you can barely boil water."

A guffaw escaped my throat. He grinned brightly at me.

"I see date nights with Kait and Adam, long weekends in Geneva with your dad, flights to Austin to see my parents, bar nights with my friends, us kissing in a corner as Rowan and Ezra make fun of us for it while Cas and Emmy bicker to the side. I see us supporting each other, through the highs and lows, always being there for one another."

I smiled, feeling a warmth spread through my chest. "I like the sound of that. And I promise to be more open, to share my fears and dreams

Chapter 40

with you."

He nodded, his eyes filled with love and determination. "We'll take it one step at a time, Alina. Together."

He leaned in and kissed me then, a kiss filled with all the promises we had for the future, and I felt the last bits of his forgiveness through it. We pulled away, our foreheads touching, our breaths mingling and for the first time in my life, my heart felt powerfully, completely, and irrevocably full.

Epilogue

One year later

The night of the grand opening of our Santoso-Reynolds Lumina Art Gallery was a whirlwind of nerves and elation. The beautiful space buzzed with excitement as guests admired the artworks and congratulated us. The gallery glowed with the soft, warm light of carefully arranged spotlights, casting a flattering illumination over the artwork Max and I had created together that adorned the walls.

Tall ceilings soared overhead, their expanse creating an airy and expansive feel. Carefully placed spotlights bathed each piece in a warm, inviting glow. Around the perimeter of the gallery, sleek wooden benches offered moments of respite for guests to absorb the visual feast before them.

My heart swelled with pride as I looked around at everything Max and I had accomplished together. It took months and months of hard work, late nights, networking at art shows, communicating, making time for each other, and dealing with Cas and Emmy's constant

Epilogue

fighting over the design of the place, but the night had finally come, and I could not be more excited for what was to come.

Max's eyes shimmered with pride as he looked around the room, his fingers intertwined with mine. "Ready?" he asked softly, a smile playing at the corners of his lips.

"As ready as I'll ever be," I replied with a nervous chuckle, trying to steady my racing pulse.

Guests trickled in, each greeting us with congratulations and admiration for the gallery's ambiance and artwork. Harper, my cousin and recent wilderness enthusiast, appeared in a flurry of excitement, her voice rising above the hum of conversation.

"Alina! Max! This place is incredible!" Harper exclaimed, pulling me into a tight hug, her blonde hair tickling my nose. "I didn't even know you were into art."

I laughed, a mixture of relief and joy flooding through me. "Thanks, Harper. I appreciate you guys driving all this way."

A gruff, broad man smiled softly at me behind her, towering over all of us with his impressive height and build. I didn't know much about him. All I knew was that Harper disappeared into the woods for six months, and when she reentered society, she brought this quiet mountain man with her. He didn't speak much, but she seemed to love him and they spent half the week in the city, the other half in his cabin in the woods.

She let go and hopped with excitement before waving her fingers at me jubilantly and pulling her man to look at some art.

Several people congratulated us on the gallery before Max and I made our way to Kait and Adam, a large smile bloomed on my face at the sight of baby Lennon Mae in a Baby Björn slung across Adam's broad chest.

"Hey, look who's here!" I exclaimed, giving Kait a hug, while Max greeted Adam with a man handshake that seemed to change every time I saw it.

Kait grinned, her eyes sweeping across the gallery. "Wow, Alina, Max, this place looks amazing! You guys really pulled it off. And the wine!" She handed me her glass and gestured at me to take a sip.

"So good right?!" Her voice raised in pitch and we laughed at her excitement. Of course, the wine was on her mind.

"But seriously, I can't stop looking at everything in here. It's beautiful." She said with a smile.

Adam adjusted Lennon's position, her tiny hands wrapped around his index fingers on either side of her, her little eyes darting around curiously. "Lennon seems to like it too. She's been eyeing those abstracts like a tiny art critic."

We all chuckled as Lennon let out a little squeal. "She's got good taste," Max said, tickling her chubby neck with a finger. She giggled, and a warm smile crossed my face at the sight. In my peripheral, I saw Kait and Adam looking at me with small smirks and I glared mockingly at them.

Kait nudged Adam playfully. "Speaking of taste, your caterer slays, this food is so good."

Adam nodded enthusiastically. "Oh yeah, those bacon wrapped fig things are on point."

Max glanced around. "It's all thanks to Rowan. I need to thank him for this."

His eyes followed a server with a tray of hors d'oeuvres coming our direction and just as they passed, his hand quickly grabbed something from it.

He turned to me, placing it in my right hand wordlessly as he joined back into Kait and Adam's conversation, and I smiled at the caprese crostini in my hand. We talked for a few more minutes before I saw my dad across the room, his eyes focused on a sculpture Max had made drunk after a night out.

Epilogue

I left them to their conversation as I made my way across the room, a smile lingering on my lips.

"Papa," I called out, drawing his attention away from the artwork. His eyes brightened as he turned towards me, a mixture of surprise and delight spreading across his face.

"Alina!" he exclaimed, his voice filled with pride. "Look at what Max has created. It's impressive."

I chuckled softly, standing beside him to admire the sculpture. Even drunk, he made pure magic.

"Yeah, he really outdid himself with this one," I replied, glancing up at my dad. "He's been pouring his heart into these pieces."

Zaki nodded thoughtfully, his gaze returning to the sculpture. "It reminds me of your mother's work," he mused, his voice tinged with nostalgia. "She had a way of capturing emotions in her art, just like Max does."

My smile faltered briefly at the mention of my mother. Her absence had shaped so much of my life, leaving a void that even art couldn't fill. But today, surrounded by loved ones and celebrating a milestone, I felt a sense of closure and healing that I hadn't known before.

After a moment of silence, he turned to me, his eyes crinkling in the corners from age.

"*Santoso*-Reynolds?" He asked, his voice tinged with curiosity and a hint of warmth.

I nodded, a soft smile playing on my lips.

"Yeah, Papa. Santoso-Reynolds. I wanted to have my parent's name so I changed it a month ago."

My mom hasn't reached out since that day in the mall. A part of me knew she never would. But my therapist told me that the fact that I wasn't numb to it anymore was a good sign. That I was able to work through my muddled emotions where she was involved was a sign of progress.

A proud smile crossed his face and he enveloped me in a strong hug. A moment passed. Then two. When he finally released me, his eyes were glistening with unshed tears.

"I like the sound of it," he said, his voice filled with quiet pride. "Santoso-Reynolds Lumina Art Gallery. It has a nice ring to it."

"Thank you, Papa."

"I'm proud of you, sayang."

He squeezed my shoulder affectionately before stepping back, his gaze scanning the room. "Go on, mingle with your friends," he encouraged, gesturing subtly towards the group in the corner. "I'll catch up with you later."

I nodded, giving him a kiss on the cheek.

Turning away from him, I made my way through the lively crowd towards where everyone had gathered. As I approached, I heard their conversation more clearly, and amusement sparked inside me.

"Those arches. Mine." Emmy pointed the arches out to the group.

"Spotlights. Mine." Cas retaliated.

"Lunettes. Mine." She glared at him.

"Horizontal windows. Mine." He glared right back at her.

The rest of the group's attention was darting back and forth at the bickering duo. Kait, Adam, Max, and Rowan looked amused while Ezra just looked around expressionlessly, sipping his wine as he paid them no attention, clearly accustomed to their arguments.

I joined them with a smile, catching the tail end of their banter. "Looks like you two really put your stamps on this place," I remarked, nodding appreciatively at the architectural details around us.

Emmy turned to me with a grin. "Of course! Thanks so much for thinking of me!"

Cas nodded in agreement. "Us," he corrected, as he look down at Emmy beside him with the faintest smile. She grinned excitedly at me, oblivious to his attention as always.

Epilogue

Rowan, standing beside them, chimed in, "Speaking of collaborations, can we take a moment to appreciate Rowan's culinary genius? These hors d'oeuvres are next level."

I glanced at Rowan gratefully. "Absolutely, Rowan. Thank you for catering tonight. The food is incredible."

Rowan smiled warmly. "My pleasure, guys. Congratulations again on the gallery opening. It's an honor to be a part of it."

Ezra finally spoke up, his voice calm amidst the chatter. "You guys did good."

He looked uncomfortable at the sight of all these people, and my heart warmed that he was here regardless of the crowd. Max patted him on the back and gave him an appreciative smile. They continued chattering, but something felt amiss to me.

I felt the back of my neck prickle with awareness as I felt someone staring at me. Turning slightly, I caught sight of Jack across the room, his vibrant eyes fixed on me with a subtle intensity that spoke volumes. Beside him, a tall man around his age was laughing with the people surrounding them, his hand holding Jack's gently.

Despite the distance between us, I could read the warmth and understanding in his expression—a silent acknowledgment of our shared history and the journey that had brought me to this moment.

He raised his glass in a quiet salute, nodding at me with a smile. He had been more than a boss; he had been a mentor, a challenger, and ultimately, a friend. I had felt horrible for turning down the promotion after the lengths he went through to help me get it, then quitting after all the time he had invested in training me. But as his eyes twinkled at me from across the room, a sense of closure washed over me, replacing the lingering doubts with a renewed sense of assurance

I returned his nod with a grateful smile and turned back to the large group.

The conversation flowed, filled with laughter and light-hearted banter. Around us, the gallery buzzed with energy, a testament to the hard work and creativity that had brought Max and me to this moment.

As I looked at our friends enjoying themselves, I couldn't help but feel a deep sense of gratitude for their support and the journey we had shared.

As the night wore on and the gallery buzzed with laughter and admiration, Max leaned close to me. "Come with me," he whispered in my ear, a mischievous glint in his eyes.

He pulled me towards the elevator and snuck a kiss before the doors opened. Intrigue blossomed inside me. We both rarely used this elevator. With the gallery only having two floors, we were more comfortable just taking the stairs. This elevator was really more to increase accessibility of our gallery.

"Where are we going?" I asked, a smile tugging at my lips as Max pressed the button for the second floor.

"Someplace special," Max replied, his voice low and filled with emotion.

The elevator ascended smoothly, the soft hum of its ascent punctuated by the rapid beating of my heart. Nerves were filling me and I couldn't help but dart my eyes at him, trying to figure out his motives.

Max's hand was warm in mine, grounding me amidst the chaos of my brain. As the ding rang at the elevator's arrival, his other hand darted out and pressed the emergency stop button.

"Max, what-"

He turned to me and took a box out of his pocket, breathing shakily like he was nervous. Oh my god.

His eyes bore into me, filled with love and determination.

"Max." Was all I could say, my eyes wide as I looked at him.

"Alina Santoso," he began, his voice thick with emotion, "My life changed the day you walked into my apartment's elevator. I was sick

Epilogue

and felt like I was dying all week, and you came in, all huffy and cranky and annoyed I sneezed on you-"

"Of course I was annoyed you sneezed on me, anyone would be annoyed at getting sneezed on by a stranger!"

He raised a brow at me and I shut up immediately.

"—and I thought I was seeing an angel."

A ball of something settled in my throat and my eyes welled up.

I used to never cry until I met him. It was like he unlocked something in me that made me feel everything more intensely.

He gave me an encouraging smile and continued on.

"You've brought so much light and love into my world, and I can't imagine a day without you in it. It hasn't been easy, but it's been fulfilling and beautiful and every day I wake up next to you, I get reminded of how much I want everything with you."

Tears poured down from my eyes as Max dropped to one knee, revealing a small velvet box in his hand. Inside, a ring sparkled, a brilliant oval-cut diamond in the center of it. Nestled against it was a stunning blue gem that I didn't know the name of that caught the light of the elevator.

"Yes." I blurted out.

He barked a laugh and shook his head.

"Will-"

"Yes."

"Will you-"

"Yes!"

He shot me a look. "Alina."

"Sorry."

He chuckled and started over.

"Will you marry me?" Max asked, an exasperated look on his face.

"No."

"ALINA."

"Yes! Sorry, I was joking. Yes."

I nodded vigorously, beaming as I felt an overwhelming rush of emotions. Relief washed over his features, and he let out a breath he seemed to have been holding since he dropped to one knee. With trembling fingers, he slipped the ring onto my finger, the diamond and blue gem shimmering with a brilliance that mirrored the love in his eyes.

"It's perfect," I murmured, marveling at the way the blue gem caught the light, reminding me of my comet.

Max rose to his feet, pulling me into his arms as we embraced tightly, lost in the moment of our engagement in the quiet confines of the elevator. His lips found mine in a tender kiss, sealing our promise to each other amidst the faint hum of the elevator machinery.

When we finally parted, Max rested his forehead against mine, his hands cradling my face gently. "I love you so much. I can't wait to spend the rest of my life with you, angel."

"I love you too," I whispered, feeling absolutely no hesitation. He was it for me. "Thank you for being patient with me all this time."

He swept me up in another kiss and I smiled against his lips as he pulled me into him. We took our time enjoying our quiet little fragment of peace inside this elevator and when his lips left mine, he placed a sweet kiss to the top of my head.

"Ready to alert the Brady Bunch?"

"Let's do it."

He disabled the emergency stop behind him without looking and softly laced my face in more kisses as the elevator made its way down and I knew then that I wanted nothing more than to bottle this moment up, put it in my pocket, and keep it forever.

About the Author

Amira Danali is a pen name for a 21-year-old girl who took up a bunch of big projects the summer after graduation because she wanted to do everything possible before starting her official adult life. She is a lover of cheesy romances, late night Taco Bell runs, spontaneous trips with friends, and trying new things. A billion new things. All at once.

Currently, she is editing her second book, writing her third book, crocheting a mandala blanket for her mom, planning her move, trying to figure out life, reading through her TBR list, researching places in Boston, and making her way through the Star Wars movies.

Also by Amira Danali

Coming out soon:

Designs on You — Cas and Emmy's Story

Emmy Bates and Cas Springer have been at each other's necks since the day they met in her older brother's senior house in college. Now, fierce competitors in the world of architecture, they somehow still hate each other. Both independent architects in the same bustling city, their professional clashes are legendary, filled with pranks, bickering, and one-upmanship.

When a prestigious client offers them both a chance to submit one design each for a new skyscraper that will transform the Chicago skyline, the stakes are higher than ever. This isn't just about winning a lucrative contract; it's about proving who's the best once and for all. Yet, beneath the surface of their rivalry lies a chemistry they both refuse to acknowledge.

Forced to work against each other in a high-pressure environment, Emmy and Cas must navigate their fierce competition while old grudges mix with new sparks. As they clash over blueprints and battle for the account, they start to realize there might be more at stake than just a professional victory. Can Emmy and Cas overcome their differences and admit what they've been denying for years, or will their stubbornness keep them apart?

Get ready for a rollercoaster of laughs, love, and architectural marvels in this dual POV rivals-to-lovers, brother's-best-friend tale where the blueprints of their story are more complex than any building they could design.

Printed in Great Britain
by Amazon